I0534611

Simon Linter

Making
Headlines

SPLINTER PUBLISHINGS

First published 2015 by Splinter Publishings

First published in paperback 2015 by Splinter Publishings

This edition first published 2015 by Splinter Publishings
Splinter Publishings, 16254 Vällingby, Sweden.
www.splinterpublishings.com

ISBN: 978-91-982368-0-4

FSC

Thanks to everyone who made this book possible.

CHAPTER 1

Smash!

Crash!

Splintered shards of glass from a shop's window lay strewn across the pavement of a dim lit winter street. The age of the shop was of no concern to the robbers. Its heritage was shown no sympathy or regard. A house brick thrown by Sneaky and his accomplice, Darren, was the weapon of choice to allow them to take what they could never afford. Kicking the loose shards of the remaining window away with his army boot, Sneaky leapt through the window, plucking items from the shelves and packed them into his bag. Darren stared idle through the smashed window and hesitated in joining his partner in crime.

'Come on. Come on. Quick. For fuck's sake!' shouted Sneaky, waving his arm at Darren.

They had met at the pool hall an hour before where the thought of robbing the shop had entered Sneaky's head over a game. Darren had been suspended from school for fighting and couldn't think of a better way to while away the hours than to shoot pool and smoke Sneaky's cigarettes. Sneaky's brainwave of robbing the photography shop had not initially enticed Darren to take part. It was Sneaky's strong grip around his throat and threatening curse words that had persuaded him.

Once Darren had jumped through the window, there wasn't a way to turn back. His nerves had started to take over his body; his hands shook; sweat soaked into his balaclava, dripping down his forehead and into his eyes as he snatched the most expensive digital SLR camera from a wall display. Sneaky watched his nervous, shaky fingered partner in crime dropped the camera on the floor. A large crunch sounded as the lens cap split away from the lens and slid towards Sneaky who stamped his foot down and trapped the lens cap under his boot, making a save an ice hockey goalie would have been proud of. Laying broken on the hard shop floor, a huge crack had ripped through the lens of the dropped camera almost mimicking the smashed shop window.

'Fuckin' idiot!' ranted Sneaky to his hapless understudy. He continued to fill up his sports bag with merchandise.

Piercing through the quiet night, the alarms sounded, echoing down the dark, cold streets that had seen much activity just a few hours before. Rare dizzy headed hopscotching drunks made their way past the wounded photography shop, pointing seven fingered hands at the action. They would never recognise the assailants through their beer goggles, making them the worst witnesses possible.

'Fuck, man. Come on. We have to go!' yelled Sneaky.

Darren struggled to pull his bag zips together, made worse by his hands that had turned from butter to jelly. The intense pressure to leave the shop before they were apprehended was proving too much. His heavy breath rebounded back from the inside of his balaclava, making his face drip with condensed sweat. Darren removed the balaclava from his head and could breath again. The cold air chilled his face, feeling as if his sweat had turned to ice.

'What the fuck are you doing? Fuckin' hell! We've got to get outta here!' shouted Sneaky.

Sneaky barged his way out of the broken shop window to the street. Darren followed suit albeit a few paces behind him.

A time and date, in bright blurred orange letters and numbers, displayed in the right bottom corner of the picture as the robbers exited the shop. Darren's glance back towards the broken window had caught the young protégé like a rabbit in the headlights. No balaclava. No disguise. The same coat he always wore. He hadn't spared a thought about being recognised. Frozen to the spot, the duo were stuck in time. They were paralysed. Suspended. The game was up. Not even the minute on the time and date had ticked over.

'Now, correct me if I am wrong. The nametag on

the inside of your coat reads Darren.'

The constable was in no mood for chavs. Hours after the raid had been declared a success by the robbers, the police had already identified them, tracked them down and brought them in for questioning. The damning evidence from the shop's video surveillance had ruined their plans to earn themselves easy money. Now they were being grilled in a warm interview room that smelt of body odour from a previous interrogatee. The nervous sweat on Darren's face had started to flow again, dripping down his cheeks. He had never been in trouble with the police before. For Sneaky, it represented his life; a life the constable was all too familiar with, as he had seen him many times before. His name was Paul but had been given the affectionate nickname of Sneaky by the other delinquents in the neighbourhood.

The constable placed his pen on the table, gave a deep sigh and looked at the lawbreakers in front of him. The baseball caps, hoodys and fresh white, probably stolen, trainers were fooling nobody. Chunky sovereign rings represented power on the hand of Sneaky. In a vain attempt to hide his embarrassment, Darren focused his gaze on the floor, not looking up, still shaken from the whole experience. The constable was shocked to see Sneaky's foot balancing on the edge of the table. Unperturbed, Sneaky had raised and rested his leg on the table, making himself at home as if he was the CEO of a major company marking his territory. The constable swept his leg off the table's edge with one almighty strike with the long arm of the law. Order had been restored. Sneaky sucked his teeth and shrugged his shoulders in a nonchalant manner.

With both of the culprit's attention caught, the constable knew that processing them would take less time that he had taken to find them and book them. Video footage had verified their guilt and if that wasn't enough, Darren had forgotten his mum had written his name on his coat's inside label.

'Darren?'

'Yes?'

Darren's inexperience made him fall for the oldest trick in the book. The constable leaned back in his chair knowing that he didn't need to go through Darren's belongings to find a valid ID. Sneaky laughed aloud and called his accomplice a 'stupid wanker'. It made Darren jump in sheer fright and look up at the constable for support. The constable remained quiet. Darren wished a hole would open up and swallow him. He hung his head towards the floor again and began to dream that he could go back to his game of Warcraft that had consumed him for hours, days, almost a year now.

'Great. Now that we are on first name terms, I'll ask you again. Take a look at this video here and tell me if you recognise this person right here, Darren.'

Darren lifted his head up and took a peek at the

freeze frame that he had looked at before. The camera had captured him sporting a wry smile looking straight at the camera. A bead of sweat swam past his eyebrow, past his eyelash and into his eye. Darren gave his forehead a nervous wipe. The deafening silence made him wonder if he had avoided the question.

'Well?'

No.

He hadn't.

Darren's cogs started to turn as he tried to think up an answer but there wasn't enough time to wait for them to turn full speed. He needed a good answer before the fear and sweat left him burnt up and saturated. Sneaky stared at his partner in crime without an inch of emotion entering his face, which only served to heighten Darren's anxiety. The first answer that entered his head, emerged from his mouth.

'Erm.. He's my twin brother!'

It was the best Darren could do in such a short space of time taking into account the constable's intense questioning and Sneaky's intimidating gaze. Sighing in disbelief, the constable relaxed and sat back in his chair and smirked. Holding back the laughter, the constable regained his composure.

'You have a twin brother with the same name as you? Two Darrens? What were your parents thinking?'

'Yeah, yeah. It's true. He's obviously wearing my

shirt for some reason.'

Sneaky folded up, bellowing out a louder laugh than the first, and almost shed a tear. He had made up some tall stories in his time but at least a majority of them were halfway to being believable. Darren had a lot to learn if he was to follow in his hob-nailed footsteps.

'Oh. I see. Well, that's alright then isn't it? You have a twin brother that just wants to frame you and get you into trouble. Perfectly understandable. We'll just go and arrest him instead them shall we?' said the constable, picking up his pen from the table.

Sneaky laughed as if Darren was a comedian that had told the world's funniest joke. He called Darren a "stupid wanker" again, further destroying any new-found confidence Darren had of making the story stick. Darren curled up in his chair and lowered his head back down to look at the same floor tile, avoiding any accusing stares. Sneaky's bout of laughing and cursing was brought to an abrupt end by the constable's fist slamming down on the table hard.

'Be quiet! I've had enough of that for one night.'

The constable didn't need any of Sneaky's abusive lip. Sneaky's face turned from laughter to rage after realising who was really in control. He had lost face in front of his trainee who still didn't have the nerve to look up.

'Did you not think about what you were doing? I mean, you robbed a photographic equipment shop.

7

What moron in their right mind would try and rob a photography shop that has their own CCTV in the form of their own cameras? Did you stop to think that some of them might actually have been turned on?' asked the constable.

Sneaky's rage had started to burn. He could feel his heart beat start to race, pumping blood from his feet through to his rough, scarred hands to his badly tattooed neck. The constable had called him a moron. Nobody dared to call Sneaky a moron.

'What did you call me?'

Sneaky leant forward in his seat and stared straight into the constable's face. Eye to eye, Sneaky was ready for a confrontation that would teach the constable not to tangle with him. The constable stared back at Sneaky and locked onto his gaze. The two opposing sides were in a battle of wills, neither willing to look away first and back down. Sneaky was adamant that he couldn't let being called a moron go. The constable blinked and withdrew back into his seat, not wanting to be pulled into a staring contest.

'Whatever you say .. Paul.'

'Don't call me Paul either,' snapped Sneaky.

The constable gave Sneaky a wry smile, picked up a remote control and turned off the TV. Darren looked up. The embarrassing picture had disappeared and it had come as a relief. He didn't have to look at it any-more. The constable waved his hand at the window behind the two criminals, prompting a colleague to enter the room.

'Process these two, will you?'

Clutching a silver ballpoint pen and holding various forms, a fresh-faced assistant sat down at the table. She pushed two blank forms towards Sneaky and Darren.

'If you could both just sign here and here, we'll all be able to go home and rest.'

Unable to conceal his anger, Sneaky batted away the assistant's arm.

'I'm not signing anything until I speak with my lawyer.'

'This isn't America….Paul. We don't do bad cop, good cop routines, Law and Order, C.S.I. or any other police programme you can think of. We'll deal with both of you when you have had a chance to cool off a bit. Some time in solitude should do the trick.'

'I said… don't call me Paul,' shouted Paul.

Sneaky lurched forwards and swung his fist in wild circles at the constable, missing each time. A passing sergeant entered the room and restrained Sneaky with a martial art's move, bending his arms into an awkward position he couldn't resist or break free from. His flurry of attempted punches and spitting had been stopped by force.

'Let me go! Argh! Fuckin' pigs!' screamed Sneaky.

The sergeant dragged Sneaky away screaming to his own private cell. The interview room's door closed behind them, leaving the constable to attend to the speechless Darren.

'If you want my advice,' said the constable, 'stay away from people like that if you want to contribute to society.'

Darren accepted the constable's advice, picked up the pen and squiggled his name on the form's dotted line. The constable placed the memory card containing the footage of the raid into a small plastic bag and sighed at the amount of paperwork he would now have to fill in just because two people decided to commit a robbery.

*****

Darren reflected on what he had done after spending a couple of hours with the police. The constable laughed when Darren asked for police protection from Sneaky who he had grassed on.

'As I said before, that's just for TV. This is the real world,' replied the constable. 'Sneaky probably won't bother you again.'

The word 'probably' distressed Darren the most.

'Probably' didn't assure Darren that Sneaky wouldn't wait for him to cross his path in the local shopping centre and strangle him again.

'It's only a matter of time before Sneaky tries another robbery of some kind, be caught again, sentenced and serve jail time. You don't have to worry about him. All you have to worry about is yourself, Darren. You still have time to turn your situation around.'

For his part in the night's crime, Darren would only have to stand up in front of a magistrate, accept what he had done, receive a fine or community service and put it all behind him. The constable accepted his confession that Sneaky had coerced him into joining him.

'A lenient judge will take it all into consideration and because you have helped us as well, it will all go for you, Darren. We've contacted your parents and I have informed them of what you did tonight. I pray that we never meet again. You're free to go.'

Darren walked out of the station never to be seen by the police again. Sneaky, on the other hand, continued to shout from inside his cell until his voice cracked and fizzled out to a murmur. His immediate anger may have been defused on the outside but he was still raging on the inside.

After the night had turned into late morning, the constable had no choice but to let him go, stating that he would be picked up again for any misdemeanor whilst waiting for his court appearance.

'You're looking at spending some time in jail, Paul. Why don't you do yourself a favour and stay away from committing crime? Book yourself on a training scheme. Get a job. Anything. It's better than what you are doing I assure you,' said the constable.

The advice fell on deaf ears. It didn't seem to matter how many times he had told Sneaky against committing crimes, he always seemed to be in and out of the station every week. Before the words had left the constable's mouth, Sneaky had spat on the floor, raised himself up from his cell bed, and walked out of the station.

'Hey, Paul,' said the constable, 'don't think of going anywhere in between now and your court appearance.'

Sneaky ignored the constable and walked on.

CHAPTER 2

Chris Wilkinson, had come home in the early hours of the morning after a pub-crawl turned binge. He fumbled his house keys, trying each one in succession before he found the right one. Once inside, Chris stomped upstairs and locked himself in the bathroom where he passed out until light.

In the morning, Chris opened one eye and heaved his head away from a new toilet roll that had doubled up for a pillow. A pulsing headache was a reminder of what he had done or couldn't remember doing the night before. Coughing up phlegm from his lungs, Chris still hadn't made the connection between his chain smoking and his bouts of irritated choking.

'I need the toilet,' said a small voice from outside.

Chris rolled to the side, lifted himself from the floor and struggled to his feet. Sunlight twinkled between the frames of his glasses that he had left by the side of an untidy sink. A large smudged thumbprint greeted Chris's left eye and a small crack could be seen out of the other as he put them on.

'Dad…'

Chuck, Chris's son, rattled the bathroom handle up and down, trying to enter the bathroom.

'Yes, yes. Ok. Ok,' said Chris.

Chris placed his glasses back on the countertop and rested his head on the cold bathroom window. A strange churning sensation welled up from inside his stomach, causing an involuntary gag reflex that hurled most of the contents of his stomach towards the floor. Chris crawled to the rim of the toilet and prayed to the porcelain god, ready for the next wave of vomit. A small stream of yellow green bile flowed from Chris's mouth, slowing to an eventual stop. Wiping his slimy mouth with a square of toilet paper, Chris felt better if a little light headed. Chris cleaned up the splash of vomit on the floor as best he could with a small hand towel that was draped over the radiator. He could feel his head throb as he rinsed the towel in the sink, washing away most the remnants of his accident.

'COME ON, DAD!' shouted Chuck, pulling down harder on the bathroom door handle.

Chris hung the sick soaked hand towel back in its place, picked up his glasses and tucked the arms around the back of his ears. He placed a firm hand on the bathroom door handle and unlocked the door. Faster than a fox chased by hounds, Chuck rushed past his dad and into the bathroom.

'Awww, Dad!! It stinks!'

Chris ignored his son and concentrated on negotiating the stairs that seemed to be trying to trip him at every opportunity. Chris ventured into the kitchen where his usual breakfast of eggs, bacon, sausages and hash browns would be replaced by the plip plop fizz of Alka-Seltzer. Raking around in the medicine cupboard, situated above the fridge, Chris flipped through the boxes of medication, trying to find the fastest remedy to appease his headache. He found a box of generic painkillers that had expired past their best before date. It was better than nothing. Chris washed them down with a generous swig of water. Although Chris's head still throbbed and dizzy spells made him feel sick, he had been here before and knew he would do it again, despite promising Kate that he wouldn't.

'Daaaad? Where are you?' asked Chuck, making his way down the stairs.

Chris had opened the back door to the garden and stepped out to spark up his first cigarette of the day. The cold air made his headache thump harder, his dizzy vision worse and seemed to stir up the same gag reflex he had failed to deal with earlier. Swallowing hard, Chris avoided throwing up again before sucking in another puff of his cigarette.

'Daaaad? What's wrong?'

It was an innocent question that Chris had to think about before replying with a good answer.

'Nothing's wrong, ok? I'm just feeling a bit sick. I've got a bellyache and a headache so I don't want any noise, ok?' said Chris.

'But weren't you ill yesterday too?' asked Chuck.

'Yes. It came back.'

Chuck accepted his answer and retreated back into the house to watch cartoons featuring robots at full volume. Exhaling the last puff from his cigarette, Chris stamped out the butt on the doorstep and kicked it into the pile of older, decaying butts.

'David? What did I say? Can you lower the volume, please? There's a good boy.'

Chuck knew that when he heard his real name, it was serious. With a flick of a button, the sound wavered away, taking away a large part of Chris's annoyance with it.

Kate, Chris's wife, had already been awoken by the sound of the robot's lasers before Chuck had had the chance to turn down the volume. The spare room had almost become Kate's bedroom in recent months. The drab moth eaten curtains, the old flowery wallpaper, the dusty sun-bleached yellow lampshade that started out orange and the off white carpet, all reminded Kate that all was not well in the Wilkinson home.

Kate placed her feet on the carpet, stretched and stood up. She still felt tired. She had not slept well after Chris had crashed through the front door in the early hours of the morning. The bathroom represented a splash of cold water and a chance to freshen up but it also represented fear. It was the fear of what she might find after Chris had made the bathroom his bedroom for the night. As she pushed the bathroom door ajar, Kate first noticed the familiar whiff of vomit, mixed with alcohol, followed by cigarettes. Kate opened the door wider, spotting the globules of sick on the floor Chris had missed and failed to mop up with the hand towel.

'Oh Jesus Christ!' muttered Kate under her breath, 'I don't know how much more I can take of this.'

Kate kneeled down on all fours, opened the cabinet under the sink and reached for a cleaning product. A spit of foam ejected from the product's nozzle as Kate squeezed the trigger, expanding into the size of an ice cream scoop as it landed on the remaining chunks of red and yellow sick. Kate scrubbed at the floor, removed Chris's accident and left it looking as good as new. The smell still remained. Kate followed her nose and spotted the abused hand towel Chris had used in his amateur attempts at cleaning.

'For crying out loud. The amount of times I have told him…,' muttered Kate.

Plucking the hand towel from its hook, Kate held it between her thumb and forefinger and placed it in a flip-top bin. Kate had cleaned as best she could considering that she had to get ready for work. It had all started to become part of her morning routine.

It hadn't always been that way.

17

They had met twenty years previous, when Chris was teetotal and treated his body like a temple. He didn't drink. He didn't curse. He had a promising career in broadcasting ahead of him. When Kate took her marriage vows, she didn't realise that she would have to take in sickness and in health so literally. Cleaning up Chris's 'accidents' and apologising to people he had insulted had started becoming commonplace.

Whilst Kate cleaned the bathroom, Chris had stomped out another cigarette in the garden and used the downstairs toilet. Chris caught a glimpse of himself in the mirror. Here stood Chris Wilkinson, the greatest local TV news reporter alive, he thought to himself. The reflection of the rough middle aged man begged to differ. Chris coughed, turned away from the mirror, walked out of the downstairs bathroom and into the living room. Chuck continued to watch the morning cartoon and ignored the heavy air of an upcoming argument between his parents. His mother had marched into the kitchen with a face like thunder and had failed to say good morning to him. The angry silence had created a thick tension that not even a knife could cut.

Chris walked into the kitchen where he could hear Kate smashing plates and cups down on the countertop. Despite the desperate cleaning, Kate still looked refreshed, radiant and almost glamourous for this time of the morning. Kate ignored Chris until she couldn't ignore him any longer. She stopped making breakfast, looked up and made eye contact with him. Chris looked back at his wife who had remained almost unchanged from the day he had married her. The flowing blonde hair accompanied her blue eyes, long slender figure, the wry smile, slight shake of the head, raised eyebrows, the daggers. Kate may have looked the same but her attitude towards him had changed. Happy smiles and compliments had been replaced by arguments and pointed angry fingers.

Chris felt intimidated and could feel his stomach start to churn again as if he had downed another vodka shot. Kate's silence made him feel uneasy and he needed an escape from her anger. He turned away, grabbed a clean glass from the draining board, filled it to the brim and started to drink.

'What a state!' exclaimed Kate, 'After last time, I can't believe you did it again. Again! You promised me that you wouldn't. Promised!'

Chris had overstepped the boundaries. She had cleaned up chunks of vomit and counteracted the stale faint smell of cigarettes with air freshener for the last time. She had tried her best to spare her son of what his dad had done but he already knew. He was old enough, wise enough and certainly not stupid, despite only being ten years old. Kate's anger had elevated to raised shouting and her son could hear her over the top of the robots. Chuck boosted the television's volume. Fighting robots vs. fighting parents.

'It's not the best example to set for our son is it? Do you want him to be like you when he grows up? Eh?'

The pounding sensation in Chris's head had returned, making him feel worse for wear again. Dry swallow after dry swallow, Chris attempted to keep the lining of his stomach where it was until he could no longer manage it. Two undissolved, eroded chalky lumps of tablet sailed towards the kitchen sink's plughole in lemon lime bile.

'Charming, Chris. I knew there was a reason I married you. I'm not dealing with this now,' said Kate,, leaving her breakfast uneaten.

The normal working day for the Wilkinsons had started in the worst possible way. Kate stomped out of the front door in a rage before Chris had a chance to try and give her a foul goodbye kiss. A short time later, a friend's knock at the door saw Chuck leave for school, leaving Chris on his own. He would have called in sick if he hadn't been out with work colleagues the night before. Chris filled a new glass with water and sent two new painkillers on a mission to numb his pain. Placing the glass down on the side, Chris adjusted his broken glasses and decided to trundle into work regardless of how he felt or looked.

The cold morning air made Chris shiver as he opened his car door. Driving to work in his state was illegal but Chris wasn't going to walk anywhere.

The news story that Chris had to cover was only two blocks away and the camera crew was already there, waiting for him. All he had to do was turn on the old Chris Wilkinson magic and the news story would be a doddle.

'Yeah, Geoff, so what is this story all about then?' asked Chris, clutching his mobile in one hand and a cigarette in the other, holding the steering wheel loose.

'It's fantastic, Chris. It's an environmental issue that affects everybody,' answered Geoff.

It was to be the most sensational story the town had ever been told in recent months. A town where the headline 'gate traps dog' had graced the front page of the local press. An environmental story didn't fill Chris with any interest or convince him that the story was anything other than the same old rot. If the truth be told, Chris had often wanted to move to London, away from the sleepy town that had been famous for making kitchen tiles and hats. London was a city that would fire up his reporting skills again and propel him to stardom as an international news reporter working for a large corporation. Chris knew what to expect from this local news story. A pointless story about a pointless cause. It depressed him.

I should be reading the News At Ten or have my own chat show or at least have won one award for journalism, thought Chris, slamming his fist on the horn, this is bullshit.

21

Chris had driven straight into rush hour traffic, joining the back of a queue of other road ragers. Chris pressed the horn again. It looked as if it would be some time before the traffic moved again.

By the time he reached the scene of the news story, the camera crew, who had been waiting for at least thirty minutes with members of the public, were bemused by Chris's lateness. A pack of frozen stiff members of the public had assembled in front of the cameras, breathing icy smoke and rubbing their hands together as they stood shivering in the winter air. They looked at Chris Wilkinson, the man they believed would highlight their cause and support them.

"Bout bloody time you turned up,' commented Geoff.

Chris had had about as much criticism as he could stand for one morning, and wasn't in the mood for a cameraman to start hurling complaints at him.

'Look. Let's just do this and get out of here. What are we doing a story about here then?'

Geoff had kept the subject of the story a secret from Chris and had insisted that it was of vital importance that they cover the story. Chris looked at the crowd for clues to what the story could be. Nobody stood out. The buildings around them all looked to be in perfect order and free from decay. Not even Chris could blame his hangover for not detecting the story. He couldn't even guess.

22

'This is what we are covering today,' said Geoff, pointing to the ground.

A small, green plant, thistle like in appearance, had sprouted from the ground where Chris was standing. Chris's blank expression gave away his lack of understanding. Geoff kept pointing to the ground until it hit him like he had eaten a large blob of wasabi.

'This? We are making a story out of this?' asked Chris.

'It's an important plant, Chris,' said one of the conservationists in the crowd. 'It's in danger of dying out because of our actions. A species of beetle is under threat of extinction if this plant dies.'

Chris now wished he had rung in ill and dealt with the aftermath the following day. The vital important news story had turned out to be nothing more than a whim to him. It wasn't important and was the least of his worries. He had bigger fish to fry, not plants to protect and have beetles eat.

Even "gate traps dog" sounds more exciting than this potential waste of time, thought Chris. This has no redeeming features at all. Nothing!

Chris recorded the report in ten minutes flat, got back into his car and drove away as fast as the wheels could spin.

*****

'…And if this shrub becomes extinct, this small beetle could also be the next species on the planet to disappear. Chris Wilkinson for Eastern View.'

The piece had been edited as fast as it had been recorded and delivered to the network. Chris's hangover had been degraded to a distant pain and he had shrugged off the angry exchange of words between him and Kate. With a piping hot coffee in one hand and a newspaper in the other, Chris walked into the TV station reading the front page.

Local screenwriter, Dexter Copeland, named screenwriter of the year.

Chris couldn't believe his eyes.

"Dexter Copeland, screenwriter extraordinaire, was awarded screenwriter of the year in a ceremony held yesterday night. He is now rumoured to be directing the movie as well."

Chris read the news report three times before he could comprehend it. His best friend, Dexter Copeland, had not only won an award but would be directing a film. Chris sipped his coffee that tasted as bitter as the headlines made him feel. They still got on well and were friends. They hung out, listened to music sometimes, talked about life in general and small problems, although Dexter seemed not to have any problems. He always spoke about happiness, the way forward being up and being rushed off his feet. He never had time for anything other than his screenwriting, the film world and his perfect family. Chris had often remarked how happy he was for his friend, how he was happy and that life had treated both of them well. Chris had always lied through gritted teeth. It wasn't how he really felt at all. In the back of Chris's mind, there was a small brain cell that wished Dexter happiness but the rest of the grey matter might as well have been green.

It's Chris Wilkinson, film guru that sounds the best. Oscar winning manuscript writer, even better, thought Chris. Spielberg bows down to Wilkinson as the world's best writer and director. Dexter Copeland? Who the fuck is he? A nobody from a poor neighbourhood that's who.

Life had thrown the ace of hearts onto the table amongst the other four aces Dexter was holding. At least this is what Chris had convinced himself of.

Slurping down the rest of his coffee up from the bottom of the cup, Chris lit up a cigarette, puffed it down in record time and walked towards Eastern View's entrance. Chris folded up the newspaper and couldn't bear to even look at the headline again, tossing it in a bin amongst the rotting rubbish.

CHAPTER 3

Dexter's awards sparkled from a rare shaft of winter sun that shone across them through the triple glazing. The latest award seemed to smile at Dexter as he sat in his chair and worked. It had joined an established club of various older awards won by Dexter from an early age to the present day. Leaning back in his reclining chair, Dexter looked at the latest arrival and a smile stretched from ear to ear. It didn't just represent a simple prize. It represented

years of turmoil and struggle growing up in an underprivileged family. His father had walked out on the family years ago after a violent argument with his mother. He didn't blame him. His mother was hard to live with. Dexter hadn't seen or heard from him since and he blamed his mother for it. It was a bitter pill he tried to swallow every day. His father had no idea that he had married Jules and that he had two beautiful grandchildren. They graced his desk in a perfect-framed professional family photograph. Dexter remembered the day the photograph had been taken. He had opted to wear a suit, which was something he rarely did. The pin stripes accentuated his brown skin and made him look almost like a gangster. His stylish looks and designer stubble had not gone unnoticed by Jules, his wife, who had spent hours with a make-up artist herself. She was still the immaculate vision of perfection and as young looking as the day the photograph had been taken. Her smooth chocolate skin had been treated with mud and oils that smelt of cocoa and mint. Her shiny jet-black hair reflected the photographic lights. The two boys had had their teeth photoshopped to cover up gaping holes and to spare Jules the embarrassment of her children's imperfections despite their teeth falling out naturally. Their curly Afro styled hair had been cut shorter than usual and as a result, they looked perfect even if unnatural. Sausage, the pet daschund, was sprawled out in front of the Copeland family and was the only one looking away from the camera. Dexter had always meant to ask if Photoshop could fix that problem and make Sausage fit in with the rest of the Copeland family.

Smiling to himself, Dexter looked away from the reassuring family photograph to take a five-minute break before plunging back into work again. He had earnt it after the phone call he had just received, confirming that he would be directing his first

feature film. He hadn't told anybody, deciding to digest and absorb the information like a sponge before squeezing it out to his nearest and dearest.

Several old newspapers littered the corners of

Dexter's mismanaged desk. Light brown rings of coffee cup stains had marked official looking letters from publishers and film companies. Confused by the pile of mounting paperwork, Dexter swept aside the top layer onto the floor and attempted to find his buried mobile. After casting old magazines and empty envelopes off the desk, Dexter resorted to ringing his mobile with the landline. A muffled ringtone followed by the vibrating sound of a bumblebee trapped in a jiffy bag marked the place where his mobile was. Dexter hung up on himself, pulled the mobile from the sea of paper and reunited himself with his gadget. One battery blip remained. It could have been two blips if he hadn't had rung himself. He dialed a number.

'Hey sweety! How's Sausage?'

Dexter always started a conversation with his wife in this way, a personal joke every time they spoke to each other.

'I got the job!'

Ecstatic jubilation almost perforated Dexter's right eardrum. He moved his phone to his left ear only to receive equal punishment. Although Jules had never doubted her husband's talent, she couldn't hold back from sounding surprised and elated. Dexter's mobile battery, that had one blip to live, had now started to beep signals to his ear, telling him that his happy conversation was going to be cut short. Dexter lifted items from his desk, looking for his charger that was usually to be found somewhere in the vicinity. It was all in vain. The slap-up celebratory dinner that they were just about to plan had been cut off. Dexter found the charger and left the phone to charge.

Dexter sat down in his seat again, returning to a short story that a magazine had commissioned. A gritty thriller featuring a detective was Dexter's current line of thought although he hadn't decided on anything yet. Dexter had only typed a handful of words when he was interrupted by his mobile ringing again. He ignored the incoming number displayed on the screen, dislodged his phone from the charger and answered.

'Hey sweety! How's Sausage?'

'It's me, you idiot!' joked Chris.

Chris had decided to call Dexter on one of his many cigarette breaks whilst dreading his next news story about gifted schoolchildren. He had heard that line so many times that he often thought that he had become Dexter's wife in some bizarre sex change operation that he had undergone without his knowledge.

'What are you up to tonight? Fancy coming down to the club tonight? Shoot a few games and get wasted?' asked Chris.

'Nah. I can't. I'm going to be out celebrating tonight with Jules because… guess what?'

There was a pause before Chris spoke again.

'What?' answered Chris.

'I got the director job. I start in a month's time here in the UK, fly out to a studio in L.A. for a while and then over to Italy to shoot some scenes and then back to the UK again.'

'Heeeey! That's great news mate. I'm pleased for you,' said Chris, who would have picked up an Oscar for best supporting actor.

'I'm on cloud nine. I'm just, well, ecstatic. It's gonna be so great. I can't wait to get started.'

Chris coughed.

'Look, mate. I'm gonna have to go. I have a story to report on. I'll speak to you later,' said Chris ending the call.

'Alright. Speak to you later,' said Dexter.

Before returning to work, Dexter made one more phone call to book an exclusive restaurant for later on that evening.

*****

Bastard! thought Chris, I should have got the chance to direct a film after sending my gold bar of a script to over thirty production companies. What has Dexter ever done to deserve a break like that? He's written a few short stories and written screenplays, sure, but none of them are any good.

After the conversation with Dexter, Chris threw his burnt out cigarette to the ground and extinguished the life out of it with heavy stamps of his foot. Chris shook his head and walked back inside the Eastern View building.

The Eastern View headquarters stood proud in the middle of the town, a purpose built modern building that projected its importance through a golden metallic logo that shone onto the opposite side of the street. The general public couldn't see beyond the facade like Chris could. They didn't see the broken machinery, decaying office chairs, desks and archaic computers that hadn't been updated for several years. The drinks machine that served up a batter of brown liquid, a type of hot mud that the company had the audacity to charge people ten pence.

Chris was trying his best to forget Dexter's good fortune whilst concentrating on a news story about a man who lost a tooth chewing on a cheese and cucumber sandwich. Halfway through an interview with the dentist, Chris was interrupted by the TV station's boss, Mr Lawson. He had been the TV station boss ever since Chris had started working for Eastern View and had been the boss for decades before that. He was close to retirement. A fluff of steely white hair accompanied a large bald spot that tended to glisten in the office lights. Looking down through his reading glasses and over his old spare tyre, Mr Lawson looked at Chris and coughed to warm up his vocal chords. He spoke with a husky deep voice that most employees thought had been caused by smoking but he had never smoked a cigarette in his life. To his side stood his polar opposite in some form of ultra slim species of human. Star struck, the teenager stood motionless, gawping at Chris, unable to keep his appreciation of the local TV celebrity a secret.

'Chris. I would like you to meet Martin. He's my grandson and just wants to sit in with you and get some work experience. I'm sure you won't mind?' asked Mr Lawson.

Chris looked at Martin's acne stained face that hadn't changed its expression since being introduced. It was the last thing Chris needed or wanted but he couldn't say no. It was either show Martin the ropes or show Martin the ropes as he was the boss's grandson. He would have to be treated like gold, be shown the finest details of the inner workings of TV news reporting and be given what he asked for however big or small. Mr Lawson looked at Martin with admiration as he introduced him to Chris. Chris wondered how Martin had the strength to raise his puny thin arms for a handshake for his first brush with somebody famous. Chris obliged and shook Martin's limp hand that felt as if he had just wrestled with the head of a dead fish.

'Nice to meet you. I've seen you on TV many times,' said Martin.

The statement moved Chris to give a wry smile. He had graced peoples' television screens day after day for twenty years. Martin couldn't have failed to have seen him. It would have been hard for anybody living in the sleepy town with a working television to not have seen Chris Wilkinson. At almost every hour of every day, a news report sporting his name was broadcast to the community, as well as numerous public appearances that took up Chris's valuable drinking time.

'Well, I'll leave you two to get acquainted,' said the boss, looking at Chris. 'Go easy on him!'

After a wink and a smile in Martin's direction, Mr Lawson trundled back to his office, leaving the enamoured Martin with the broadcasting master who would divulge all of his media knowledge. Martin sat on a vacant chair by the side of Chris and looked at him expectant, waiting for the first words of professional advice. A small amount of uncomfortable silence fell between the two as Chris sighed, rubbed his face and composed himself. Chris looked at Martin's blotchy complexion, homing in on a large zit that had caught his attention. It was red, ripe and ready to explode.

'So how did you get into local news reporting? How did you get on TV? How long have you been doing it? I loved your story on the shrub, by the way. I want to do this job when I leave college. Is it easy to find news stories all the time?'

An ambush of questions rattled out of Martin's

mouth in quick fire succession without any time in-
between for Chris to launch a counter attack. He had
met work experience students before but they hadn't
been as enthusiastic as Martin was turning out to be.
Drifting in and out of the one sided interrogation,
Chris choose to part ignore Martin's rampant questioning. He wasn't going to learn anything from his
expertise if he wasn't going to listen. As Martin's questions changed to conversation, Chris continued to ignore him until a compliment struck a nerve.

'I have to say, actually, that you are a bit of a role
model to me. I mean, you are the guru of Eastern
View.'

Chris's ears pricked up like a startled horse's and
took the opportunity to soak up the praise that inflat-
ed his ego. It had been some time since he had heard
positive comments from anybody and although they
came from the boss's grandson, Chris lapped up the
acknowledgement that he was now a "guru".

'Well, you know, you have to study hard, play hard,
take no prisoners, you know what I'm saying? It's not
your typical nine to five job. You might get a call in
the night and have to cover that story right there and
then. It keeps you on your toes. It just never stops,
you know, it's a rush,' said Chris. Martin looked on in
admiration.

Chris placed his hands behind his head, leant back
in his chair and began to fill Martin's mind with stories

35

about his most difficult, most daring, most dangerous news stories in his career.

'Then, there was the time when the zoo's lion almost bit me through the railings. I was lucky to escape injury actually,' quipped Chris, 'and then the time when I chased a couple of bank robbers through town. That was hair-raising but what a rush! I can't describe everything that happened. It was just too quick, you know.'

Martin's bottom lip drooped open in sheer astonishment. A silent 'wow' dropped out. He listened to the near misses with death, the apprehension of hardened criminals and a multitude of daring charity fundraisers. His admiration for Chris seemed to grow by the second.

'But the scariest of all was the bungee jump I did for charity. Freezing cold day. Gale force winds and there I was at the top of this bloody crane waiting to jump.'

'And.. Did you?' asked Martin, on the edge of his seat.

'Well, you know, I just thought of the charity and knew I had to do it.'

A work colleague, who had been lingering behind Chris by the coffee machine, twitched. He had been listening to Chris's tales and looked disgusted by the blatant lies he expected Martin to eat and digest. The colleague shook his head behind Chris, attracting Martin's attention.

'Don't you mean the time that I took part in a charity bungee jump?' piped up Chris's colleague. 'If I remember right, you chickened out and walked off in the other direction. You didn't even climb up the ladder! Don't listen to him. He lies all the time. ALL the time!'

Chris gave out a nervous but controlled laugh and batted away the derogatory comments.

'I don't think so. Ha! Ha! He's just having a laugh,' said Chris.

'Yeah, right!' replied the colleague.

'Oh that guy! Just one laugh after another. Just ignore him and he might go away!' said Chris.

The colleague walked away, passing the cup of napalm liquid he had just bought from the vending machine from one hand to the other, and through the double doors that led into a department. Chris looked at Martin, hoping he had not lost the admiration of his new buddy. Martin smiled, laughed and remained hooked to Chris's conversation, blowing off the colleague's remarks as a mere office joke. Chris breathed a silent sigh of relief.

A news story based on the footage from the failed camera store robbery was to be Martin's introduction to the world of video editing. Chris laughed at the submitted police footage and shook his head at the antics of the town's dumbest criminals, particularly at the criminal who had his name written on the inside of his coat.

'OK. All we need to do here is record a voice-over, describe what happened, what happened after.. Blah de blah de blah. Compile it and bang it out to the punters,' said Chris.

Chris continued to speak about the process of recording a voice over whilst Martin rummaged in the bottom of his rucksack for a notebook and pen. By the time Martin had found a pen that worked, Chris had finished his voice over in two minutes flat. The news article was ready for the network and Martin had missed the production process in the blink of an eye.

'Oh sorry. Could you take me through what you did again?' asked Martin, in hope that Chris would erase and re-record.

'Sorry pal! You have to wake up early in the morning to keep up with me! Don't worry! There will be a chance tomorrow to edit another report.'

Chris yearned for the day when a significant news story about a tragedy would happen just so that he could go and cover it. A compelling story of a local turned national tragedy that would boost his career and make him a hero.

Chris broke away from his daydream when Martin popped his think cloud with a sharp question.

'Are all news stories this quick to compile?'

'It takes years of experience to get to this level. I

make it look easy but I can assure you, it takes raw talent and the heart of a true reporter to get it spot on. You need to turn the mundane into the remarkable,' said Chris, raising his eyebrows.

'Wow! I want this job. I can't wait to get going and record a story with you!'

Chris looked at Martin, paused for a second and started to evaluate him.

There isn't any way Martin the stick insect would be able to become a face at Eastern View, thought Chris. The acne would have to be treated. His voice would have to be fully broken. His greasy hair would have to be washed and conditioned. Finding a suit with drainpipes for sleeves and trouser legs would be near nigh impossible. He would have to have one tailor made. He has absolutely zero potential and if he weren't the boss's grandson, I would tell him that but obviously in a nice, constructive way. There's no damn way he's recording a news story with me.

Chris wrenched himself away from his thoughts, shook his head and knew that he needed to reduce Martin's thirst for news reporting.

'One thing at a time, Martin. One thing at a time. We'll go out tomorrow and cover the story about an old wool and knitting shop closing down. I just want you to watch. Work-shadow if you will. It's the best way you'll learn anything.'

Martin's smile faded and his line of questions had

39

come to a halt. So long as Chris the guru was in control, Martin would be just a mere spectator.

CHAPTER 4

Dexter had his nose to the grindstone, working hard to the point where a migraine had developed. The letters of his manuscript had started to dance around in front of his crossed eyes, forming a magic eye pattern he couldn't decipher. Dexter shut his laptop and had taken his fill of punishment for the day. He checked the time. He hadn't noticed that he was late. Dexter figured an hour and a half wasn't enough time for him to slice his way through traffic congestion, get home and create the perfect man Jules had married.

Jules had beaten him home by two hours, had dropped the kids off at her parents, fed Sausage and was halfway through her make-up regime when she heard the front door slam.

'Hey there! You'd better get moving!' said Jules, peeking into the bathroom.

Jules stood with a slight hunch towards the mirror, applying powder with an imperfect used circular pad. There wasn't a hair out of place. She had perfect elongated eyelashes stroked with black mascara that accentuated her brown eyes. Dexter smiled and looked at her reflection in the bathroom mirror. She looked as beautiful as the day they had got married if not better.

'I'm sorry hun'. The traffic was just diabolical. They are digging up the motorway again and reduced it to one lane at Luton. It should only take fifteen minutes but today..'

Dexter opened his wardrobe and flicked through his clothes, choosing the same pinstripe suit he had worn in the professional photograph.

'Well, I'm ready!' said Dexter, walking into the bathroom.

Jules looked up from the washbasin and caught a reflection of Dexter in the bathroom mirror.

'What have you done to your tie? God! Come here!'

Jules fiddled the knot into a pleasing symmetrical shape.

'There! Perfect!' said Jules, returning to her make-up, 'I'm almost done.'

After putting on their shoes, coats and hats, the Copelands left their house.

The calming traffic and the taxi's ability to roll through amber to red lights shaved valuable minutes off their journey time, pulling up outside the restaurant five minutes early. Le Fromage Puant was the restaurant of choice in the town, with three stars to its name. The evening's dinner was going to be an extra special celebration. A tanned waiter with slicked back hair, who greeted the arrival of the happy couple at the entrance, ran his thin boney finger down the list of booked patrons.

'Copeland, Dexter?'

A candlelit table for two, decorated with Rosa Canina created the ambience for the special occasion. Jules was the first to be presented with an unfolded lavish designed menu that featured an exquisite menu and extensive wine list. Dexter's eyes bulged out of their sockets at the extortionate prices.

Dexter remarked on the shocking three-figured price for a bottle of vintage wine. 'One hundred and twenty five pounds?'

'Don't worry, Dexy! It's a special occasion. We can order what we want,' said Jules.

Dexter closed his eyes and could see the pounds leaking out of his bank account through an open wound in his wallet. Three figures would have fed the Copeland family for a whole month when he was growing up. Weeks of stringent budgeting meant the difference between a warm, cosy house and an igloo when Dexter was a child. Not even budgeting saved the Copelands from cutting off the phone, electricity and, sometimes, even the water.

One hundred and twenty five pounds.

Three figures for a bottle of wine? Dexter thought.

Dexter questioned if he could justify paying the exorbitant asking price. The principle of paying a small fortune for a luxury when some people were poor and destitute bothered him but he convinced himself that he deserved it, if only on this special occasion. He would hold aloft his glass and toast to everyone who wanted to climb the ladder of success and that it was possible regardless of a poor background.

Dexter nodded his head to the waiter and ordered the expensive bottle of wine. The waiter complimented Dexter on his fine choice and tapped his heel on the floor and walked away to fetch it.

Dexter looked at Jules through the candlelight. She was the picture of perfection, like a valuable artwork that Dexter could never tire from looking at. He remembered the first time he caught a glance of her from across the school playground. It had hit him like an electric shock that jolted him sideways and turned his insides into liquid. It was love and had known it was the first time he ever felt it. Nobody apart from Dexter and Jules could quite believe that their so-called childhood crush was serious until both families were standing in a church, watching them walk up the aisle.

The waiter returned with the bottle of wine and started to wrestle with it, extracting the cork with an expensive looking corkscrew. After a satisfying pop had echoed across the restaurant, the waiter tipped the bottle over Dexter's glass for the obligatory taste. Dexter swirled the wine around in the bottom of the glass, took a sniff and sipped. The hairs on the back of his neck stood on end. Goosebumps started to form and disappear, creating a flowing sensation down his back. Despite it being the best wine Dexter had ever tasted, he still questioned whether it was worth the money. Dexter marked his approval with a nod of the head to the waiter who poured the Copelands each a glass before placing the bottle down in the centre of the table.

'And what would you like to eat?' asked the waiter, raising his nose in the air.

'We would both like to try the three course set menu – here,' said Dexter, pointing to the menu.

'Very good, sir,' replied the waiter and removed the menus from the table.

The waiter clicked his heel on the floor again before walking away with the menus tucked under his right arm. Dexter sat back in his chair and admired Jules.

'You look beautiful,' said Dexter.

'Here's to my successful husband,' replied Jules, raising her glass.

They took a sip of wine each, absorbed the expense on their tongues and gazed into each other's eyes. The candlelight reflected the beautiful couple, flickering light across their faces like a hazy film noir. The aroma of garlic and tomato from the gazpacho soup broke the hypnotic trance between them when the waiter placed the starters in front of them, served in tall thin glasses with basil leaves balanced on the rim. Dexter picked up the long spoon from the table hoping the starter would taste as rich as it smelt. Dexter skimmed the surface and collected a small amount of soup on his spoon. The sound of Dexter's mobile ringing in his trouser pocket made him jump. He dropped the spoon into his glass and breathed out an irritated sigh.

'Typical! Who the hell is calling me now?'

Dexter knew he should have left his mobile at home or at least put it on silent.

'Hey, mate. I'm at the club szhooting some fwames and hitting szome balls. You wanna join?'

It was Chris. He had forgotten all about Dexter's celebratory dinner and Jules could hear his loud slurred voice from across the table. Her squinted screwed up face cut through the romantic candlelight. Dexter tried his best to ignore Jules's annoyance but couldn't ignore her pouted lips that moved and spelt the words "hang up now".

'No. Sorry, Chris. I can't. I'm out celebrating with Jules, remember?'

Jules rolled her eyes to the sky and swiped her glass of wine from the table.

'Zzelebrating? Yeah. Yeah. Yeah. That'z right. Yeah.

Zzelebrating. Ha! Ha! Yeah. Now I wemember. Look, wonz you're done with that, you can meet me yeah? You gotta man. I need my pool par'ner. Ha! Ha! Yeah?'

Dexter pulled his mobile further away from his ear and could have sworn he felt a globule of Chris's spit hit him in the face. Although he should have taken the advice of his wife's body language, he couldn't just hang up on his best man. They had been friends right from the first day of university. Dexter couldn't believe the drunken man on the other end of the phone was the same Chris. The Chris that didn't play video games through fear of getting arthritis. The Chris that didn't smoke or drink. The Chris that didn't take drugs. Dexter often wondered whether Chris had started taking drugs. It would have explained the odd behaviour but Dexter didn't want to believe it. It was hard enough to believe Chris was an alcoholic let alone a drug addict too.

'Chris. Chris. Look, I can't come and meet you, I'm having a VERY special dinner with Jules. Do you understand? VERY special.'

Jules had finished the gazpacho soup and licked the spoon, clinking it down hard on the plate. Dexter glanced at the empty tall glass, stained with the slither of garlic tomato. His starter still stood almost untouched. Jules's pretty smiling face that had started the evening had turned to a thundering grimace.

'Yeah. Yeah. Yeah. But you'll be here later on yeah?

Come on, you know you want to, you know you want to man.'

'Listen, mate. I really have to go. We'll speak soon, OK? Bye!'

Dexter hated hanging up on Chris but feared Jules's reaction if he had continued the conversation. After Dexter had tucked his mobile into his trouser pocket, he dived his spoon back into the gazpacho soup and tried his best to gloss over the interference.

'Mmmm. This is really good. How do they make it taste as good as this?'

Dexter looked at Jules, hoping that he had deflected an upcoming argument about Chris. Jules remained silent and watched her husband polish off the starter before opening her mouth.

'I don't know why you bother,' said Jules, 'he's not worth it. He needs help.'

Dexter sighed in resignation.

'Jules. Please. He's my friend. My best friend. Don't friends help each other?'

'Yes but the problem is that he can't help himself.'

Dexter drank his wine glass down to the stem, leaving a small pool of red wine to form a filled circle in the bottom. The reappearance of the slicked back haired waiter acted as a blessing for Dexter. He breathed a sigh of relief when the waiter took away the empty gazpacho soup glasses.

'Everything ok?' asked the waiter, looking at Dexter.

'Yes. They were really good.'

The waiter nodded at the couple and walked off towards the kitchen to fetch the main courses. Jules rested her hand on her wine glass and continued to let off steam.

'He just doesn't seem to want to change. I mean, have you seen him sober in the last six months because I haven't.'

'Ok. Ok. Look. I've hung up on him. Let's just enjoy this evening. It's not about Chris. It's about us, isn't it?'

Jules shrugged her shoulders and took a sip of wine. Dexter reached for the bottle in the middle of the table and filled his glass. An uncomfortable silence fell between the couple and Dexter hoped the argument wouldn't turn the special evening into just an evening.

The waiter approached the table with the main courses, placing them between the knives and forks. The powerful aroma from the pepper-root, coupled with the halibut coated in garlic breadcrumbs, reminded the Copelands of their appetite. Dexter took the first mouthful, and looked at Jules for her reaction to the masterchef meal.

'This is great.'

The Copelands relaxed, eating mouthful after mouthful of the best food money could buy. The exquisite quality of the main course had diffused the argument they were having. Dexter was relieved that the special evening was back on track. After finishing the main course, Dexter and Jules kissed, toasted their successes and plotted their children's future careers as train driver and astronaut. Dexter smiled at Jules feeling elated at his success as writer and now film director. He was as happy for Jules as he was with himself when she announced a possible promotion to manager at the bank. Dexter felt a high that he had not experienced before. He was on top of the world with his perfect wife by his side. By the time the crème brûlées arrived at their table, the restaurant had reached full capacity. The slicked back hair of the waiter had come unstuck and small strands of hair had started to windscreen wipe across his sweaty forehead.

'Bon appetite!' commented the waiter, as he rushed away, failing to click his heel.

Jules plunged her spoon into the hard shiny surface of the chocolate crème brûlée. It cracked revealing velvety smooth liquid chocolate underneath. Jules paused from eating and looked at Dexter.

'Well, I feel sorry for Kate. That's all I can say. I've a good mind to tell her to just walk away and take Chuck with her,' said Jules.

Dexter thought he had escaped. The meal had only acted as a temporary distraction from the topic of Chris. Jules had caught him off guard and made him feel as if the evening had the potential to be ruined once again.

'I thought we said we wouldn't talk about this.'

'Yes. We did but I'm just saying… I think she either needs to leave or Chris needs some help or both.'

The revelation of Jules's marital advice stopped Dexter from devouring the last spoonful of dessert.

'Well, I can see what you are saying,' said Dexter, 'but I just think he needs help. He can't do it without Kate and Chuck.'

'How many chances does the guy need? He screwed up rehab, he walked out of AA after just one meeting and he just continues to drink, party and god knows what else. It's got past the stage of help, Dexter.'

Dexter played with his dessert spoon, spinning it by the handle and then placed it into the empty bowl. Maybe his wife was right.

'Look. I know what you are saying but maybe just one more try. Maybe an intervention or something similar. I don't know. He's my friend, Jules. I don't want to desert him. He was the best man at our wedding, remember?'

'Do you really think he deserves another chance?' sighed Jules.

'Yes. Just one more chance. If he fails to come to his senses then that'll be it, I guess.'

Jules took another sip of wine and remained quiet. Dexter looked out of the restaurant's window to avoid the conversation. A patch of condensation from Dexter's breath hit the window. Heavy raindrops had started to hit the window signaling the start of a torrential downpour. The fluorescent street lights flickered in the puddles as cars drove past.

'Great! Rain!' said Dexter.

Dexter continued to look through the window, and caught sight of a dark figure standing on the street. Dexter watched the figure stagger from side to side, pointing a finger at him. The figure continued to stumble across the road towards the restaurant where a passing car beeped its horn and swerved to avoid hitting the shadow. As the figure continued to

walk like a toddler towards the restaurant, Dexter recognised who it was.

'Oh God!' remarked Dexter.

It was Chris.

CHAPTER 5

A day at Eastern View was drawing to a close and Chris felt shattered. It had been time spent with Martin sat by his side, asking question after question. It had worn Chris down to the point where he had started to ignore him.

'When you started, how long did it take you to reach the level you are at now? When do you wake up? When do you normally have lunch? When do you leave? Do you get paid for overtime and is expected that you work more than eight hours a day? Do you think you will go national? International? Are you married? Single? Kids?'

Chris had even avoided going to the toilet in fear of Martin following him in and comparing sizes.

'So what do you do in the evenings?'

'What everybody else does, mate. What everybody else does.'

Any answer that failed to satisfy Martin's mind with correct information made him ask even more questions. Chris continued to try and fob him off. Despite Martin's frail, thin and almost grey complexion, he seemed to have a thick skin that protected him from Chris's sarcasm towards him.

'What are you doing this evening?'

Chris didn't want to answer Martin's direct question. He had already spent a working day with him and he didn't want that to spill over into the evening. Chris had made plans to go to the pool

hall, shoot a few games and drink. The earlier conversation with Dexter had soured him. As far as Chris was concerned, Dexter was turning his back on their friendship, his best man, and on Chris Wilkinson, the guru.

Chris thought back to old times. The pool hall had always been the place where Chris and Dexter had met after a hard day at university. Dexter wasn't good at pool and was easy to beat. It wasn't a competition, just friendly games between two friends. When Dexter ordered the occasional beer, Chris had always been the one to offer health advice.

'You should watch what you drink. Do you know what it does to your insides?'

It was a line Chris repeated often and a line Dexter tended to disregard.

Chris longed for the old days to return but Dexter now had responsibilities. Family responsibilities. His career. It was rare that he agreed to meet Chris at the pool hall anymore. Chris missed the days were they would relax, talk and have a laugh.

'What are you doing this evening?' repeated Martin.

'I'm going home. I'm going to eat, sleep and then wake up tomorrow morning to go to work again.'

Martin nodded. Chris hoped that the abrupt answer would dam up Martin's constant flow of prying questions.

'Well, that's it for today,' said Chris, turning off the monitors, 'I've had enough.'

Martin remained in his seat looking as if he was waiting for further instructions. Chris raised himself from his seat, put on his coat and Thinsulate thermal hat, tapped a cigarette from its packet, trapping it between his fingers and looked at Martin. He wondered if he had a home to go to.

'We're done for the day, mate. You're free to go.'

A knee-jerk reaction sprang Martin into collecting his belongings in a frenzy. Chris walked away from his desk, unwilling to wait and left Eastern View's building. He walked outside past the main entrance and was hit by minus degree wind chills. He had not succeeded in ditching Martin who had followed him out of the building. The condensation fogged Chris's glasses, slowing his pace to a stop. The small break in Chris's pace allowed him to attempt to light the cigarette clenched between his fingers. Chris pressed down on his lighter's button several times, creating sparks that flew into the wind and were lifted away from the gas that would light his stick of nicotine. Frustrated and desperate for a smoke, Chris needed a solution to his problem.

'Martin? Come here for a second.'

Jumping at the chance to get closer to the man he had called a guru, Martin stepped up to Chris and smiled. Was Chris about to offer Martin some expert advice for working within the media industry? Praise for the work he had done today? Martin was expectant of some expert advice. Chris crouched over, cupped one hand over his cigarette, lit a flame with the other and used Martin as a human windbreaker. One puff of smoke later and Chris had eased his addiction into submission.

'Thanks mate!' said Chris, walking away fast.

Martin half-skipped the distance it took to catch Chris up, inhaling second-hand cigarette smoke. Chris couldn't lose Martin no matter what he tried.

'So. What are we going to work on tomorrow?'

'I don't know, Martin. I don't know. Look, I don't want to talk about work. It's been a long day and I want to relax, you know? Relax?'

Martin didn't ask any further questions for the rest of their walk. Chris was glad for what he called dead air, a muted silence that only a disc jockey would hate. The pool hall would dissuade him from spending the whole evening with him. It had one of the roughest reputations in town highlighted by broken windows, a lack of security and suspicious looking clientele. It wasn't a place for Martin.

Chris walked into the pool hall with his new protégé, wondering when Martin would turn tail and run. Hooking his jacket on a stand, Chris struck up a conversation with the owner of the hall who stood behind an opening in a wall. Chris was a regular customer and the two would quite often exchange pleasantries. The owner chewed gum and sat under a dim light that accentuated his yellow wrinkled face.

'The same table?' asked the owner.

Chris nodded his approval as the owner handed him two warped cues, sporting nicks and divots.

'I hope you play,' said Chris, looking at Martin.

'I sometimes play at college,' replied Martin, 'but I'm not very good.'

The owner scanned Martin from head to toe and failed to raise a smile. Chris took the cues, walked into the main hall and towards his favourite table that was still in good condition. An earlier fight had left one of the table's baize ripped and splintered with glass from the smashed overhead light. A gang of uncouth looking youths stopped playing and looked in Chris's direction. Tipping his head back, Chris acknowledged them as if he knew them. Sneaky, who used the pool hall as his own backyard, flicked cigarette ash onto the floor, turned away and readied himself for his next shot.

'Don't they have a non-smoking policy here?' asked Martin.

Sneaky interrupted his shot, broke away from his game and scowled at Martin.

'What the fuck did that shithead say?' asked Sneaky of his friends.

The gang of friends stood up and started to hurl insults at Martin who gulped. His arms and legs started to shake.

'I think you need to leave, Martin,' said Chris, tilting his head towards the exit.

It had worked better than Chris could have planned it. If Martin wanted to live to see his nineteenth birthday, Chris knew he would have to leave. Sneaky started to edge towards their table, thumping the wrong end of his cue into his grubby hands. Martin gave his cue to Chris in a flurry, summoned his jellied legs to half run out of the exit and down the street, not daring to look behind him. Sneaky continued to approach the table.

'Who was that scrawny fuck?' asked Sneaky.

'He was nobody,' replied Chris.

'More like a fuckin' nobody,' shouted Sneaky. Reducing his voice to a normal volume, Sneaky jerked his head back slightly and continued. 'I've got something for ya.'

Chris rested the warped cues on his favourite table and followed Sneaky into the toilets. An overpowering odour of urine, feces, sick and disinfectant filled the air. Scribbled profanities defaced each toilet cubicle door as if the world had run out of writing paper. One of the toilets had been blocked by hand towels causing it to overflow and line the floor with light brown polluted water. A broken window allowed the howling wind to breeze in through the cracks, freezing the room.

Chris looked into the mirror above a blocked cracked sink. Sneaky had his back towards him until he turned around fast and clutched Chris hard by the throat.

'What the fuck was the story on the camera shop raid doing on the news? You little shit. I fuckin' told you that I hate publicity. You made me look like a fuckin' idiot. I ain't no fuckin' idiot,' spat Sneaky.

Chris had seen the demonic, evil look on Sneaky's scarred face before. It had been when they had first met.

*****

Chris and Dexter walked into the pool hall with the intention of playing nine frames, gulping down a beer to relax after a hard day's work.

'I can only stay for a couple of games, mate. Jules and the boys are expecting me home.'

Chris shrugged his shoulders in a nonchalant manner as if Dexter's family were unimportant.

Dexter fired the cue ball into the triangle of spots and stripes, and Chris noticed two men playing in a corner of the hall. Chris whispered his concerns to Dexter as they exchanged turns. Sneaky, the roughest looking of the men, continued to stare his disapproval at Dexter, which made him miss every shot.

'I think I might leave after this game. I don't like the look of him,' whispered Dexter to Chris.

'I don't blame you. I need to take a piss anyway,' said Chris, finishing another beer, 'see you later!'

Dexter grabbed his coat from a chair by the pool table and left. Chris placed his cue on the table, walked into the toilet and stood by the urinal to relieve himself. Sneaky entered the toilet shortly after Chris, carrying a cue. He stood beside Chris, snorted and splashed him on purpose with his piss.

'What the hell are you doing?' remarked Chris.

Sneaky forced the pool cue up against Chris's windpipe and prevented air from entering his lungs. The force of Sneaky's attack knocked his glasses into an unusable angle.

'What the fuck were you whispering about earlier, eh? Tell me. What were you fuckin' whispering about?' snarled Sneaky through gritted teeth and a clenched face.

'Nothing. Nothing. I promise. We usually use that table,' squealed Chris.

'Yeah? Well, we're using it. Got it?'

Two tattooed teardrops under Sneaky's right eye could have been the last image Chris had seen if he hadn't acted as fast as he did.

'Look, you can take what I have in my back pocket. T..t..t..take it all. If you want money…'

Sneaky loosened his grip on the snooker cue and copped a feel of Chris's back pocket. The redness on Chris's face started to mellow and return to a normal human colour. Sneaky removed a zip lock bag from Chris's pocket containing a clump of greenish brown hash and his wallet.

'So you like drugs, eh? Fuckin' junky!' said Sneaky, dropping his cue on the slippery floor, 'I think we can come to some arrangement here, you know.'

'Arrangement?' said Chris, securing his glasses.

'Yeah. I'm your new dealer.'

'Ok. Yeah. Erm..'

Chris looked Sneaky in the eye and could sense that he wouldn't leave the toilet alive if he dared to say no. Sneaky grabbed Chris by the shirt lapels and tightened his grip. Sneaky flipped open Chris's wallet with his other hand and spotted Chris's driving licence.

'Yeah... Chris Wilkinson,' said Sneaky, 'because if you don't agree to my fuckin' terms - I'll find you!'

Sneaky slapped Chris across the chops. The impact made Chris jump backwards and almost slip on the floor. Sneaky took the notes out of his wallet and tucked them into his trouser pocket, along with the haul of hash.

'You'd fuckin' better come back here otherwise you won't be fuckin' coming back at all. You fuckin' got me?'

Sneaky threw the wallet at Chris, watched Chris catch it and left the toilet. Chris breathed hard through his crushed windpipe that felt as if it had been permanently damaged. He had never been threatened at the pool hall before and didn't want it to happen again. The thought of using another pool hall crossed Chris's mind but was snubbed out by the small promise of Sneaky appearing on his doorstep with a Molotov cocktail in one hand and a match in the other. It didn't bear thinking about. Sneaky had reassured him that he could find out where he lived. It could have been a ruse but Chris couldn't take that risk. He decided to keep on visiting the pool hall out of blackmail and pure fear.

*****

'I didn't even know it was you. Honest. If I had known, I would have suggested to pull the story completely,' said Chris, 'I have to report on these things. It's my job.'

'Well, I don't give a fuck if it is your job, you make sure you don't do it a-fuckin'-'gain.'

Sneaky released his tight grip and reached into his pocket.

'Here. I got this.'

Chris took a bag from Sneaky's choking hand and looked at it. The light brownish tinge to the leaves looked odd and Chris could tell that the hash was well below par quality.

'I haven't got all fuckin' day. Where's the money?'

Chris knew that he was paying for dried up banana skins and handed over several crumpled notes without an argument. The money looked as if it had been through the wash, tumble dried and left for dead. Sneaky unravelled the notes and checked the amount.

'Where's the rest?'

'What?'

'Yeah, the fuckin' rest. This isn't enough. My price has gone up since last week.'

'Come on....'

'Come on? What the fuck?'

Sneaky leant forwards and started to choke Chris again.

'I'll show you fuckin' come on...'

'OK. OK,' gurgled Chris, 'take another twenty, take another twenty.'

Chris fumbled his fingers through his wallet, extracted another twenty and waved it in front of Sneaky's eyes. Sneaky snatched the twenty and released his grip.

'That'll fuckin' do.' Sneaky slipped the money into his back pocket and walked out of the toilet.

Chris looked into the new toilet mirror. Tired, drawn out bags had formed and rested under each eye. Chris adjusted his glasses, wiped the sweat away from his forehead and left the toilet and the pool hall with haste, avoiding any further contact with Sneaky.

*****

Chris settled his lips on the side of a beer glass and sucked up the remains of his sixth beer. A small, distorted, jaded logo of a ghosted bird marked on the bottom of the glass told Chris that it was time for a seventh or maybe something stronger. He hadn't decided.

'What will it be Chris?' asked the barman, collecting the empty glass.

'I dunno. I dunno. Watcha got? Watcha got? I'm thinking…. Brandy… yeah.. Brandy. A lil' fire.'

The barman was familiar with Chris who had inhabited The Belvedere almost every evening for the last month. The brown stained beer mats, plastered to the bar through fermented soft drinks and beer, had not been replaced since the pub opened. Sticky footprints, squelching from the feet of new customers, were the result of every cleaner that had quit the job after two days. Batches of Jurassic food, usually accompanied by the sound of laughing kitchen staff, were served at a snail's pace if served at all. Health and Safety had given the pub three months to clean up their culinary act or face closure amidst hails of protests from loyal drinkers who were responsible for keeping it afloat. The pub had often been described as a spit and sawdust pub, not for the likes of Kate and Chuck. The barman served Chris a dubious short measure of brandy, who assumed the drunken Chris was too far gone to realise the missing millilitres.

'Here's mud in your eye,' said Chris, holding the glass aloft.

Chris downed the shot, which made him grimace

as the two differing worlds of fading beer and hot brandy collided. Displaying the ability of a Russian gymnast on the beam, Chris jerked himself back onto the edge of his seat, saving himself from falling onto the floor. The barman rang the bell for last orders and served Chris another dubious low-level shot of brandy. Throwing the shot down the back of his throat, Chris ejected himself from his ripped bar stool, threw a tenner down on the bar and staggered towards the exit.

Chris couldn't feel the freezing air when he left The Belvedere. The last shot of brandy and copious amount of alcohol he had consumed had made him immune to the chill. Chris stood in the middle of the street and pondered over the conundrum of making his way home. The heavy rain pelted him, soaking through his less than waterproof coat. The familiar town centre, that had filled up many of his news reports and where he had lived since birth, had become a blurred labyrinth of street corners and fuzzy street lamps. Chris stepped out into the street, splashing his foot down into a deep roadside puddle that went up his shin. An angry horn sounded from a crazy taxi driver who swerved to avoid Chris stumbling across the street. A gust of wind lifted the rain away as Chris made it across to the other side of the street. Chris stuttered and came to a halt at a street corner where a bakery had stood for many years. The right leg of his rain soaked trousers had started to chill his shin. The rain bounced off the thick painted black and white stripes of a pedestrian crossing that stretched out before him. A red man seemed to wave at Chris as he looked up. A green man danced to the sound of the mechanical clicks. Chris took a step backwards and tried to comprehend what he thought he could see through his beer goggles and the rain. The fancy restaurant on the other side of the street and pedestrian crossing had caught his attention. Chris squinted his eyes and could see two hazy figures, one of which looked like Dexter. Chris was certain it was Dexter but couldn't recognise who he was with. The red man of the pedestrian crossing blinked again, reducing the sound of the mechanical click to a steady slow rhythm. Chris lingered on the edge of the pavement before deciding that it wasn't Jules that Dexter was having a romantic dinner with. It was another woman. Chris squinted again to make sure but came to the same conclusion. It was definitely another woman.

The szheating baaztard, thought Chris, I'll giz him a piz of my mind. A real talking to. He needzsh it.

Chris ignored the red man and stepped onto the pedestrian crossing, placing one uncoordinated foot in front of the other, wobbling backwards at regular intervals.

He'z not gonna get away with thiz. You'z not gonna ezcape from thiz. You'z ain't so perfect after all, thought Chris.

An emergency stop screeched an approaching car

to a standstill. Black tyre marks painted the road with the spot where Chris stood in the middle of the street.

'What the hell is wrong with you? Arsehole!' shouted the motorist through a gap in his wound down window.

The less than sympathetic chants of the angry motorist failed to make Chris move. Out of frustration, the motorist turned his steering wheel, drove around Chris and continued to shout as he passed by. Chris remained unmoved. He squinted at the restaurant window again and tried to focus.

'Baztard. Baztard. Baztard,' spluttered Chris, 'You're not worthy of Jules, mate. You ain't.'

Chris walked closer to the restaurant window, he recognised that it was Jules after all. How could he have got it so wrong? Chris lowered his accusing finger and muted the volume of his drunken chants. Chris slumped to a sitting position on the curb, held his head in his hands and started to roll his cheeks like pastry dough. He could have sworn it was another woman.

'I don't believe it.. I juzt can't...'

The noise of the angry car horn and the screech of tyres had attracted the attention of the restaurant's guests. It had got Dexter's attention. Shocked and appalled at what he was seeing, Dexter left his warm restaurant seat to attend to his friend. Jules looked to the heavens, shook her head and turned away.

'Chris? Chris? What the hell are you doing?' asked Dexter, 'God! Look at the state of you.'

'Dexter to the rescue. Ha! Ha!' said Chris, leaning on Dexter for support.

'For God's sake. I'll call a taxi. You need to go home Chris. You hear me?'

'Yeah. Yeah. Go home. Go home, ha ha! Yeah.'

A taxi stopped by the roadside after Dexter had called for it. Dexter guided Chris to the taxi's open door and shoved him onto the back seat.

'He'd better not puke. I just had this cab valeted yesterday,' stated the driver.

'I'm sorry I can't guarantee that but he doesn't live too far away from here. I don't think he'll vomit in that short space of time. Here, take this,' said Dexter handing the taxi driver twenty pounds, 'keep the change.'

Blurred street lights flashed by as Chris looked out of the taxi window on the way home. The taxi driver glanced at him at every available opportunity in the rear view mirror, checking for any signs of a gag reflex.

'Fuck it. Fuck it,' said Chris, over and over.

'Do me a favour mate. Could you please be quiet? I know it's a small drive home but I'd rather drive safely, especially in this bloody weather,' said the driver, peering out at the rain-drenched road through his frantic hi-speed windscreen wipers.

Chris crawled out of the taxi as soon as it had stopped outside his house, walked jagged towards his front door, fumbled the key into the lock and slithered into a comfortable position on the sofa. It would be his bed for the night.

CHAPTER 6

Chris awoke to a blurred rectangle that he could see on the coffee table. A wet patch of dribble stained the sofa where his head had been resting. Another late night binge had been the last straw for Kate. He tried to remember the events from yesterday evening. He remembered standing in the middle of the street. It had been raining. Somebody from the restaurant had helped him but he couldn't remember who the person was. Chris lifted his head from the sofa pillow and adjusted his glasses. The blurred rectangle was an envelope with his name written on it in Kate's handwriting. The Wilkinson house was eerily quiet.

'Kate? Chuck?' shouted Chris to the empty air, 'Kate?'

Chris waited a minute before the lack of replies confirmed he was alone. He assumed that Kate had gone to work and Chuck had left for school. He picked up the envelope, opened it and began reading a letter.

You bastard. After you promised you wouldn't get

drunk again - what do you do? Go out and get drunk again. Just in case you are wondering, I've left you and taken Chuck with me. Don't even bother trying to contact me.

We're done.

Chris shook his head, read the first sentence again, and tried to comprehend what he had just read.

Left me? thought Chris, I am Chris Wilkinson, top TV reporter for Eastern View, a pillar of the community who has served it for the last twenty years, bringing everybody important news stories. A person people can trust. A guru. Left me?

In haste and anger, Chris screwed up the letter with both hands, forming a tight compact paper ball and threw it into the kitchen. He watched it bounce before landing next to the rubbish bin. Chris plucked his filthy glasses away from his eyes, breathed on the lenses and gave the lenses a quick rub with his shirt. An evanescent neon light from his mobile reflected off the glass of the living room table. He had missed a call from Dexter.

Dexter. Of course, it was Dexter who helped me last night. He's probably calling me to see how I am.

Chris returned Dexter's call.

'Chris. I was wondering when you would call. What the hell were you doing yesterday night?'

'Kate's left me.'

A brief silence fell. Dexter breathed a despondent sigh into Chris's ear. Chris ignored it and waited for Dexter's reaction.

'Well, what did you expect Chris? What is wrong with you? Have you any memory of yesterday night at all? Yesterday night? Any memory? What the hell are you playing at?'

The barrage of short stabbing questions took Chris by surprise. He had expected his best friend to be more supportive towards him and show him some pity. Chris had had enough of Kate's constant nagging over the recent months and now Dexter had taken up the mantle. It was wearing Chris out.

'You almost ruined our special evening yesterday. I don't know what is wrong with you Chris. You were never like this before. You could have been run over yesterday - Christ!'

A mumble emerged from Chris's dry mouth, forming an apology that Dexter couldn't hear. Every statement Dexter barked hit Chris like a boxer connecting a right hook with his chin.

'You need some help.'

Smack!

'You need to sort your life out.'

Wallop!

'You've got responsibilities. Be a responsible adult.'

Out for the count. Chris Wilkinson felt that he would never get up off the canvas.

'Look, we've known each other for years, Chris. We're good friends. You can talk to me and if you can't do that, go and talk to a professional.'

Chris listened to his friend's rant, sucked in a deep breath and held it.

'Don't you think Kate and Chuck deserve better? Well, don't you? And…..'

Chris exhaled the large breath into the phone's receiver, hung up and cut Dexter off before he could finish his next sentence.

Dexter has kept all the praise for his writing and screenplays to himself. It hasn't even crossed his mind to even mention my perfect screenplay to any of his contacts like a true friend would. He's too busy becoming successful. Too busy filming. Too busy travelling to the USA and Italy. Too busy for me, thought Chris.

As Chris moved from the sofa and into the kitchen, the pulse from his hangover became a hard throb, making him stop and collect himself. He needed a painkiller. He reached into a cupboard and found an empty box. He would have to put up with his pulsating headache for the time being.

Chris looked down at the floor. Kate's crumpled letter had started to uncurl, revealing the words Chris couldn't understand. Chris snatched the letter up from the floor, squeezed it into a Ping-Pong ball sized pebble and threw it out of the back door as hard as he could. Driving rain from dismal heavy black clouds pelted the letter as it flew through the air and landed in a muddy puddle.

The deafening silence of the living room reminded Chris that Kate and Chuck were gone. Chris sat down on the sofa and and lit an earlier prepared joint, blowing smoke rings into the living room. Kate wasn't around to nag him. Chuck wasn't around for Chris to set an example of a good father. Chris would not be punished for his filthy habits. Chris leant back in the sofa, feeling mellowed and relaxed. He was sure Kate and Chuck would be back. The joint burned halfway towards Chris's fingers before his mobile rang. Chris cursed, stubbed the joint out and saved it for later.

'Chris? Is that you?'

'Yes?' Chris didn't recognise the voice.

'Thank God I have reached you. We have a breaking news story about a farm that is the home of the first hen in the UK to lay a double egg.' Martin paused between words to catch his breath through the excitement. 'A Siamese egg. Can you believe it?'

It was the enthusiastic voice of Martin, a voice Chris didn't want to hear at any time, let alone this morning. Chris sighed at the prospect of covering yet another pointless local news story about a Siamese egg, especially in his state.

'The term is conjoined, Martin. Conjoined.'

Chris twiddled a cigarette between his thumb and fingers and wondered why a simple intern would be calling him. Who had given him permission to ring him and who had divulged his mobile number? Martin was already at the news story's scene. He had beaten him to it. Although Chris thought the story to be pointless, he was the man in charge, not Martin.

Martin Lawson, the stick insect with about as much charisma as a potato, is after my job. That jumped up little upstart. I'm going to have to nip this in the bud, thought Chris.

Chris didn't care less about the conjoined egg unless it was going to improve the future of his full English breakfast. Chris thought a story about a two headed chicken may have made a more interesting news story if the egg were to hatch, but it would only fill up a broadcast before the weather report.

'Look. Don't do anything yet. Wait until I get there.'

Chris hung up on Martin, lit the cigarette he had been toying with, walked into the kitchen and locked the back door. Kate's letter had vanished from the muddy puddle. Chris looked from left to right and

76

couldn't spot it in the garden at all. Had the wind blown it over the fence and into the neighbour's garden? Chris hoped not. His professional reputation would lay in tatters if any of the neighbours found out.

Give up drinking? That starts today. No more alcohol for me, thought Chris, That's right. You heard me brain. Career? What do I do about that? I have Martin to take down a peg or two. He has that coming to him. Siamese egg! I ask you! He doesn't know what makes a good news story in the same way I do. I don't want that spotty geek muscling in on my job. But he is the boss's grandson. Damn the boss. The future? I've written the best screenplay that's ever been written or will be written but Dexter, the so-called good friend I've got, won't put in a good word for me. Says he is too busy. Arsehole.

Chris left the family home, jangling his car keys in front of him. Chris pulled away and had puffed his cigarette into extinction by the time he reached the farm's address.

Chris pulled up outside the small farm and parked. A combined smell of putrid sheep dip and festering manure made Chris heave and almost vomit the instant he opened his car door. A buoyant Martin bounced towards him, waving his arms around in excited semaphores, wanting Chris to follow him as quick as possible. Chris paid little attention to Martin as he trundled behind him.

'Ar! I s'pose you want to see the egg do you, me duck?' asked the farmer.

An elderly farmer with a grey steel beard, old green army hat and manure stained clothes, outstretched his hand. Martin greeted the farmer with a smile and a shake of the hand. Chris managed to produce a half smile and avoided the handshake.

'Ar! Come with me. Come with me.'

Chris and Martin were shown the way to the hen-house that promoted free-range hens.

'Tasty ecological eggs. Ar! You won't find better!'

'Fantastic!' said Martin.

The farmer guided Chris and Martin to the Siamese egg that had been placed in a cordoned off area, away from the other hens. The film crew had set up their gear and had been ready for an hour. They all stared at Chris when he took a quick look at the egg.

Christ! This is boring. This reminds me of a nativity scene but with only one wise man - me! thought Chris.

'How should we do this, Chris? Should we just film the egg first and then the farmer or maybe start with the hen that laid it? I was thinking of starting with a pan shot across the barn, showing all the chickens in action and then cut to the mother hen here, then the egg and then the farmer. What do you think, Chris? What are your thoughts? What would you do?'

Martin's relentless quick fire questioning irritated Chris as it had done the day before.

'Well, first, I think you need to take it easy, ok? We don't want to upset the hens or make the egg hatch prematurely, do we?' answered Chris, 'I think you really need to watch what I do for this report, so maybe, if you can, could you stand over there somewhere?'

Chris pointed to a spot outside the security zone and in amongst the brood of pecking chickens. Scowling lines wrinkled Martin's bitter disappointed face. He was just a mere spectator. Geoff, Eastern View's veteran cameraman, shrugged his shoulders as Martin walked over to the other unimportant chickens.

'Right. What I think we should do here is to focus on the egg for a start and then pan across the barn. We'll then interview the farmer, what does it mean to hmm, blah, blah etc, etc, and then cut back to me making a witty remark at the end. How does that sound?' asked Chris.

Martin looked at Geoff who raised his eyebrows aghast at Chris's stage directions. They were Martin's ideas. After fifteen minutes of filming, Chris had had enough of talking to the smelly farmer that spoke with a strange accent.

'We'll just wrap things up here now,' said Chris.

Martin continued to watch from the sidelines as Chris finished the report.

'A miracle has happened here at Brickley Farm today. An egg laid by Henrietta the hen has caused quite a stir…'

Martin turned his back away from the action and plodded towards the entrance to the barn with his head down. Chickens flapped away from his shuffling feet, upset at him for breaking the rhythm of their constant pecking. Chris watched Martin walk into the distance as he wrapped up the report and the camera crew lowered their cameras. Chris hurried to catch Martin up and placed a hand on his shoulder, pulling Martin backwards.

'Did you see that, Martin? That's how to compile a report. What did you think? Did you learn anything from me today?'

Martin bit his tongue and tried to ignore Chris's condescending attitude towards him.

'Yes. I think I have learnt a lot today. More than I thought I would,' snarled Martin.

'That's great! We'll go through and edit it all when we get back,' said Chris.

Thumping his hand on Martin's shoulder twice, Chris walked on ahead of his deflated protégé, knowing he had put him back in his place.

*****

'Chris! Come in. Make yourself comfortable,' said the boss of Eastern View, pointing to an executive leather chair in front of him, 'How are things going with Martin?'

'I think it's going well. He said to me that he has learnt more than he thought he would, so you can't get better praise than that!' replied Chris.

'Well, Martin has spoken to me about his experience so far and he feels that he isn't getting a fair shot at compiling a report.'

'Oh? Really? Are you sure? He didn't say that to me.'

Chris shifted in the leather seat that blew a raspberry every time he moved.

'He wants a fair crack at compiling a report and as far as understand, that hasn't happened. I don't want his eagerness and passion for television news to evaporate before he's even had the chance to do anything. You must remember what it was like when you first started here.'

Chris had got the job at Eastern View straight after leaving university. His qualifications and work examples had been enough for the boss to employ him right then and there. No work experience. Martin, on the other hand, was being shown preferential treatment.

81

Mr Lawson pulled the shots and Martin was his grandson. Even though Chris believed he had been generous in giving Martin all the editing work he could, it wasn't enough. Martin wanted more. He wanted to report. He wanted Chris's job.

'Sure. I guess. There's no harm in that I guess, sure,' said Chris, grinding his teeth together.

'Good. That's all.'

Chris left the boss's office with his feathers ruffled.

That spotty idiot will not get my job. No way! thought Chris, Who does he think he is? So, he wants to report on a news story does he? I'll make sure he gets all the boring stories. There are plenty of them. He'll want to give up his dream of being a news presenter after that.

Chris got into his car, revved the engine once, pulled away and continued to think.

*****

By the time Chris had reached The Belvedere, he had already decided to break his own promise of abstaining from drinking. Hailing the bartender to pull the tap on his favourite stout, Chris made himself comfortable on a bar stool and waited for his pint to settle. He hadn't forgotten about the day's events. Martin had started to tread on his toes. It was dangerous territory for a person who was on work experience.

During a lull in the background noise, Chris heard his mobile ring. It was Dexter who had tried to reach him several times but without any success.

'Yesh?'

'Chris? It's Dexter. Where are you?'

'I'm at The Bellydeer. The Bevvydreer…'

'I can't believe it. I simply can't Chris. What the hell are you playing at? I was calling to see how you are and to talk to you about your drinking problem but I guess the drink has got to you first. What's going on with you Chris? You never used to….'

Chris saved his ears from the deluge of Dexter's righteousness by ending the call. Chris slurped down the malty remainder of his sixth pint. The evening still had some hours left for Chris to order a seventh, eighth, or maybe even twelfth pint.

Boy! I could hit Dexter if he was standing right here in front of me. I could. I know I could. How dare he reel off advice as if he knows best. A sodding expert. I am the almighty Chris Wilkinson who knows best. It should be me in the limelight, the famous film director, writer, author. Not him. Not Dexter. I could kill him right now if he was sitting here beside me, thought Chris.

Chris revelled in the first sip of his seventh pint

of stout that he always believed tasted better than the last few drops. As Chris tipped the glass back, his dark thoughts started to return. The prospect of actually murdering Dexter started to take hold.

I should be the rich and famous one. I was the one who wrote the screenplay. THE screenplay. The screenplay that he stole and recycled into something else. Bastard. Yes. I'll show him. I'll kill him. Get him out of the way. It'll be the best story Eastern View would ever report on. If I could actually film the murder taking place, I would be famous overnight. I would be in demand. Presenter of the News At Ten. My own chat show. God!

It had been the best idea he had had for days, months, years, maybe even a decade. He had always known that he was smart but this, he thought, was a work of a pure genius. Chris finished his seventh pint and scanned the array of bottles behind the bar.

'Hey! Can I get a whizky? What's the most expenshiv one you have?'

'Well, this one here,' said the bartender pointing upwards.

A small glass cabinet containing a bottle of mature whisky hung above the bar. The door had a small padlock attached to it, highlighting the whisky's value. The yellowing label featured an old styled font that Chris could see was at least one hundred years old, if not more. It looked expensive.

'I'll take a shot.'

'Are you sure? It costs thirty-four pounds a shot. Most people try to steal it rather than pay for it!' quipped the barman.

'Yeah. Yeah. Gimme. I have money.'

The bartender poured out a thin slip of dark yellow liquid into a shot glass. To Chris, it was a small price to pay to celebrate the definitive answer to most of his problems. Clutching the glass in his shaky hand, the bartender watched Chris with interest as he threw the liquid nectar down the back of his throat in one swift action.

'What's the occasion?'

Chris smiled and shrugged his shoulders.

'Just because…'

The whisky tasted sensational and smooth. Chris could feel its powerful warmth rise up from his chest and up into his throat. A small hint of almonds remained on Chris's tongue. It was the perfect celebration of the best idea he had ever had. He'd got it. The master plan that would solve everything.

CHAPTER 7

Unable to sleep through the night, Dexter felt he had woken almost every hour. He started to count the specks on the ceiling in the hope that he would drift into a deep sleep. The events of the ruined special evening and Chris cutting him off had irritated him. Dexter threw the tip of the duvet away to form a triangle and stepped out of bed.

Dexter made his way to the kitchen and switched on the kitchen lights, keeping them dimmed. He poured himself a glass of water from the filtered kitchen tap and swallowed it down all in one go. His face reflected in the window as he looked out into the garden. Dexter breathed a sigh, placed the glass on the granite surface worktop, and took a seat next to his laptop.

Dexter powered up his laptop, the glare from the screen brightened the room. The familiar jingle of the operating system sounded and Dexter hit the mute key with the reactions of a preying puma. He hoped that it hadn't woken any of his family as he settled down at the keyboard. The brilliant white glare from the word processor presented Dexter's unfinished screenplay where he had left it.

DETECTIVE CHASE

I don't know what we shou…

Delete.

DETECTIVE CHASE

I think we should hand…

Delete.

DETECTIVE CHASE

I'm not sure what we should do but I think we shou…

Dexter wasn't able to write and he couldn't sleep either.

'What's the matter, hun'?' said Jules who stood behind her husband.

'Christ!' said Dexter, almost jumping out of his seat, 'Nothing. I can't sleep. I thought I would try to write something but it's just not working.'

'Well, it's four in the morning.'

Dexter looked at Jules in the eye and then at the line he had written numerous times.

'It's Chris, isn't it? Is he the reason you can't sleep? Please tell me that it isn't.'

Dexter looked into his laptop's screen and tried to avoid the question.

'No. No. It's not. I don't even want to talk about him.'

'I don't know why on earth you are wasting time on him, Dexter.'

Jules's patience for Chris had run out. Dexter couldn't squeeze a word in between Jules's pauses for air as she continued to vent.

'I feel sorry for Kate and Chuck. They are the ones who are suffering. Chris isn't doing anything. He's made no attempt to sort his problems out and you still want to help him?'

'You've said all this before. I know.'

Jules frowned, bending the lines on her forehead downwards.

'Shhh! You'll wake the kids!'

Dexter shut down his laptop and closed the screen, reducing the room to dimmed light.

'Let's just try and get some sleep,' said Dexter.

'I'm awake. I won't be able to sleep now. I came out to go to the toilet and you were gone.'

'Ok. Ok. Let's just try and sleep, eh?'

Dexter and Jules returned to their bedroom, hissing whispers to each other as they walked down the hallway.

*****

An unwelcome alarm woke the Copelands after a troubled night of sleep. Dexter had managed to doze but Jules had remained wide awake. Dexter silenced the alarm, rolled over in Jules's direction and looked at his wife's back.

'Well, I got some sleep at least,' commented Dexter.

'Good for you,' snapped Jules. She was still angry, tired and irritable. 'I don't want you to have anything to do with Chris, maybe ever.'

'Now come on, Jules…'

'Don't 'come on' me, Dexter. Don't even go there. I don't want that drunk anywhere near us, near our kids, infecting us with his swearwords or alcoholism or god knows what else he does. You understand me? I don't want it.'

Dexter ignored his wife's last comment, raised himself out of bed and headed to the bathroom to brush his teeth. There was a short pause before Jules entered the room to do the same thing. The sound of the brushing cut through the silence. The large bathroom mirror made it hard for the couple to avoid exchanging glances. Everywhere they turned, they had to face each other. Jules returned her brush to its holder.

'I don't know why you want to support him. It's Kate and Chuck who need that. Not him. Not that loser,' spat Jules.

'He's not a loser. He's a friend in trouble. He needs help,' pleaded Dexter.

'He's had help, Dexter. He's had help. He's been to rehab so many times and been kicked out each time. We've been more than lenient, Dexter. I'm sticking to what I said. He's not welcome here and that's it.'

The constant bickering echoed down the halls of their modest designer house as the couple moved from the bathroom and into the living room. Their children, who had been awake for some time, both looked up and smiled at their parents. There was an immediate halt in their argument when the sight of their offspring caught them by surprise. The older of the two ran up to his parents clutching a drawing that he had been busy working on. The younger son followed two steps behind.

'What's this? Looks like we have an artist in the

91

family!' said Dexter, complimenting his son on his drawing of stick people with long necks.

The drawing had been set as homework by the private primary school that cost a small fortune. Dexter knew it would be time for the school run soon, a chance to escape the argument and change the subject from Chris to the kids. The morning's breakfast was going without a hitch. No bickering. No argument. Not even a mention of Chris Wilkinson. The focus was on the kids and what the day had in store for them.

'Come on. Time to get ready,' said Dexter, patting his son on the head.

The eldest son left the kitchen table and darted to the bathroom to get ready. Dexter placed his dishes in the dishwasher.

'I have a TV interview later so I don't know how long it will take,' said Dexter.

Jules nodded her head and picked up the youngest son. They stood by the front door and waved goodbye.

The journey to school was fraught with traffic problems. When Dexter pulled up outside the school, his son had missed registration by twenty minutes. In turn, Dexter was also twenty minutes late for his television interview. He pulled with haste away from the school with a screech of rubber, desperate to make up time.

Dexter drove into the studio's car park, dumped his car into a vacant parking space, ran into the studio's reception and announced his arrival.

'Hi! I'm Dexter Copeland,' spluttered Dexter.

'Mr Copeland. Yes. We have been expecting you. We are running slightly late so if you could take a seat over there, we'll be with you shortly. Would you like a tea or coffee or something?' said the receptionist.

'Erm, a tea, thanks.'

Dexter made himself at home, happy that he could relax, take a load off and put his feet up after his erratic driving. Dexter checked his mobile and had missed a number of calls from Chris. He rotated the mobile around in his hands and contemplated calling Chris back. Was it to apologise? Had he rung him by mistake? Against Dexter's best judgment and Jules's new anti-Chris law, he decided to call him back.

'Chris? You called? What did you want?' snapped Dexter.

A small cough after a few seconds of silence was the only sign that Chris was on the other end.

'Yes. Yes. I did call Dexter. Yes. A few times actually. I really called to say.. Erm.. Well.. What I wanted to say was…'

Dexter couldn't tell if Chris was suffering from his usual hangover but his nervous shaky voice made him assume that Chris had carried on where he had left off on the night of the special dinner; flat on his face, doubling up as a bear rug on the floor of The Belvedere.

'I'm sorry, Dexter. I'm sorry. I don't know what else to say,' apologised Chris.

The shock of a sincere sounding apology made Dexter's eyes open wide.

'I didn't mean to hang up you, you know, I was just..'

'Hungover?'

'No. I wasn't. Well, I guess, yeah, well, I…'

Chris's awkward conversation seemed to be a sign of some sincerity and it had been some time since Dexter had heard him sound like the best friend that he knew. Dexter stayed on the line waiting for Chris to apologise and really mean it.

'Look, I shouldn't really be calling you. I'm sorry,' said Chris.

'Say what you have to say.'

'I'm no good over the phone. Are you busy tonight?'

'Tonight? Yes, I think so. There is a lot going on. Why?'

'I was thinking of coming over to your place if that's ok? I think I need someone to talk to.'

Dexter thought about Chris visiting his house after Jules had stated that he was banned from their social circle. If Chris could make it to Dexter's house without being sidetracked and pulled into the nearest brewery by his demons, he had a chance of being saved. He had been given these chances before but Dexter had never heard him be so apologetic.

'I can't do tonight but how about Sunday? Jules will be at her parents with the kids. It was supposed to be my writing day but I can cut that in half. Sunday evening?'

Dexter had made an executive decision that went against everything Jules wanted. It would be hard to keep the meeting a secret. If she ever suspected or found out about any meeting, the spare bedroom would be prepared followed by an unspecified amount of cold shoulder.

'Sunday sounds great. Thanks, mate, I appreciate it.'

Dexter ended the conversation with a goodbye and wondered if he had just made a good decision. There wasn't any guarantee Dexter could fix Chris's problems but it was a good sign that he wanted to talk about them.

'Mr Copeland? They are ready for you now, if you could make your way down the corridor here, the studio is right at the end and through the double doors. The crew will give you instructions.'

The receptionist broke Dexter away from his dream of utopia and reminded him of the interview about his rags to riches life story. Dexter took a deep breath and felt nervous about his first national television appearance. He collected himself, adjusted his tie and walked towards the double doors.

CHAPTER 8

Martin looked through the spots of rain and into the camera lens, holding an old microphone sporting a blue misshaped foam cover. Chris had given him full power to compile a news report about a tannery that was laying half of its workforce off. The crew positioned Martin in front of the tannery's entrance, aware that the story was not important enough to feature on Eastern View's news programme. The rain started to drip over Martin's effective jacket hood, pelting droplets onto the damp microphone. Chris paid Martin no attention and was more interested in freeing up some memory on his mobile phone. By the time Martin had finished the report, he had only freed up half of his memory card.

'How was that, Chris?' asked Geoff, 'Chris?'

Chris looked up from his mobile and scowled at Geoff, annoyed by the disturbance.

'Oh? Yeah, I thought that was perfect, Martin. You've got a future for sure,' said Chris, returning to his phone.

Geoff tutted, shook his head and called the news story a wrap. Martin shook the excess water from his jacket, squelched the microphone back into the equipment box and stepped away from the tannery. He wanted to leave the scene of his first news report behind him. Not only had he got soaked standing in the pouring rain, he had also been told that the other more important reports would be broadcast. A robbery, a small charity gig and a school scandal were all stories that had happened that day but Chris had kept them all for himself. Martin had been a bystander in all of them and watched all of his chances to be on the news go down the drain.

As the day at Eastern View headquarters drew to a close, Chris reflected on his successful day of news reporting. He particularly liked his coverage of the school scandal where he had forced a microphone up the nose of the accused but it wasn't enough. The report would only be seen by a small percentage of the UK population. Chris wanted more. Martin snatched his damp coat off the hook and left the building, ignoring Chris on the way out. Chris didn't care. He had thought up a brilliant idea; an idea of such genius that couldn't fail to propel him into the spotlight in front of adoring fans.

The rain lashed down on Chris's windscreen as he made his way home. He pulled into the driveway of the empty Wilkinson home feeling calm, collected and unfazed by any hindrances. Chris slammed the front door behind him, ran up the stairs into the spare room and booted up his desktop. The wallpaper displayed an image of a Japanese cartoon character carrying a laser gun with folders dotted around the confines of the flat screen. Chris clicked through a folder of photographs until he found one that would serve his purpose. It was a year old photo of Dexter and Chris together after a rare night out at the bowling hall. Chris had drunk a few beers. Four strikes and three spares. He remembered winning a game that night. Chris picked up a pair of novelty scissors from an organiser on the desk and jabbed them through the photo, cutting it in half. Chris threw the image of himself into the bin, glanced at the photo of Dexter and flipped it over to write on the back.

Chris stuffed the photograph into his wallet without waiting for the ink to dry. He couldn't wait. He rushed down the stairs, out of the door, into his car, reversed out of the drive and towards his destination—the pool hall.

'You need two people to play a game of pool, you know!' joked the pool hall owner as Chris entered.

Chris reacted with a wry smile and refrained from removing his coat, passing the owner by.

'You also need to pay!'

The club was unusually busy for a weekday night. Chris looked around for Sneaky but couldn't spot him, only his accomplice, Jock.

'What the fuck do you want?' asked Jock as Chris approached.

'Where's Sneaky?'

'How the fuck should I know?'

'Look. I might have something that he would be interested in, if you know what I mean.'

'Well, he's not here is he?'

'Can you give him a call and get him to come down here?'

'What do I look like? His fucking secretary?' snapped Jock.

'Look. It would be worth your while too, if you know what I mean. Can you call him?'

Jock breathed through his lips, making a sound as if he was trying to spit out an orange pip. Jock called Sneaky on his mobile and stared at Chris who stared back.

'Hey, man. You coming down tonight?'

'No. I've got shit to do.'

'I've got Chris here. He says he has something for you.'

'Something? What's something?'

'I dunno. Something.'

'Fuck that. Tell him I've got shit to do.'

Jock shrugged his shoulders and relayed Sneaky's message.

'Please. This is important. I promise. It's worth his while,' said Chris.

Jock relayed the information back to Sneaky.

'Fuck's sake. Alright. I'll be outside the garages in Sitten's Mill.'

Chris had heard Sneaky's meeting location, before Jock could say anything, and had left the pool hall in a rush.

Smash!

Thump!

It was the noise of a football being hit against the garage door.

Smash!

Thump!

The police had been called for countless times for disturbance but it didn't make any difference.

Thump!

Sneaky didn't care. Sneaky didn't care because he didn't have much to care about. He didn't care for his jobless father that drank. He didn't care for his mother

101

who had an awkward reputation. He didn't care about his weakling brother whom he beat on a daily basis. Cigarettes. Drugs. Drink. Sex. Money. He cared about them.

Smash!

Crash!

It had come to this. Kicking a football against the garage doors of paying owners. This was the shit Sneaky had to do. As Sneaky left yet another dent in the garage door, a car entered the road and pulled up beside him.

'What the fuck do you want? What's so fucking good that I'd be interested?' barked Sneaky.

The speed at which Sneaky wanted to know about the plan took Chris by surprise. Chris delved into his wallet and retrieved the photo of Dexter, complete with a time and location on the reverse. He didn't want to waste any time.

'I want you to break into this address and kill this guy,' exclaimed Chris.

There it was. Chris had laid it out as a matter of fact. He hadn't hesitated or stuttered from nerves. Sneaky took the photograph of Dexter and glanced at it. He looked at the time and location when the murder should take place. Sneaky looked at Dexter's face again before throwing the photograph to the ground in disgust.

'Why the fuck would I do that? Why?'

'Money. A lot of money. In fact, almost all the money you've ever dreamt of.'

'Yeah? Why should I trust you? Why would I fucking do this?'

The meeting wasn't going as smooth as Chris had imagined. He thought Sneaky was a moron who would jump at the chance to make some easy money.

'That man's wife is the manager of the ANA bank. That's why. I want you to break into his home, kill him, and in return, you can steal her work laptop that she keeps on the kitchen table. It contains all the key codes to all the doors and vaults in that bank. Can you imagine how much money you could get away with?' pleaded Chris.

Chris had spoken with a bold authority. He hoped it would be enough to dupe Sneaky into the proposed job. Sneaky picked up the photo from the ground, remained silent and seemed to be really thinking about the hit on Dexter.

'I'll be in the house that evening. I'll leave the back door unlocked. All you have to do is the job.'

This was it. This was his ticket to success and Dexter's demise if Sneaky agreed. Sweat had started to drip down Chris's neck. Sneaky continued to look at the photo and then at the date and time again. He had beaten people up, not killed them.

'Why don't you fuckin' do it? What's in it for you?' asked Sneaky, throwing the photo to the ground again.

'Of course, I will take a small cut from the bank raid, which, I will add, can't fail with all that information on the laptop. You'll be the one taking the risks but the one taking most of the cash.'

Chris's voice had started to waver and show signs of nerves.

'Nah way. Fuck that. You're a fuckin' nutjob!' said Sneaky with a half laugh.

Sneaky started to walk away, leaving the football behind him, muttering expletives. Chris shook his head and was shocked at Sneaky's refusal to take the job.

'Just think of the money!' shouted Chris at Sneaky's disappearing figure, 'You'll be set for life! FOR LIFE!'

No reaction. Sneaky continued to walk away until he was out of sight. Chris lit a cigarette, choked on the first puff, leant against his car and reflected on what had gone wrong.

Now what do I do? Kill Dexter myself? I'm no murderer. I just wouldn't be able to bring myself to hit or stab Dexter. Now Sneaky knows my plan and what's in my head. Maybe it's good that he walked away. I guess that was a no. But he didn't say no. He didn't say yes either. What did he actually say? He walked away and turned my deal down, didn't he? He didn't attack me. He usually attacks me. He didn't. Does that mean a yes in criminal code? What do I know?

Chris climbed into his car and breathed out a cloud of smoke over the dashboard.

I should be a successful screenplay writer working in the movie business. The chat show host that every celebrity would want to talk to. A superstar. That's what I should be. Not Dexter. He stole my screenplay idea and made it his own. Damn him. I thought we were old friends. Memories. That's all they are. What's left when they get old?

Chris drove away from the dented garages, out of the rough neighbourhood and hoped he would see Sneaky on his way home. He would stop and talk some sense into him. Chris would convince Sneaky of the advantages of stealing the bank vault's contents. He could buy all the drugs he wanted. He could buy all the drink he wanted. Hookers if he wanted. Sneaky would have the possibility to do anything. Anything.

Chris didn't see Sneaky on his journey home.

CHAPTER 9

The light that seeped into the Copelands' bedroom hit Dexter across the eyes, waking him to the sounds of his children rolling their toys across the hallway floor. Jules continued to sleep, oblivious to it all. Dexter got out of bed and made his way to the kitchen, followed by the children who had stopped playing. Sausage, who had been plodding around the kitchen for hours on end, was pleased to see a figure of authority who would replenish his water bowl and slop out some food from an open can in the fridge. By the time Jules awoke from her deep slumber, Dexter had arranged a healthy breakfast, persuaded the kids into their seats and had fixed a coffee press full to the brim with de-caff.

Jules sat down at the table and started to fill her plate with food.

'I'll be meeting Kate later,' said Jules.

Dexter nodded his head and avoided speaking with his mouth full.

'She's not feeling good right now and needs a friend

to talk to.'

Dexter nodded again and turned his attention to a small dribble of cereal that dripped down the chin of Marcus, the younger of the two boys.

'I'll drop the kids off at 5 with my parents. Can you pick them up later? About 10?' asked Jules.

'Sure,' said Dexter through tight lips.

'So, what you will be doing tonight?' asked Jules.

'Well, I thought I would... probably work on... go over my script one last time. You know, make sure that it's as good as it can be.'

Dexter thought about the meeting he had arranged with Chris as he lied to Jules. It caused him to stutter.

'I thought you had been through that already, lots of times,' questioned Jules.

'Yeah, well, you know, I, erm, know how fussy these film executives can be.'

Jules stared at Dexter and noticed he had not made eye contact with her while answering. 'Is there anything wrong, Dexy?'

'Wrong? No. Why would there be?' replied Dexter, 'It's just.. I'm not really sure about my own work to be honest. You know, is it really that good?'

'Of course it's good, Dexy. I love it and I'm sure the film executives love it. They're making it into a film after all aren't they?'

'Well, I would feel better just reading it over one more time. Maybe it's just me being too self critical but I think I need to do it.'

'Well, you do what you want to do. I don't understand personally.'

Jules started to clear away the breakfast table as Dexter ushered the children to the bathroom. They had a trip to the supermarket to make.

The darkness of the evening had started to draw in. Miles and Marcus were resisting Jules's efforts to dress them up in their best clothes for the trip to see their grandparents.

'Look, a special day like Sunday would cease to be special if we didn't make an effort. Now put on your shoes!' demanded Jules.

Jules had lost count on how many times she had said that statement but the more she said it, the more she believed the boys would come around to her way of thinking. Dexter edited his screenplay, trying to ignore his children's tantrums. Jules walked towards the front door with the children following her.

'Now, I'll be back late, Dex. I'm not sure how long I'll actually be. Are you sure you don't want to come with us?'

'Naahh. I think I need to work on it a bit more. Just be on the safe side.'

'Ok.'

Dexter and Jules embraced and gave each other a goodbye kiss. The teary eyed children looked on and continued to moan their protests about leaving. As soon as the front door slammed, Dexter stepped into the living room, looked through the window and watched his family pull away. Dexter looked at his watch and realised that it wouldn't be long until Chris arrived.

He had to prepare.

Dexter cleared away every single bottle of liquor from the drinks cabinet and placed them in the cupboard under the stairs. The drinks were usually reserved for guests who didn't have drinking problems.

*****

Chris stood on the doorstep of the Copelands' home, ready for the evening that would make him a star. He felt a nervous sensation welling up inside his stomach as if he his was due to take an exam. He didn't know whether Sneaky would go through with the plan; if he would turn up. He might have been working himself up for nothing. He didn't know if it was going to happen but he had to believe that it would.

'Chris! Hello. Welcome. Come in,' said Dexter with a smile.

Chris hung his jacket on a hook, took his shoes off and walked into the kitchen.

'Tea or coffee?'

'Oh, erm, tea thanks.'

'What kind? We have black, white, green, red or some kind of herbal shit that Jules likes.'

'Black, I guess.'

'I'll bring them through to the living room.'

As Chris entered the living room, he noticed some new additions since his last visit. A new expensive looking three-piece suite in black leather. A new TV that seemed to take up one wall. A display case that displayed family photos, certificates and an award featuring a bronze quill. Chris examined the award close up. It was an award for "Best Newcomer In Screenwriting". It made his teeth itch.

I was the one that had wrote a screenplay first. I was the one who sweat for months on end, making sure it was perfect and he gets all the awards, thought Chris.

Chris shook his head and sat on the leather sofa that seemed to swallow him up.

'Here you go,' said Dexter, entering the room, carrying two cups of tea, 'So….'

Chris sipped his cup of tea and burnt his tongue.

'So,' replied Chris, 'here we are I guess.'

Chris bounced his left leg up and down in a fast rhythm as if he had a muscle spasm he couldn't control.

'Easy, Chris. Please! You'll wear a hole in the carpet.'

Chris realised what he was doing and stopped twitching his restless legs.

'So, what's up then? You wanted to talk,' said Dexter.

'Yes, well, I do. I do. I need your advice really.'

'Yes, sure. Shoot.'

'How do I get Kate back? You're good with women, well, one woman.'

'Chris. I don't think you understand. You've been drinking every day and every night. You've been coming home late, drunk and stinking of god knows how many cigarettes you've smoked. You don't get it. Can you imagine how Kate feels coming home to a drunk, waking up to a drunk, cleaning up after a drunk? You want to know to get Kate back? Stop drinking. Stop smoking. Start acting like a husband.'

Chris didn't answer. As far as Chris was concerned, he didn't have a problem. He liked to have a drink now and again. So what? He wasn't unlike anybody else that inhabited The Belvedere. Chris placed his tea close to Dexter's, took his glasses off and rubbed the bridge of his nose. The restless leg syndrome kicked in again.

'Chris! Please. Listen to me. I know you don't like to hear it but it's the truth.'

Chris put his glasses back on and looked at Dexter.

'I don't think I have a problem.'

'Really? Well…'

Dexter started to hammer home the fact that his friend was an alcoholic, mentioning the incident outside the restaurant a few days previously. Chris didn't care to listen. He wasn't there to be lectured. He was there for another reason. His master plan. Chris checked his watch.

19:21

Dexter continued to talk.

Chris checked his watch.

19:25

19:30 and forty-two seconds.

Chris kept checking his watch until Dexter twigged.

'Are you listening to a damn word I'm saying? Do you need to be somewhere else?' asked Dexter, annoyed by Chris's constant time keeping.

'No. No. I'm listening. I'm just trying to give up smoking. You know, I have to do something with my

113

hands.'

Dexter smiled.

'Congratulations! At least that is a step in the right direction.'

Chris checked his watch again.

The excuse may have succeeded in fooling Dexter into thinking the evening was nothing more than old friends having a serious conversation but Chris had one more person to fool. Sneaky. Chris had prepared a memory stick containing the fake bank security information.

The time was fast approaching 8 'o' clock.

'God! I'm sorry! I've just remembered something. I need to check my emails? It's work. I'm sorry. Can I use the computer in the kitchen?' asked Chris.

Dexter lifted his tea off the table, took a sip and nodded. Chris booted the laptop and waited, tapping his foot on the floor. The wait seemed to last for half an hour before the laptop displayed a password screen. Chris sighed, swore under his breath and tapped the space bar out of frustration. It was a hold up he didn't want.

'What's the password?' shouted Chris.

'I'll give you two guesses,' shouted Dexter back.

Chris thought for a moment and typed in S-A-U-S-A-G-E. The operating system's jingle played. Chris plugged the memory stick into the laptop and waited again.

Cut file.

Paste.

Chris had transferred the file sensitiveinformation. doc to Jules's laptop desktop in a matter of seconds.

Chris checked his watch again. He didn't have much time left. Chris shut the laptop, dashed to the toilet and smiled at Dexter on his way past who was on his way into the kitchen. Once inside the bathroom, Chris waited, simulating the time it would take for him to take a leak. Chris opened the lid to the toilet, plopped the memory stick into the water, flushed, washed his hands and dried them on a fancy looking hand towel. He checked the time.

19:53

Chris had seven minutes left to set everything up. Chris opened the toilet door where Dexter was waiting outside. Chris jumped, startled at seeing his best friend looking back at him. Had he heard the memory stick being flushed away? Had he checked Jules's laptop? Had his plan been twigged?

'I need to go now too,' said Dexter as he brushed past Chris and locked the door behind him.

Chris breathed a sigh of relief.

Chris took the opportunity to open the back door that linked to the kitchen whilst Dexter was in the toilet. The stage had been set. Everything was ready for the main event. Chris still didn't know if Sneaky would show. Had the bait been substantial or believable enough for Sneaky? If he didn't show up, Chris imagined killing Dexter himself but he knew that it wouldn't achieve anything. He needed it to look as if he was the hero at the scene of the crime, filming evidence to be used in court. A film that would appear on social media sites and beamed across the world. Chris would be an overnight star and hero but an important detail had been forgotten that would prevent him from that hero.

The password.

The password to Jules's laptop.

Without it, Sneaky wouldn't be able to access the fake information. Chris looked around the kitchen and ripped a pen and pad fridge magnet away from the fridge door. Chris scribbled down the password and threw the piece of paper onto the laptop's keyboard. Chris shut the screen, sandwiching the piece of paper between the screen and the keyboard. He heard the sound of the toilet flush.

Chris looked at his watch again. It was time but where was Sneaky? He could feel his heart beating fast; the nervous butterflies fluttering around in his stomach; the restless legs. Chris took off his glasses and rubbed the lenses with his shirt.

Where was Sneaky?

'Are you ok?' asked Dexter.

Chris stood close to Jules's laptop and looked at Dexter whilst trying to act normal. The master plan had started to become harder for Chris to hide from. Every minute the clock ticked past 8 heightened Chris's agitation.

'Yeah. Yeah. I'm, I'm ok. I'm ok. Th-thanks. I'm ok,' stuttered Chris.

Chris glanced at the back door as Dexter watched his friend act in a peculiar way.

'Are you sure you are ok?' asked Dexter again.

Chris looked back at Dexter. A sick would be killer stood under a light bulb like a lizard. If he continued to shake and stutter, Dexter would start to ask more probing questions and the plan would be ruined.

Where was Sneaky?

'I think you should go and see someone. Look at yourself. You never used to be like this.'

THUMP!

The back door almost derailed as it slammed against

117

the rubber stopper. Sneaky and Jock entered the kitchen, wearing disguises and carrying weapons including a bat. Dexter turned around with an open mouthed shocked expression on his face. He was speechless at what he was seeing. Two intruders in his safe family home. Chris remained rooted to the spot through fear and could feel his heart beat faster and faster. Sneaky had taken the bait after all. Chris fished around in his trouser pocket and grabbed his mobile with trembling fingers. Chris scrambled to select camera mode and started to film, hoping he hadn't missed any of the action.

Sneaky threw a mean right hook, which connected with Dexter's nose with the sound of a small crack, producing a stream of blood that dripped onto the kitchen floor. Dexter stumbled backwards, reeling from the intense pain. The stream of blood continued to flow out of Dexter's nose, splattering the brilliant white floor tiles with dark red spots. Dexter raised his hands to his face and tried to protect himself from the continuous beating. Kicks to the legs. Punches to the stomach. Right and left hooks to the head. Dexter ducked and dived as best he could but he was outnumbered. Chris shuffled his feet backwards towards the end of the table where the prize, Jules's laptop, was waiting for Sneaky and Jock. He continued to film and watched the vicious attack; watched the blows land; watched Dexter's face grimace in pain as he felt each hit.

'HELP! CHRIS…,' cried Dexter.

Jock lunged forwards, raised the baseball bat up in the air and smashed down with full force, striking Dexter on the corner of his forehead. Dexter crouched down to the floor and held onto a kitchen chair for support.

Chris continued to film.

A plethora of smeared bloody red footprints marked the floor. Dexter couldn't hold onto the chair any longer, lost his grip and slumped to the floor. He started to twitch, laying in a pool of his own blood.

'Chris….'

Dexter's whispered moan was a plea for his friend to help but Chris continued to film. The attack had gone to plan and Dexter was a goner but it hadn't finished. Sneaky dealt two final fatal looking blows to Dexter's torso with a kitchen knife he had pulled from his jacket.

Stab.

Slice.

Chris was shocked and aghast at the brutality. He gasped at the bloody imagery on his mobile's screen.

119

An overriding sense of guilt hit him sharp like the stabs had pierced Dexter. Nobody deserved to leave the earth in this way.

'HEY! STOP! Stop! What the hell?' shouted Chris.

Dexter's body lay stricken and still. Blood poured out the wounds. Chris could almost smell the iron in the air. Sneaky looked up at Chris and noticed that he was holding his mobile out in front of him.

'YOU'RE FUCKIN' FILMING US?' shouted Sneaky.

Sneaky's putrid angry face moved fast towards Chris's mobile screen. Sneaky wrenched the mobile out from Chris's hands, threw it to the floor and stamped on it in fury. The combat boots ground it into a pulp of splintered glass and mangled components. Chris backed himself further into the corner of the room, fearing for his life. His master plan had turned into his worst nightmare. Chris waved his sweaty, nervous hands at Sneaky and Jock who looked hell-bent on making him their next victim. They snarled, grunted and hurled swearwords at Chris, raising their weapons to attack.

'No. No. No. Listen, don't hurt me. I've done nothing to you. Just…,' murmured Chris.

The pleas bounced off the ears of the newborn killers. Sneaky's first punch knocked Chris's glasses clean off of his face. They flew through the air and bounced on the floor coming to a standstill at Sneaky's feet. Sneaky crushed Chris's glasses under his boots and reduced them to fragments. Jock's baseball bat smashed into the side of Chris's head, sending him crashing to the kitchen floor. A shard of the broken mobile phone tore into Chris's right cheek and created a large gash.

'That'll fuckin' teach you,' yelled Sneaky.

Sneaky kicked Chris in the side. The pain made Chris grit his teeth in agony. The two attackers stood over him and breathed hard as they stared at him. Chris decided to shut his eyes and play dead as if he was being attacked by grizzly bears. Chris could feel his attackers' breath down the back of his neck or at least he thought he could. They were standing close to him, looking for signs of life. Chris took shallow breaths and hoped the combat boot footsteps would walk away from him.

'Is this it?' asked Jock, pointing to the laptop.

'Yeah. Fuckin' grab it and whatever else,' replied Sneaky.

Chris didn't dare to flinch an eyelash. Sneaky and Jock proceeded to turn the house upside down. A drawer crashed to the floor with a bump; glasses smashed; boxes opened and overturned. The noise stopped. Chris heard the heavy clomp of boots grow closer until Sneaky and Jock were back in the kitchen. Chris held his breath and heard them leave through the back door. Chris wasn't sure if they had left or if they would return to steal everything in the house. Chris continued to lie still, taking small breaths. After some time had passed, he assumed the coast was clear.

Chris started to lever himself up off the floor with an outstretched arm. The pain from the blow to the side of his head pulsed. Chris raised his arm to his head and felt a moist patch of hair soaked in blood. He looked at his bloodstained hand in shock. Chris adjusted himself to an upright position and felt the floor in front of him. He could feel the frame of his glasses in front of him. He picked them up only to realise that it was just an arm.

Chris raised himself to his feet. He felt light headed and the room began to spin. He reached out at a blurred chair in front of him and used it as a support. The fuzzy outline of Dexter's body lay on the floor in front of him. Chris couldn't tell if he was alive or not.

'Dexter?' No reply. Chris gulped. 'Dexter?'

No reply. No moans. No gasps for air. Silence.

Chris was sure that Dexter had been murdered. He squinted at the floor, trying his best to focus on his mobile that had been crushed under Sneaky's boot. A broken rectangle of plastic and shattered screen lay on the floor in front of him. Chris kneeled down and picked up the remnants in his hands. Half of the phone had remained intact. Chris opened the compartment to the memory card and wrestled with the catch and released it. Chris placed the memory card in his pocket and stood up again. He hoped that the footage had survived. His future depended on it.

Chris started to shuffle his feet forwards across the kitchen floor towards Dexter's lifeless body. Chris stood by the side of Dexter as his shuffling came to a stop. He squinted and looked down at his friend. Not a sound could be heard. Chris continued to stare at Dexter's battered bloody face and knew it was the last image he would see of his former best friend.

I'm sorry, Dexter. We had many good times when we were younger but things changed. Things changed when you stole my idea, you bastard. You made me do this to you. You made me do it, Chris thought.

Chris turned his face away and continued to shuffle forwards, through the pool of blood that felt as thick as treacle. A trail of dark red shoe prints marked Chris's walk to the phone. Chris squinted at the dialing pad, lifted the receiver and pressed in a number.

'Hello. This is Martin Lawson. Eastern View.'

Chris was bewildered by the voice on the other end of the phone. Martin? What was he doing working so late? He was only on work experience.

'Martin?' spluttered Chris. 'Something terrible has happened.'

'What's happened? Are you ok? What's going on? Where are you? What can I do?' rambled Martin.

'Martin! ….Listen! I've been attacked. We've been

attacked. Come right away.'

'My God! Are you ok? Do you need an ambulance? Have you called one? We'll be there as soon as we can. My God!'

Chris gave Dexter's address to Martin and didn't answer any of his questions. Chris pressed the receiver button down, hung up on Martin and dialed for an ambulance.

Chris sat down on the nearest chair close to Dexter's body and reflected on what had happened. Dexter's corpse continued to weep blood onto the kitchen floor. Chris smiled as he thought about the evening's footage that would shape his future.

A local TV news reporter caught in an attack that had managed to film it all.

He would be famous.

He would get an award for bravery.

An award for brave news reporting. For being in the line of fire and surviving.

Become a senior reporter for the BBC.

Get his own TV chat show called Wilkinson.

It would all be within reach.

A new celebrity had been born.

CHAPTER 10

A trace of red lipstick stuck to the rim of Kate's wine glass as she took a sip. She had been sitting for twenty minutes, anticipating the arrival of Jules who was late. Kate flipped a page of a magazine, which made her wedding ring sparkle in the bistro's lights. Jules entered the bistro and sat opposite Kate.

'Sorry I'm late. I couldn't tear myself away from my boys and my parents. You know how it is. How are you?'

'I'm ok, I guess.'

Kate watched Jules arrange her coat and winter hat on the back of the seat. She hoped that she wouldn't mention Chris's problems. A waitress appeared by the side of the table, clutching a pad and pen ready to take their orders. Kate picked up a dog-eared menu and started to read down the list of appetisers.

'Two potato pancakes with goulash, a white wine and did you want another, Kate?'

Shocked by the speed and the nerve of Jules ordering her dinner for her, Kate nodded her head and agreed to another glass of white wine.

'Two white wines please. Thanks,' said Jules.

Kate looked at Jules as she handed the menus to the waitress. Her dinner had been hijacked and now she would have to eat a potato pancake instead of a pasta dish she had set her heart on.

'I'm sorry, Kate. You just have to try the potato pancake. Trust me. It's the best meal on the menu.'

Kate's fake smile camouflaged her annoyance. The waitress placed two glasses of white wine on their table. Their conversation continued with small talk about make-up and the best hair preparations until there was a gap.

'Have you heard from Chris?' asked Jules.

Kate hadn't heard from Chris and hadn't spoken to him either. She had had no desire to ring him or answer her mobile if he had tried to call. She couldn't face it. She believed it had been a good decision to move out, taking Chuck with her and, without being unreasonable.

'I'm sorry. I just don't know what to do, Jules. He's changed over the past few months and I've had enough.'

Kate wiped the tears away with a used tissue she retrieved from her handbag. As the waterworks continued to flow, the tissue started to shrink and reduce to a mushy pulp in her hand. Jules unwound the small red plastic thread on a packet of new tissues and offered Kate a replacement.

'Chuck really doesn't understand what is going on. He thinks his dad has an illness that won't leave him alone. I don't know what to say to him and I hate lying. I don't know what else I can do. I just don't know Jules. I'm sorry, I shouldn't burden you with all my problems.'

Jules shook her head. Kate's mascara had started to run through her tears, streaking two pale grey lines of speckled black substance down her cheeks. She wasn't the self-assured, confident Kate who always looked perfect even on a bad day. This was a broken Kate. Jules handed Kate the packet of tissues and urged her to keep them.

'You know, Dexter and I were considering something. I don't know what you'll think about the idea but here goes. What about an intervention?'

Kate stopped weeping and looked at Jules for a sign of sincerity. An intervention? Kate had always thought them to be a product of American psychiatrists who preyed on the weak and vulnerable to make a quick buck. Jules continued to smile at Kate, awaiting an answer. Were the Copelands the knights in shining armour that would take control of the Wilkinson's lives and save them? If someone else could fix their problems, Kate was willing to let them try. She was

127

willing to try anything.

'Here you go,' said the waitress, offloading two potato pancake dishes onto the table, 'enjoy your meals.'

A piping hot dark brown semi-circle of crispy batter sat in front of Kate. The pancakes smelt as good as Jules had described but they failed as artwork.

'Just what the doctor ordered,' said Jules, closing her mouth around her first bite.

Kate cut and pronged a small piece of pancake and lifted it to her mouth.

'I think it would be a good idea. Just to talk through the problems. Make Chris confront them. He obviously has a problem and a reason for doing what he is doing.'

Jules gulped down a second piece of goulash soaked pancake and starting telling Kate what she needed to hear.

'We can't live with Chris in our lives the way he is at the moment escpecially with two small children to consider. I think you have made the right choice to move out,' said Jules, 'I've seen miraculous things happen with interventions. They can only do good but I will say this - Chris has to want to do it himself otherwise…. He has to give it a chance. What we should do is get everybody together, with the therapists I know, and arrange for Chris to turn up at a certain time and at the same place. Arrange something like a birthday party. Something like that.'

Kate nodded until a negative thought stopped her head from bobbing.

'Would I have to be in the same room as Chris?'

'Of course. It won't work without you,' replied Jules.

'Not right now. Maybe in a week or two. Not now. I can't do it. I simply can't do it.'

A fresh batch of tears rolled out of Kate's eyes and followed the tracks of old mascara streaks.

'He's not the man I married, Jules. Where did the promising man with a future go? He was at our wedding. I can't do it now. Maybe in a month or two.'

'A month would just give Chris more drinking time. You need to tackle the problem head on, while the iron is hot… before he gets worse,' pleaded Jules.

Kate looked at Jules.

An intervention.

It had a chance of working.

Would Kate give him a chance?

Did he deserve a chance?

Did she love him? Of course she still loved him. She had asked herself that question at every available opportunity and the answer was still the same. She still loved him.

'I mean, I don't know what his problem is but if anyone can find out then it's this guy,' said Jules, handing Kate a business card.

Kate looked at the black business card featuring a white embossed dove in one corner and the name of a therapist, centered with perfect equal distance from every edge. Kate's face reflected back from the glossy black card that resembled a funeral director instead of a therapist.

'Thanks.'

The waitress returned, collected the plates and balanced them on her right arm.

'Can I get you something else?'

'A coffee and strawberry cheesecake for me,' replied Jules.

'Just a coffee,' said Kate.

Kate leant back in her seat. Jules was going to save the Wilkinson's relationship, save Dexter's best friend and all through watching television shows and reading articles in women's magazines. Jules took a swig of coffee and changed the subject.

'The boys are doing really well at nursery and school. One teacher said that they could be child geniuses. Dexter is working really hard and it's paying off as I am sure you have heard. Sausage has been awarded a certificate at obedience school and... guess what?'

Kate shrugged her shoulders.

'I'm in line for the managerial position at the bank!'

'Congratulations. I'm pleased for you.'

Jules stopped talking as she noticed Kate's lack of an enthusiastic reply.

'Oh! I'm sorry, Kate. I didn't mean to brag. I'm sorry. I just get caught up in everything that's happening. You know what I'm like. Look, we'll turn your situation around, I promise.'

Kate gave a wry smile and spooned some milky foam out from the bottom of her cappuccino cup. It made a change for Kate to hear something positive even if it was vague.

The dinner date had been going well until a phone call changed everything.

'What?' answered Jules, placing a hand over her shocked face, 'Oh my God. I don't…. I'll.. I mean, we'll be there..Kate is here with me.'

'Jules?'

'There's been some sort of accident. They're at the hospital. In hospital…my God.'

'Jules? Who?'

'Dexter and Chris. They're in hospital. I've… We've got to go..my God, my God.'

Jules couldn't look Kate straight in the face. Her

whole demeanour had changed and her body had started to shake. Her arms could barely pick up her coat from the back of the chair and her legs buckled. Kate readied herself with the same haste and followed Jules.

'Hey! Come back!' yelled the waitress.

The women left the bistro without paying.

CHAPTER 11

The hospital was awash with a number of waiting patients when Kate and Jules rushed up to the reception. A middle-aged receptionist, stressed under the weight of administration, failed to look up from her desk.

'Dexter Copeland. Where is he?' asked Jules.

'And you are....?'

'Jules Copeland.'

'And I'm Kate Wilkinson. Chris Wilkinson?'

'One name at a time! One name at a time! Copeland. Copeland. Copeland... yes, Copeland. He's in the neurology ward. Go down this hallway to your right, keep going until you get to a cross section, then take a left and keep going. The reception is....'

Jules had already sprinted away from the receptionist's help before she could finish her sentence. Her beloved Dexter needed her. Jules hurried down the corridor to her right, creating a draft that wafted the tainted air of surgical spirit behind her. Confused and desperate, Jules was lost in the labyrinth of cloned hallways, polished marble effect flooring and dim fluorescent lighting. It all looked the same.

"Scuse me. 'Scuse me,' said Jules, getting the attention of a nurse, 'Where's the neurology ward?'

'Go down there and it's to your left.'

Jules continued to walk down the hallway and felt her weight buckle her legs as if they had turned to rubber. A large sign marked 'neurology' above a front desk acted as a beacon. Jules approached it, breathless and pouring with sweat.

'Dexter. Where is her? Where is he?'

'Dexter Copeland?' asked the receptionist.

'Yes. Where is he? I want to see him. I'm his wife.'

'Please could you take a seat and I will call for the doctor on call.'

'But I want to see him now.'

'Yes, I know you do but he's not allowed any visitors at this time. I've bleeped the doctor and she'll be here in a moment or two.'

Jules tapped her knuckles on the receptionist's desk. She took a seat amongst the other people waiting and started to tap her foot on the floor. A man sitting in a chair opposite lowered his magazine and stared at her. Jules continued to send out Morse code with her shoe, oblivious to the annoyance of the other people waiting.

'Jules Copeland?' asked the doctor.

'Yes. Yes. That's me. Dexter…'

Jules gulped.

'Dexter.. Where.. How is he? What happened? My god….'

'Please. Could you follow me?'

The doctor led Jules to a small office that had a large colourful medical poster of a brain on the wall. An old beige skeleton, lurked in the corner of the room. It caught Jules's eye as she panned the room. Its obligatory smile disturbed her.

'Please. I think you should take a seat,' said the doctor.

Jules sat down and started to tap her foot again. The doctor could see the concern in her panic stricken face. The quivering open mouth. Her anxiety that made every fibre of her body shake. The tears.

'I'm afraid I have some bad news.'

Jules gasped, raised a hand to her mouth and started to cry.

'Your husband has suffered a severe skull fracture, a stab wound to his abdomen as well as a large surface cut to his stomach and has been badly bruised.'

'Oh my God.. Oh my God.. Stab? Oh God.. Is he….?'

Jules stopped tapping her foot, held her breath and feared the worst.

'He's in critical condition,' said the doctor.

Jules breathed out, relieved that her husband was alive.

'I have to warn you that he is in a coma and has sixty percent chance of survival.'

Jules couldn't process sixty percent with her upside down mind. Sixty percent was better than ten but it also meant Dexter had a forty percent chance of dying. Jules started to cry. She had never had to cope with something as serious as this before.

'Sixty percent? But that's like fifty-fifty. He's going to die isn't he? Just tell me straight.… I …'

Jules sobbed. The doctor extended her arm, ripped a tissue from a box on her desk and offered it to Jules.

'We're doing everything we can, Mrs Copeland. Dexter is in the best possible hands. I can assure you of that.'

Jules looked up, nodded and mopped up some of her tears.

'Can I see him?'

'Of course.'

The doctor led Jules to a private room where Dexter lay comatose in a bed.

Blip!……………Blip!…………..Blip!

The sound from a machine was the only sign that Dexter was alive. Jules looked at her husband. She barely recognised him. Black, yellow blotches surrounded his eyes. A large bandage circled his head. Thin plastic tubes connected to an intravenous sprung out from his arms like tree branches. Jules couldn't see the extent of the damage caused by the stab wounds under the bedsheets.

Blip!……………Blip!…………..Blip!

At least he was stable.

'My God…' cried Jules. 'What happened to you.. I don't understand….'

'I'll leave you alone, Mrs Copeland,' said the doctor and left the room.

Jules brushed her hand down Dexter's cheek. There was nothing she could do. She felt helpless. The fate of her husband was out of her hands. She wanted him to open his bruised battered eyes and say 'How's Sausage?' but instead, he remained locked in sleep, unable to blink an eyelid.

'What have they done to you? Who did this, Dexy? Don't leave me. Please. Don't leave me,' cried Jules, clawing at the bedsheets, 'You hear me? You will not leave us.'

Jules lowered her head onto Dexter's bed and wept.

*****

Kate had found Chris in casualty. Chris had not noticed her standing by the doorway. The doctors had given him two crutches to help him hobble around the room. His injuries were not as bad compared to Dexter's injuries but looked worse. The gash across his cheek glowed red whilst the baseball strike to the side of his head had left a mark in a shade of magenta. Chris clutched his side where Sneaky had kicked him. The doctors had confirmed that he hadn't broken any ribs but would still feel some pain. Kate was shocked at his frailty. He had trouble walking and grimaced every step he took. Kate had some reservations about entering the room after the arguments they had had but the situation had changed. Kate took a deep breath and entered the room, deciding to put their marital problems to one side for the time being. The hobbling stopped. Chris looked at Kate and had nothing to say.

'Chris? Where are your glasses?' asked Kate.

Chris remained silent and squinted towards Kate's direction.

'Kate? Kate! I'm ok. Yes. I'm ok. I'm getting used to these things. Arhhh!'

As Chris tried to point to his crutches, the pain from the kick to his side reminded him not to point at all.

'I think I'll sit down,' said Chris, lowering himself down on the bed.

Kate rushed to his side and sat down beside her injured husband. Chris's hand crept onto Kate's knee and gave it a pat.

'Thanks for being here Kate. I would hug you but…'

Kate smiled as a tear fell from her eye. She leant over towards Chris and rubbed her head up against his shoulder.

'Who did this? What happened?' asked Kate.

'I don't know. It all happened so fast. One minute I was talking to Dexter, the next, I was watching two masked men beat him to a pulp. After they had finished with him, they started on me. I tried to stop them.'

'My God!' exclaimed Kate.

'My head is still spinning from it. I don't know, Kate. They broke my glasses too!'

Kate raised a half smile at the reason Chris had lost his glasses. He had always made light of serious situations in the past until the drink had disabled his ability to do it in the present.

'Oh! But what about Dexter? I, er, don't know what happened' asked Chris.

139

'Dexter. I don't know. I left Jules to visit you. She only mentioned an attack and then we made our way here as quick as we could. God, Chris! I don't believe this!'

Kate nestled her head up onto Chris's torso. Chris smiled and rested his chin on the top of Kate's head. It felt as if Kate had forgiven him for everything.

'I was thinking………….maybe we can make a go of it again. You know, perhaps you can move back in,' suggested Chris.

Kate froze. She had put the marital issues to one side. This wasn't the time or place to discuss happy families. Kate pushed herself away from Chris's chest and sat upright, shocked at the mere suggestion that they should reunite.

'What? Did I say something wrong?'

'I don't know, Chris. You need to sort yourself out,' urged Kate.

'But I thought…'

'I might be here, Chris, but it doesn't make our, or more to the point, your problems vanish all of a sudden.'

'Oh…Sorry, I just thought…'

Kate started to cry again.

'I'm sorry, Kate,' said Chris, trying to calm her with an apology.

Kate wiped her tears away with a used tissue. Leaning over, Kate placed her head back up against Chris's shoulder and allowed herself to feel comfortable. Chris beamed a half moon smile from ear to ear.

'Here he is! In here,' cried Martin, making his way into the room with the film crew, 'we got here as fast as we could. The police had shut down the address you gave me and said you'd be here. How are you? What happened? Who did this? How is Dexter Copeland? Where is Dexter Copeland? Can you relay everything that happened?'

Kate moved her head away from Chris and looked at the intruders. A puzzled expression filled her face with a question mark. Chris grabbed his crutches and lifted himself up from the bed, leaving Kate perplexed.

'I'm glad you are all here. Just set up right here. We'll make a report here,' said Chris.

'Are you sure you are up for it? Maybe I should interview you instead of it being a typical report?' asked Martin.

'No. No. I just want to speak. Make it an appeal to the camera.'

Chris let go of one of his crutches, delved into his pocket and found the memory card he had taken from the wreckage of his mobile. Kate watched his every move in shock. It didn't appear that his head was still spinning from the attack as he plugged the memory card into the crew's laptop, squinted at the footage and edited with one hand.

'You filmed the attack?' asked Martin, staring in awe at the violent jerky footage.

'Yes. I thought it best to try and capture these bastards on film. They should be easy to find for the police once this footage goes public.'

Kate remained stunned. The moments of tenderness she had shared with Chris before the film crew arrived now seemed superfluous. The crew fluttered like busy bees around the room, setting up lights and cameras.

'Ok. Here's how we play it, Martin. I'll just talk to the audience. A monologue if you will. I'll do the voice-over for the actual footage of the attack. After that, I'll write down how you should get Nige' to edit everything together,' directed Chris.

Chris took the memory card out of the laptop and placed it back in his pocket. Chris hobbled around and back towards the bed. Kate didn't say anything. She just looked bewildered.

'Are you ok?' asked Chris.

Kate said nothing.

'Ok. Chris. Just stand where you are and we'll film whatever…whenever you're ready,' said Geoff.

Chris turned his back on Kate and faced the cameras. He leant with his full weight on his crutches to accentuate the fact that he was a wounded victim. It would make good news. People took pity on wounded journalists and correspondents who had been injured in the line of duty. They were treated like soldiers. Like heroes. Chris had seen it before.

In an act of generosity, Geoff moved away from the camera and pointed at Martin to take over. Martin counted down from three and pressed REC, signalling the beginning and the end of his evening's work.

'Today, I was attacked by two unknown assailants when they broke into the home of Dexter Copeland, the film director and writer. Copeland is currently receiving treatment. During the attack, I managed to capture vital seconds of the robbers before being violently beaten myself, leaving me with concussion and on crutches. If anybody recognises or can name them, we urge you to come forward,' reported Chris.

'Ok. That's it!' said Martin, pulling his face away from the camera's viewfinder.

'Do you have the footage of the attack saved on your desktop? Don't forget that. That's the most important thing,' urged Chris.

'Yes. I have that,' said Martin.

Martin unplugged and packed away Geoff's camera. As the film crew left the room, Chris turned around and lowered himself down next to Kate again.

'There. That had to be done. The footage should

make catching these bastards a whole lot easier.'

Kate smiled and rested her head back up against Chris. The footage from the raid had to be shown to catch the perpetrators. An appeal from one of the victims would only boost the profile of the attack. It would all lead to the attackers being caught, prosecuted and thrown in jail. Kate looked up into Chris's eyes, took a deep sigh and hugged him tighter.

'I promise - no more drinking. This has woke me up. I know you've heard this from me before but this time I mean it,' promised Chris.

Kate had heard it all before but there was sincerity in Chris's voice this time. He seemed to be on the level. Kate was convinced. She nodded her head towards Chris and they kissed passionately. Kate looked at Chris in admiration as she pulled her lips away from his.

CHAPTER 12

Blue lights from multiple police vehicles bounced off the windows of the Copelands' house. Nosey neighbours twitched their curtains aside as they replaced the evening's television with real time drama. Yards of plastic blue and white tape had been wound around trees to cordon off the area. According to the police, there was nothing to see although there was. There was a reason why Detective West had been called to the scene, on a late Sunday evening, disturbing his day of rest.

'What have we got here then, hmm?'

He ruffled his white fluffy balding hair with his hand while he reviewed the notes and statements collected by the first arriving officers.

2 victims. Victim 1: Chris Wilkinson. White. 43 years old. Trauma to the head and bruising to his legs and abdomen. Victim 2: Dexter Copeland. Black. 42 years old. Found comatose and badly beaten. Skull fracture. Two stab wounds to the stomach. Cuts and

bruises to the face and legs. Both victims were beaten with a bat that caused the head injuries. Victim 2 was stabbed with a standard kitchen knife with an approx. 8" blade. The robbers gained unforced entry through the back door.

Detective West rested the clipboard by his side and stood up, extending himself to his full tall height, his spare tyre thrust outwards for all the world to see. His colleagues called him Friar Tuck but only behind his back.

'It looks like a simple break-in,' said a constable.

Detective West raised the clipboard to his eyes and tapped his pen on the fake gold clip. Detective West liked to chew, swallow and digest the evidence before making one remark. If the arriving officer's report had been the starter, Chris's statement proved to be the main course. It made Detective West raise his eyebrows with numerous twitches that sent ripples of skin racing towards his receding hairline and back again. The constable, who had been waiting for an answer to his statement, broke the silence.

'They took everything of significant value. Upstairs and downstairs. They came in through the back door. Unforced entry.'

Detective West lowered the clipboard towards his oversized belly without uttering a word. It was if the constable was talking to an apparition.

146

'Something's not right here, hmm. It doesn't sit right, hmm.'

The constable stared at Detective West who was still looking past him and towards the Copelands' house.

'Sir?'

'I'm having a problem with the details, hmm. The details. The robbers targeted a house that had an un-locked back door. Stroke of luck wouldn't you say, hmm? And why stab one victim and not the other, hmm? Hmm? Why?'

'Well, I guess where the door is concerned, they got lucky. As for the stabbings, maybe they were disturbed by something and rushed.'

Detective West tutted and shook his head in disbe-lief at the constable's theories. He had seen too many crime scenes of this type before and none of them had been resolved with simple guesswork. Thirty-four years on the force told him so. Detective West could feel something in his heavy gut, an intuition that had never failed to steer him wrong before.

'What about this Chris character, hmm? What do we know about him?'

'Well, according to him, the robbers entered through the back door, rushed in and attacked Dexter. He claims he tried to stop them when they turned on him and beat him to the floor. He heard them ransack

147

the house and leave. After that, he called for an ambulance,' answered the constable.

'Really, hmm?'

The constable turned away to look at the house when he turned back again.

'Oh yes! I almost forgot. A film crew turned up from Eastern View wanting to cover the story.'

'Nothing unusual about that, hmm. The media is the media.'

'They said that Chris had called them to cover the story. We sent them on to the hospital.'

'Chris called them you say? How did he manage that, hmm? According to this report, he was hardly in a state to do anything, hmm. Do you know when he made the call and from where, hmm? Hmm?'

'No sir. We'll check the phone records.'

Detective West watched the constable duck under the police tape and walk towards the Copelands' house. Unforced entry. Chris's lack of any serious injury. The phone call. Detective West wasn't buying the simple break-in and entering crime. He couldn't put his finger on what was out of place but he knew it would eat away at him while he tried to sleep that night.

*****

The following morning had failed to turn Detective West's suspicions into anything concrete. The constable had retrieved the phone records and found the phone call to the news team had come from the Copeland residence. It wasn't enough. Detective West had been scratching his head so much that he had collected a large amount of scalp under his fingernails. The station's coffee was not helping and neither was the evidence that lay strewn across his desk.

Detective West picked up a pencil and twiddled it with his thumb and finger, placed it between his nose and upper lip and gurned it in place, forming a wooden moustache. A statuette of a golden airplane weighed down some paperwork that balanced on the edge of his desk. Detective West looked at it. It reminded him of the time he had spent in the Royal Air Force, serving missions in the Falklands amongst others. He was proud of his achievements but had decided policing was his call in life after the Royal Air Force. He had won awards for his police work but regarded his desk was for police work only and not for awards; a workspace to lay out the evidence to enable him to catch the bad guy or bad guys. The walls were pinned with so much evidence from cases that his office had turned into a paper cocoon.

Detective West looked down over the brim of his reading glasses and looked at the notes again. Chris had called his film crew first rather than the emergency services. It was an odd decision that made Detective West murmur to himself. At first, he considered that Chris, under the circumstances, didn't know what he was doing and just phoned the film crew first. It was possible but Detective West still had a niggling doubt. Everybody's initial reaction would have been to phone for an ambulance. Everybody, thought Detective West.

'Sir. You need to come and see this,' said the constable, who poked his head into the Detective West's nest.

A small team of police colleagues had collected around a television screen situated in the main open plan part of the station. Detective West walked towards the television and was in disbelief at what he was seeing and hearing. The Eastern News report featuring the mobile phone attack footage and Chris's appeal from the hospital was being premiered.

'HEY! STOP! STOP! WHAT THE HELL?'

'YOU'RE *bleep* FILMING US?'

It had been something forensics had not found at the scene of the crime. Chris had not declared that he had filmed any of the actual attack and attackers. Chris had not been asked. It had been an oversight.

'Well, that's interesting, hmm? He failed to tell us that he had filmed some of the attack. That's vital evidence that we should have been privy to, hmm. Devious behaviour. Devious, hmm.'

Detective West tutted. He deplored how Chris had made himself out to be the real victim while Dexter Copeland clung to life. It reinforced his hunch that was evolving into a monkey on his back.

'What's Mr Wilkinson's number? I need to speak to that young blaggard, hmm.'

Detective West punched the number into the nearest phone and waited for an answer.

'Chris Wilkinson, Eastern View.'

'Yes, hmm. Mr Wilkinson. This is Detective West. I've just had the odd experience, hmm, of watching your entertaining news report on the attack that left you injured, hmm, and your friend near death, hmm,' quipped Detective West.

'Odd?'

'Yes, Mr Wilkinson, hmm, odd. You failed to mention, hmm, the mobile phone footage that you shot. Do you have anything to say in your defence, hmm?'

'Erm, yes, well, I found the memory card in my pocket. I forgot all about it to be honest until my film crew started to talk to me. I took what was left of my phone as I thought I could fix it. That's when I remembered that I had filmed some of the events of that terrible night. I didn't have time to call you and thought it best to use it on my report to help catch my

151

attackers.'

Detective West scratched the stubble on his chin, loosening the particles of scalp that had collected under his fingernails earlier.

'I appreciate that you want to see, hmm, justice done for you and your friend, hmm, but you have to leave the police work to the, hmm, police. That's why we are called the, hmm, police. We police. You do not. I would very much appreciate, hmm, that you turn over that memory card to myself, hmm, as evidence in an ongoing investigation,' said Detective West.

'Erm, yes, of course, yes. I will get it to you.'

'No need. I will send a, hmm, constable over to get it.'

Detective West hung up and without saying goodbye. His irritation did not go unnoticed by his work colleagues who also shook their heads in contempt at the news report.

'What shall we do, sir?' asked the constable.

'Well, you can go and collect, hmm, that memory card. At the moment, we should still concentrate, hmm, on the Smythe abduction. The Dexter Copeland attack does not, hmm, have sufficient evidence to conduct a full blown, hmm, investigation as of yet.'

It had been the first time that Detective West had referred to the case as being the Dexter Copeland attack. It had been named the Wilkinson Copeland attack up until now. A new light had started to shine down on the case after Chris had kept his memory card to himself. Detective West's intuition still told him something was out of place. If Chris had made one mistake, he would make more and when he did, Detective West would be ready to arrest him.

CHAPTER 13

Jules returned to Dexter's bedside for the third day in a row. The doctors had told her to get some rest but she had ignored their advice. The compassionate leave that the bank had given Jules was being well spent and her parents didn't mind looking after the boys under the circumstances. Jules hated telling her sons a white lie when they asked about the whereabouts of their dad. She had told them that he had been in an accident and would get better. Jules didn't like to think about the possibility that he wouldn't.

Blip!

The noise from the machine had stayed the same but Dexter's appearance had not improved. The yellow blotchy bruises that had lined his eyes had turned a darker shade of maroon brown and looked as if they had spread across his face. The doctors had assured Jules that he was recovering despite his awful appearance. Jules respected the doctor's opinion but it didn't console her every time she looked at her frail husband. He looked one step closer to the grave every day that passed.

Jules reached out and held Dexter's limp hand.

'Hello, Dexy. I'm here again. I have so much to tell you. The boys are doing fine. Don't worry about them. They are doing well at school and my parents are helping me look after them. They ask about you every day.. Well, almost every minute….,' Jules paused to wipe away tears that welled in her eyes, 'I know you can hear me. The doctors say you can. I'll be here every day until you get better and come home. You will come home, Dexter. You will..,' Jules blew her nose and tucked away the tissue in her pocket, 'I can't do this without you, Dexter. This thing called life without you. I'm not geared up to deal with it. Please, Dexter. Wake up! Please. Wake up!'

Blip!

Jules's pleas fell on deaf injured ears. There was no reaction. No flinch. No twinge. No flicker of life to indicate that he had heard what his wife had said. Nothing. Jules lowered her head towards Dexter's bedclothes and sobbed. Jules realised, after a few moments, that her tears were also failing to provoke a reaction. She pulled herself together, raised her head and held back the tears.

'I have been in touch with the police. A detective called West is handling the case. He said that he will bring those responsible to justice. He's quote old fashioned. A what-ho type if you know what I mean,'

Jules gave a small laugh, 'He's the type that goes out clay pigeon shooting. A rain jacket with patches on the elbows. Probably a pipe too. But I guess that's not important really. He said he would make it his responsibility. One less thing to worry about, eh Dexy?'

Blip!

'Kate seems she has moved back in with Chris. I told her that it's a bad move but she won't listen. I mean, I didn't phrase it in those exact words but I said she needed more time away from him. To give herself perspective. But she won't listen to me. She's still besotted with him. Did I tell you about his news report? I did. I'm sure. The nerve of the guy. He didn't consult me before he put that disgusting, that revolting, repugnant footage....'

Jules stopped her monologue and tried hard to resist picturing the mobile phone footage of Dexter being beaten and stabbed. Jules had been chatting to a neighbour when the video came up in conversation. She turned off the television every time she thought she would be exposed to it on the news. She couldn't imagine who would want to watch the footage. Even the most ardent newshound would have turned their head away if it was as bad as people made it out to be. The footage had not only been shown on television at various times, it had also hit social media, causing massive attention and racist comments amongst well-wishers.

157

Blip!

'Detective West said he would look into it. He's a good man,' said Jules.

Jules regained her composure and looked at Dexter. She squeezed his hand tight. He didn't move. His eyes remained stapled shut. Comatose. Jules wept a single tear and wondered if Dexter would ever open his eyes again.

CHAPTER 14

Kate awoke and rolled over to face Chris snoring beside her. They had taken full advantage of their time without Chuck who was staying with Kate's parents. It had been weeks, probably months, since Kate had felt any love from Chris. It almost felt as if they had just met, fallen in love again and started a new relationship. Kate felt a new page had been turned and order had been restored. Chris had avoided spending evenings at The Belvedere, and instead, spent them with her. It was a sign that things were on the mend.

Kate gazed at Chris who continued to snore aloud. She didn't want to wake him. He had been through a traumatic experience and needed the blissful rest. Kate kissed Chris's forehead, flapped the edge of the duvet aside and got out of bed. A tune that she had heard on the radio the day before hummed from her mouth as she walked to the kitchen. She had realised that the house was in bad shape when she walked over the threshold the day she moved back in, dragging her travel bag behind her. Overflowing ashtrays peppered ash onto the living room table and floor. Old beer cans had been thrown into a new black refuse sack as the plastic rubbish bin was full. The fridge contained half a litre of unintentional yoghurt, a small slither of cheese and a slab of butter polluted with burnt black toasted breadcrumbs. Kate took the last slices of stale bread from its polythene wrapper and plunged them down into the toaster. She couldn't ignore the state the house was in. Kate knew it could all be fixed and she was confident the new Chris would help to clean it up. The slices of toast sprung up out of the metallic chrome toaster at the same time as Chris yawned and entered the kitchen.

'Too-aaast?' groaned Chris.

'It's all that's left. Can you go out and buy some food?'

'Later. Later.'

'What are you going to eat for breakfast then?'

'I don't know. I can eat that banana, I guess.'

Kate looked at the fruit bowl that contained a once healthy yellow banana that had turned black, attracting the attention of zigzagging fruit flies.

'You can't eat that. Go out and buy something and while you are at it, chuck the rubbish out too. We need to clean this house.'

Chris's shoulders slumped towards the stained lino.

'..But I have a television appearance to make today.

I have to get ready and prepare. I don't have the time to clean the house.'

Kate breathed out a deep sigh. She hated living in filth and hated the fact that she would be the one to wage the war against it alone. Chris stepped closer to Kate and put his arms around her waist.

'..Look, we can sort this house out tomorrow. I promise. I've had a lot on my plate and the attack has left me feeling drained to be honest. We'll do it tomorrow. What do you say?'

Kate raised a wry smile and hugged Chris back. The house could wait another day but Kate knew she wouldn't be able to live another day with fruit flies circling her head. She would have to clean regardless.

'I should get ready. I'll eat something out,' said Chris.

Chris kissed Kate on the lips, walked out of the kitchen, upstairs and into the bathroom. Kate placed her unappealing toast on the counter top, walked to the bottom of the stairs and looked up at the bathroom door.

'Chris? I've just thought of something. Why don't I come with you?'

The toilet flushed. The door unlocked. Chris stood by the doorway and looked down at Kate.

'Come with me? What are you talking about?' asked Chris.

161

'I thought it would be nice. Take a trip to a TV station - together.'

'Together. Yes. Well. I don't think you would get a seat in the audience. They have all these things booked well in advance. I mean, you could come with me but you might be bored,' stuttered Chris.

'It sounds as if you don't want me to come with you.'

'Kate? As if! It's just the logistics, that's all… erm, ok, well, if you want to come with me then, ok.'

Chris reached into the bathroom and grabbed his toothbrush that sported a parting. Kate climbed the stairs and neared the bathroom. Chris spat a foam ball of toothpaste into the dull off-white sink. Chris didn't pay any attention to Kate as she walked past the bathroom door and into the bedroom. He slammed his bottle of aftershave down on the sink and muttered something under his breath.

'Are you ok?' asked Kate.

'Yeah. Yeah. I'm ok. I'm ok. I'm just rushing, that's all.'

'Ok.'

After Chris had finished splashing his face with potent aftershave, he stomped downstairs and waited for Kate. Chris's impatience and urgency made Kate skip washing her hair and conceal her blemishes with rushed strokes of make-up.

162

Kate could see Chris standing by the front door looking at his watch. She hopped down off the last stair. He leaned on the hospital crutches that he hadn't used for a couple of days. Kate stopped and looked at him in astonishment.

'Crutches? I thought you were feeling better?'

'Nah! I'm still feeling the bruises. Better safe than sorry.'

'Do you want me to drive?'

'I think that might be best.'

Chris pronged the crutches over the doorstep and onto the driveway. Kate was in shock. She had assumed Chris had recovered from the worst of his injuries but instead he stumbled towards the car door as if he had been attacked an hour ago. Chris grabbed the back passenger door with one hand and threw the crutches onto the back seat, climbed into the passenger seat and waited for Kate to drive to their destination.

*****

'And now we are deee-lighted to have with us tonight a hero. Chris Wilkinson might appear all too familiar to you if you live in the Easthampton area as a local TV journalist but for the rest of you, you'll probably recognise him from the clip on YouTube that has had a staggering number of hits so far.. ..and that number will only rise. Please welcome, Chris Wilkinson!' shouted the host.

Kate clapped along with the rest of the audience who had been told to keep their gazes fixed on the monitors. Kate could see several empty seats that the studio had managed to make it look as full as possible. Chris hobbled his way towards centre stage on the crutches he hadn't used for the past few days. The host smiled and waited with an extended hand. Kate half-clapped as she watched Chris's struggle to walk. He had climbed the stairs to the bathroom without any problem and made love without any moans of pain. Kate looked at the audience on her left and to her right. Their enthusiasm for her husband could not be faulted.

'Welcome Chris. Please, take a seat,' said the host with a guiding hand towards an empty seat.

Chris shook the host's hand and sat down with his full weight behind him. The chair tipped backwards and forwards again. The studio lights illuminated the stage whilst the monitors showed a close-up of Chris's composed and relaxed face.

'Welcome, Chris Wilkinson, a hero. How do you like the sound of that?' asked the cheerful host.

'I don't know really. I wouldn't say I was a hero as such.'

'Ah come on! You put your own life at risk to save

164

your friend. We have the footage if we can show it?'

'Sure.'

The audience gasped as they watched the mobile phone footage on the monitors. Whispers filled the studio air. Kate shut her eyes to avoid watching the footage again. A tear trickled down her left cheek when Chris's harrowing cries blasted from the sound system. After the clip had finished, the host raised his eyebrows and looked at the audience for a brief moment.

'Yes. How do you feel after seeing that?'

'It all happened so fast. I know that sounds like a cliché but it's true. One minute Dexter and I were talking about our lives and the next, we were having our lives taken from us.'

'It must have been scary.'

'Well, you know, what can you do in these situations? I just had to ride it out and hope that both of us came out the other side smiling. I tried my best to stop the attackers but they overpowered me as you saw,' exclaimed Chris with pride.

'Yes. You were very brave, I have to say.'

The audience clapped hard. Whistles and uniformed chants of 'CHRIS!' echoed around the studio. Kate clapped but couldn't celebrate the violent footage that showed her husband and friend being butchered.

'How…' The host waited a moment for the noise to subside. 'How are you feeling now? I see you are using crutches.'

'Oh these? Yes. They are just a precaution. I had so much trouble walking after those thugs beat me that the doctors gave me these to help. I feel fine though to answer your questions. I don't stay down for long!'

The audience clapped and whooped once again. Chris turned to them and bowed his head, acknowledged the praise and sucked up every last moment until the last clap had lost its reverb.

'And Dexter? Do you know if his condition has improved?'

Chris looked at the host in shock. The host had asked a question he had not expected and couldn't answer. Kate had mentioned Dexter's condition had improved on the journey down to the studio but Chris had chosen to turn a deaf ear. She had kept in touch with Jules whereas Chris had not even been to visit his best friend since the attack. It was if Dexter no longer existed. That he had, in fact, died. Kate looked at the monitor closest to her and could see the cogwheels of Chris's brain turning behind his empty eyes.

'N..n..no. There is no news unfortunately,' stuttered Chris, 'he's still.. still in a coma.'

Kate shook her head. She had told him that Dexter's condition had improved but he had ignored her as was so often the case. The audience cried out a universal 'aw' as Kate sat motionless. Chris looked towards the audience puzzled by their reaction. Dexter had stolen the limelight and he wasn't even in the room.

'Well, you can tell him from all of us here that we wish him a speedy recovery,' said the host.

Chris nodded his head towards the host, indicating with a reassurance that he would wish Dexter a speedy recovery but it couldn't have been further from the truth.

'Chris Wilkinson, everybody!' shouted the host.

Kate, along with the audience stood and gave Chris a standing ovation. Chris grabbed his crutches, levered himself up from his seat, shook hands with the host and hobbled off the stage.

'Thanks Chris,' said the studio manager who had been waiting backstage, 'Good job! Good job! Listen, listen.. We have this thing tonight, you know, kinda like a party thing going on. We always throw one every month. I happen to know, actually, I do know, you know, that there are some interested people that want to talk to you. Can you be there, come to it, this evening, like today? It would be great if you could, if you want to, only if you can, you know.'

The barrage of fast spoken words bounced off Chris's ears as if they were part of a beautiful symphony. People were interested in him. The media. Very important media professionals. Important media professionals that wanted to offer him a job, offer him a break into national, maybe international television.

'Yes. I wouldn't dream of missing that for the world,' replied Chris.

'Good! Good! I'll add you to the list. You can find out where it is from reception, the front desk, the powers that be. They have all the gumph!' joked the studio manager.

The studio manager turned her back on Chris and walked away. Chris held both crutches with one hand, adjusted his glasses and smiled.

'Chris? Who was that?' asked Kate, approaching Chris from behind.

Chris turned around. 'The studio manager. She said there are a lot of people who also want to talk to me. This is it, Kate!'

Chris grabbed Kate by the upper arms and squeezed down hard. He looked at Kate who seemed perplexed. She didn't know what 'it' was. Chris was euphoric and talking riddles that only he seemed to understand.

'Chris! Please. You're starting to hurt me,' squealed Kate.

'Oh sorry. I didn't mean to, I was just, well.. Anyway, they have a party this evening and I've been invited! It's going to be great. A lot of important people will be there.'

Kate lowered her head and looked at the floor.

'What's up? Kate?' asked Chris.

'What about Chuck?' replied Kate.

'What about him?' asked Chris back.

'We have to pick him up tonight. My parents leave for the Lake District tomorrow. He can't stay there tonight,' argued Kate.

'Oh Christ!'

Chris couldn't hide his disappointment. There had been a handful of occasions when Chris had cursed Chuck's existence for spoiling his fun but he had never resented him. Not until now.

'Look. I really have to go to this, Kate. I really do. This is it, Kate. This could be the break I have been looking for. I mean, the boss of this television network is going to be there and a whole host of others. Imagine how many contacts I could make. Imagine what it could mean for me, I mean, us. Can't you pick him up by yourself?' asked Chris.

Kate angled her head up and looked at Chris with pursed lips. A party would mean alcohol; alcohol would present temptation; temptation would become a drunken Chris; a drunken Chris would suffer the following day from a hangover and the disappointment of Chuck who had been promised his time.

'But you promised you would spend time with him. Do fatherly things. Help with his homework. Go out somewhere. Swimming. Cycling. Whatever. What am I

169

supposed to tell him? That his father is ill, more likely hungover - AGAIN?' snapped Kate.

'Don't be like that, Kate. I haven't touched a drop since… since.. three or four days now. I'll go to the party, speak to who I need to speak to and be back in time for the midnight news. I promise. This is important, Kate. REALLY important,' pleaded Chris.

Kate breathed a deep sigh. He had avoided the booze since they had rekindled their love and she believed that he was on the level. Kate looked at Chris again who had the expectant look of a teenager who wanted to borrow a parent's car. Kate blanked her expression and agreed.

'Thanks, Kate, you are a star! You'll see. This could be it. I'll be back later.'

Chris placed a crutch in each hand and walked in the direction of the reception without hobbling.

'You'd better remember your promise,' growled Kate.

Chris turned left at the end of the corridor and disappeared without responding to Kate's warning.

*****

'So you are Chris Wilkinson? How are you? There's nothing quite like being a television journalist and being injured in the line of duty.'

A man dressed in a fetching grey suit stood beside Chris at the bar. The barman had served him a whisky with one rock that the man swirled around until it had almost melted. Chris adjusted his glasses, picked up his beer and downed the remaining contents.

'Do you want another? It's on me,' said the man with some insistence.

'Sure. Thanks.'

'I should introduce myself. I'm Rod Parkton. I'm glad I bumped into you but not literally of course! Ha! Ha! I wouldn't want to injure you further! Ha! Ha!'

Chris assumed Rod's upper class accent and guffaws made him one of the very important people he had described to Kate. Chris had met many people that night but none of them had seemed keen to part with their business cards. Chris clasped a new pint of beer in his hand and lifted it to his mouth. Rod put the bill on his tab. Rod had a tab. Now Chris knew Rod had to be of some importance.

'I have seen the footage that has been zapping its way across the cosmos, Chris. Dastardly things happen sometimes but there's always a silver lining to any black cloud or at least that is what I say. You're starting to become notorious. You're popular. Starting to become seen. A man of the moment. Correct my assumptions if I am wrong.'

'Yes. I guess you are right. Over one hundred thousand people have seen the clip on YouTube and the number seems to keep going up. I've had so much support and I'm on the mend,' commented Chris.

'Jolly good to hear. And what about that friend of yours, that Dexter character?'

Chris froze and started to choke on a gulp of beer.

'Oh dear. Are you ok?' said Rod, slapping Chris on the back.

'I'm fine,' said Chris, forcing the speech past the trapped fluid stuck in his throat. 'It went down the wrong hole.'

Rod looked away from Chris and scanned the room until a silence marked that Chris had recovered.

'I've done some research on you,' stated Rod.

Chris remained quiet. His heart rate started to increase and butterflies started to take over his stomach. What research had Rod undertaken? Was he a private detective hired to get to the bottom of Dexter's attack? Chris gulped.

'Why, you look as if you have seen a ghost, my good man. Here's my business card. I'm not from the Inland Revenue if that's what you are thinking,' said Rod, handing over his card.

Rodney Parkton. HTN. Chief executive.

Chris relaxed. Rod was one of those important media executives after all.

'I've seen your curriculum vitae and a selection of your news reports and I am suitably impressed with you. I happen to know that my network is looking for a presenter for our new show Sunny Days. You know, it's one of these relocation shows. We find customers properties abroad, show them around and get them to buy one or at least that is the plan. It involves a lot of travel but I also happen to know that we offer a lucrative wage, perks and you might even come away with a sun tan. What do you say? You don't have to say yes right now but give me a call either way.'

Chris tipped Rod's business card backwards and forwards in the spotlights. The bold silver letters flashed by one after the other, including the phone number.

'HTN?' asked Chris.

'Holiday Television Network. We're owned by this station but I am the chief in command.'

It wasn't one of the networks Chris had hoped he would be contacted by. It wasn't a large network but was larger than Eastern View. It was a step up. A step up towards presenting the News at Ten. A small step towards Wilkinson, his own chat show where he would ask all the questions. Chris tucked the fancy looking business card into his jacket pocket, took a sip of beer and extended his hand towards Rod.

'I don't have to call you. Yes! I'm saying yes!' exclaimed Chris with a large smile.

'Well! That's fantastic! I like spontaneous people like myself. It's a deal. Do you have a business card by the way?'

Rod left the bar as soon as they had shaken hands and planted Chris's information into his mobile. Chris smiled, raised his beer glass to his lips and sucked down the remaining froth. His plan had started to work and predicted Sunny Days would only be the start of his rise to fame.

Chris looked at his watch. It was late. The promise he had made to Kate had been forgotten, clouded by the job offer he had just received and the beers he had drunk. Chris shrugged his shoulders and ordered another beer. This was it.

CHAPTER 15

They were waiting. They had been waiting for almost nine minutes. The time on the dashboard seemed to add another minute every thirty seconds. The view of the bank was obstructed by a large deep crack that had spread up the windshield.

'What the fuck are you doing? Stop fuckin' revving the engine. Do you want everyone to know we are fuckin' here?' said Sneaky.

Jock stopped revving the car and let his foot rest on the accelerator. Sneaky plucked the cigarette lighter from under the radio, lit a cigarette and threw the lighter out of the window.

'Hey! Why did you do that? This is my cousin's car!'

'Was your cousin's car. It's our fuckin' car now,' said Sneaky, puffing a cloud of smoke across Jock's face.

Jock pulled his face away from the cigarette smoke and looked straight at the bank. If all went to plan, Jock would be able to replace the car not just the cigarette lighter. They could both live the life of luxury like Ronnie Biggs, dodging the law and spending cash as if it would never run out.

'No fuck ups ok? We get in there and get out quick, yeah?' said Sneaky.

Sneaky flicked ash over the inside of the Jock's cousin's car with disregard.

'You got the codes?'

Jock lifted one hand off the steering wheel and showed Sneaky the back of his hand. He had written down the codes onto his skin with a ballpoint pen. The ink had started to expand and smudge but the numbers were still visible.

'What did you do with the laptop?' asked Sneaky.

'Sold it.'

'What? You did what? You sold it? You fuckin' spac. That could be traced.'

'What was I supposed to do? I needed some shit, you know. Look, the geezer I sold it to is sound. He'll wipe the drive clean. Strip the machine down to parts. No fuckin' problems man. I took care of it.'

Sneaky swore at Jock. He did not want to get caught again and be made to look stupid. Sneaky looked at the dashboard clock.

08:47.

Thirteen minutes. Thirteen minutes until the bank

opened. Thirteen minutes to get ready. The job needed to get underway at 09:00 on the dot. Fewer customers. Minimum fuss. Perfect timing. Sneaky had imagined the raid in his head. The bank clerks all complied. The sparse amount of customers all lay on the floor. Bundles of bank notes dropped one after another into their sacks. Sneaky had predicted that it would all take less than five minutes.

Sneaky reached across, grabbed a bag off the back seat, unzipped it and removed two fake guns. As long as people kept their distance, the guns would not be able to be distinguished from the real thing. Sneaky passed one of the guns to Jock. Jock threaded his finger through the trigger and held the gun in his right hand. His foot balanced on the accelerator, forcing the engine to turn over and splutter.

'Do we have to have the fuckin' car on?' asked Sneaky.

'Yeah. The car's fucked. It probably won't start again,' exclaimed Jock.

'Fuck's sake! I thought you said the fuckin' car was alright.'

'Yeah… and it is alright.. It's just the soddin' motor.'

'Fuck's sake! Just turn it off. We'll nick another if we have to or push start it or.. fuck's sake!'

Jock turned the key in the ignition and took his foot

off the accelerator. The car shuddered to a silence and an ominous grinding sound of mechanical failure emanated from under the bonnet. Sneaky started to sweat with worry, puffed down the remainder of his cigarette and threw the butt out of the window to join the lighter that had given it life.

'Where's the disguises?' asked Sneaky.

'Disguises?' remarked Jock.

'Yeah. The fuckin' disguises. You know, so we don't get fuckin' recognised.'

'I thought you were bringing them.'

'Oh for fuck's sake! We don't have any fuckin' disguises? Fuck's sake! What's wrong with you? I told you. Pack the fuckin' disguises - I'll bring the guns.'

Jock shrugged his shoulders, avoided eye contact with Sneaky and looked into the passenger side wing mirror. A couple, deep in conversation, walked past the car without looking at either of them. Jock breathed out a sigh of relief.

'Now what do we fuckin' do?'

'There's some shit in the boot that my cousin keeps there.'

'Fuck. Well, go and have a fuckin' look then. I'll wait here. Make sure you open the fuckin' boot first. Idiot.'

Jock stepped out of the car mumbling insults at

Sneaky under his breath.

'I'll teach 'im. That son of bitch. Fuckin' arsehole,' muttered Jock.

Jock imagined the day when he could stand up against Sneaky, throw a right hook and floor him. He would stand victorious and would never have to endure his insults again. Perhaps that day had arrived. Jock opened the car's boot.

A reel of duct tape.

A pair of roller skates.

A bag of (probably stolen) DVDs and CDs.

A skateboard.

Jumper cables, car jack and a tyre pump.

'Shit!' thought Jock as he looked at the junk.

Jock picked up the reel of duct tape, looked at it and then at the remaining items. It was the only item that could prove useful in the bank robbery unless they wanted to skate in through the open doors. Jock closed the boot and got back into the car.

'What… the fuck.. is that?'

'Duct tape.'

'I know it's soddin' duct tape, you tosser. What do you want me to do with it?'

Sneaky looked at his partner's blank expression and started to think that he had bitten off more than he could chew. The Copeland job had gone well. They had done what they had been told to do and got away with more than they had bargained for. The bank job, however, was starting to fall apart before it had started. Sneaky sucked his teeth and looked at the duct tape. He didn't want to give up. They had the codes to the bank vaults. It would be a quick job. The planned bank job he had imagined would take less than five minutes. In and out. Simple. Sneaky grabbed the duct tape from Jock's sweaty hands and tore off a large strip and started to wrap it around his head.

'Ok. This is what we'll fuckin' do. Get in and out as fast as fuck right? We'll just have to make do with this shit. You all clear, arsewipe? I'll keep the punters calm. You nip in and fuckin' use them codes. Pack this bag with what you can get and then we'll fuckin' leg it. Got it?'

Jock absorbed yet another insult, sighed and started to wrap a strip of duct tape around his head, leaving a gap for his eyes. Once they had perfected the make shift disguises, they were ready. Sneaky and Jock looked at each other one last time, nodded, opened the car doors and sprinted towards the bank.

'EVERYBODY DOWN ON THE FLOOR. I'M NOT AFRAID TO USE THIS. IF ANYONE MOVES, THEY'LL BE FUCKIN' SORRY,' shouted Sneaky. The bank doors shut behind them.

Beads of sweat started to drip from Sneaky's head.

The warm moist breath exhaled from his nose started to loosen up the duct tape. He couldn't scratch his skin that had started to itch. Sneaky concentrated his stare on the frightened, shivering bank clerks before him. A dozen customers had thrown themselves to the ground with their hands behind their heads. The bank clerks remained rooted to their posts with their hands in the air. A man sitting behind the counter slumped off his seat and crawled into the space under his desk.

'GOOD! Good. YOU.. The gay in the blue shirt. Out from under the fuckin' table NOW! Keep your hands where I can fuckin' see them. I hate alarms. I get very nervous when I hear alarms. You'd better not have pressed the fuckin' alarm. If I hear one, I'll start unloading this mother fucker at you all.'

Sneaky glanced across at Jock who stood outside a locked door with a key coded lock. Jock looked at the back of his hand. The door was the entrance to the clerks' desks and workspace, an area that separated them from the customers outside. The sweat had caused the numbers to lose their form making them almost impossible to read. Jock squinted his eyes and punched in a sequence of random numbers into the code pad. A red L.E.D flashed: access denied. Sweat started to pour down from Jock's forehead and into his eyes, stinging them and blurring his vision. The more Jock tried to focus on the keypad, the dizzier he felt. The room started to spin. He could feel his heart beat thump faster and faster as sheer panic started to take him over.

'Mmmmmm… muuuh… Maaaaah,' screamed Jock out from under the duct tape.

Jock waved his hands much to the amazement of the bank staff. Sneaky, distracted by Jock's impression of a windmill, turned his guard away from the customers and bank clerks.

'What the fuck are you doing, cockhead?' shouted Sneaky.

A bank employee, who had noticed Sneaky's lapse of concentration, moved behind a customer bench and rang the police with her mobile. Sneaky's head was still turned in the direction of Jock by the time she had returned to her original position.

'What the fuck is wrong with you?' shouted Sneaky.

'MMMMMAAAAHHHHH!' mumbled Jock.

Sneaky turned towards the bank staff and customers. They were still laying face down on the ground where they were supposed to be or had their hands in the air. Sneaky's plan of getting away within five minutes looked to be dashed. Jock clawed at the edges of the duct tape, scratching at the sides and pulled at the gap for his eyes in sheer panic, trying to free up an airway to his nose and mouth that he had taped over by mistake. Jock fell to his knees and could feel the strength in his arms fading away as he continued to pick at the duct tape.

'You stupid bastard. You stupid fuckin' bastard,' shouted Sneaky, looking aghast at Jock's stupidity, 'Fuck this.'

Sneaky turned around and ran towards the bank's entrance. As he opened the doors, he was confronted by blue flashing lights and a mass of black and white uniforms.

'DO NOT MOVE,' shouted one policeman in Sneaky's direction, 'put the gun down and we'll leave in a calm manner. Understand?'

Sneaky, stunned by the number of police looking at him, put the gun down on the ground and raised his hands in submission. A constable rushed forwards, pushed Sneaky's torso forwards and clicked on a pair of handcuffs faster than a formula one pit stop mechanic changing a wheel.

'Where's your accomplice?' asked the constable.

Sneaky remained silent. The constable looked up and signalled to another to enter the bank. The bank staff, who had raised themselves to their feet, pointed in Jock's direction when the police entered the bank. Jock lay on the ground; his feet twitching; his hands raised towards his head. The police rushed towards him and sliced away some of the duct tape from Jock's face.

'We need a doctor here,' stated one of the police.

After Jock had been secured on a stretcher and carried out of the bank with an oxygen mask attached to his nose, he was transported to the police station separate from Sneaky. The eyes that stared out from behind the duct tape did not give the police any clues to whom they had arrested or how significant they would be.

*****

Detective West flipped a hash brown over on his breakfast plate. The underside revealed itself to be as badly burnt and black as the other side. The yoke of his fried egg had also been overcooked and resembled a fake rubber toy than something edible. Chief Super-intendent Bryant sat opposite, putting large pieces of toast into his mouth that he almost almost seemed to swallow without chewing like a snake.

'So how is this Wilkinson case going anyway? Has that Copeland fellow improved any?' asked CS Bryant.

Detective West flipped the hash brown over again and watched it plop to a halt in the thick tomato sauce.

'Would you look at this? Hmmm? What is the world coming to when you can't.. Hmm.. get a decent breakfast to start the day, hmm? I'm sorry. What did you say?'

CS Bryant stopped shovelling his food into his mouth and looked up at Detective West sensing that he was irritated. CS Bryant accepted Detective West's adopted zero tolerance to some degree but complaining about a cheap, greasy hash brown was over the top.

'Wilkinson. How's that going?'

'Hmmph! Where should I start, hmm?'

Detective West placed his knife and fork on the plate and leant back in his seat. The Wilkinson case had slipped and found itself on the back burners whilst other cases took precedence. It was something Detective West hated. He also hated the lack of evidence against Chris Wilkinson. The memory card hadn't provided any further clues despite the footage being edited and the file's information displaying a time and date after the attack. Chris had edited the footage at the hospital claiming it was just initial, shaky, blurred footage that couldn't be used. To Detective West, it was crucial evidence that could have been sent to the recycle bin without any thought to its importance. It annoyed him.

'No new developments, hmm. I still believe Chris Wilkinson is our main suspect, hmm, but so far the evidence is weak.'

'Did you see him on 'Logan'? He's still using crutches!' exclaimed CS Bryant.

'The likes of him wouldn't get on the force, hmm. Crutches, hmm, Crutches. He'd never survive the way we had to sometimes, hmm. I don't like him. He's smug, hmm, overconfident, hmm, egotistical, hmm.

Hmm. No. Untrustworthy. He had something to do with this break-in and attack, hmm, and he'll slip up and when he, hmm, does..'

A waiter, who was busy wiping down the tables, approached Detective West's table and picked up their half empty plates.

'Excuse me, hmm, my breakfast was inedible. When I ordered from the menu, I'm sure I read "hash browns" and not "hash blacks", hmm? I could quite easily take part, hmm, in a art class specialising in drawing with charcoal, hmm, hmm, with that sorry excuse.'

The waiter looked at the incinerated hash brown and then at Detective West with a gormless expression.

'Two minutes a side, man, hmm, two minutes a-bloody-side, hmm.'

The café's customers paused their conversations and looked across at Detective West's table. The waiter stood still, rendered speechless by Detective West's rant.

'You wanna refund or somefink?' coughed the waiter.

Detective West tutted, turned his back on the waiter and waved him away with a flippant gesture. CS Bryant nodded at the waiter, picked up a serviette and rubbed his hands clean.

'What was all that about?'

'It was about a badly cooked breakfast, hmm. The most important meal of the day, hmm. Now I'm feeling unprepared for the day that is about to unfold, hmm.'

'Really?'

Detective West paused and looked at CS Bryant. They knew each other well enough to know when there was a problem with each other and Detective West's outburst at the waiter had spoken volumes to CS Bryant.

'The problem I have, hmm, is with this element that we call the general public, hmm. Nobody has come forward with any useful information, hmm. Pranksters mainly. False leads. Red herrings. It just makes our job more difficult, hmm. It buggers up nearly every investigation.'

'I can sympathise there. I haven't had a case that didn't attract false information from the general public,' said CS Bryant, wiping his nostrils with a serviette.

Detective West's mobile rang with a call from the station.

'Yes, hmm? .. Really? Well, that's interesting, hmm, interesting indeed. Yes. Goodbye.'

Detective West raised himself from his chair, put on his tweed jacket and ran his hand through his white fluffy hair.

'Good news?' asked CS Bryant.

187

'There's been a development, hmm, a major development. The net seems to be closing in, hmm.'

Detective West left the café without acknowledging the waiters and staff who had served him the worst breakfast he had encountered.

*****

'You're not going to like this, Sarge,' said the constable, as Detective West walked into the police station.

Detective West's stomach growled in protest of being subjected to a substandard breakfast and then being forced to digest a cheap sandwich bought from a newsagent. The day had not started well but Detective West knew that it was going to get better after being told of Sneaky and Jock's arrests. Detective West approached the constable and looked at his computer screen that had a social network page displayed. The uploaded video of the Copeland attack had received a substantial amount of attention and had spread across many of the social network and video sites on the Internet.

Detective West grumbled and rubbed his hand across his mouth, brushing away stubborn crumbs left over from the sandwich he had quickly gobbled down.

'Hmm. Hmm. Well, what can you expect from this generation, hmm? I don't really understand, hmm, this new fangled Internet. Anything that involves people being hurt, blood, accidents, hmm, seems to fascinate. I cannot fathom it out. I find it all terribly morbid hmm? Can these clips be taken down hmm? They are impeding our investigation, hmm?'

'We are trying, Sarge, but as soon as we manage to take one down, it seems that five new versions appear. We're fighting a losing battle.'

Detective West breathed a heavy sigh, ran his fingers through his white, sweaty hair and flapped his arm down by his side.

'Hmm. Well, hmm, if that's the case then maybe your time might be best spent focusing on the case itself hmm? Go through the evidence again, hmm. Look for anything we may have overlooked, hmm?'

'Yes, Sarge.'

Detective West turned away from the screen and looked around the police station. It was full with activity even though the day had only just started. The arrests of Sneaky and Jock and their statements had shone a beacon of light onto the Copeland attack and thrown Detective West a lifeline to hold onto.

'Sir? Sir? Paul is in interview room one and Jock in interview room five. They have both issued statements that I think make interesting reading,' said a sergeant.

'Can you give me the basics? Hmm? I want to talk to each of them myself, hmm.'

'Both have implicated Chris Wilkinson as being the mastermind behind the attack on Dexter Copeland.'

'Hmm. Why would they say that, hmm? And more importantly, why should we believe them, hmm?'

'Jock is the one who is being most cooperative after we did the 'your friend has told us' routine. Neither one of them wants to be made look foolish,' said the sergeant.

'Hmm. I find that most amusing considering their tomfoolery, hmm. Preposterous! Hmm. I'll start with Jock first.'

'The last time I checked, he was resting his head on the table and falling asleep,' said the sergeant with a smile.

'Well, I will have to wake him up then, hmm.'

Detective West walked away from the sergeant and entered interview room five. The force of the door slamming behind him made Jock jump back in his chair in shock. Detective West looked at Jock who reminded him of a mole popping his head out of the ground with screwed up eyes. His face was red raw from the removal of duct tape.

'James McCracken, hmm? My name is Detective West. I would like you to start from the beginning if you would be so kind, hmm?'

'Wha? For fuck's sake! I have already told you everything.'

190

'Excuse me. I will have less of that, thank you very much, hmm? I won't tolerate any foul language hmm. Manners. They don't cost anything hmm? Start from the beginning.'

Detective West stared at Jock who looked back with a half frown.

'We.. We went into the Copeland house and did it over. We took a laptop and some other things..'

'Why did you, as you so aptly put it, hmmm, do over the Copeland house? Was there something specific about that particular house or family hmm?'

'I've already fuckin' said, it was the fuckin' laptop, for fuck's sake!' said Jock waving his hands at Detective West.

Detective West's anger boiled up inside him like an indicator on a thermometer on a roasting day. He raised his hand and gave Jock a hard slap around the face. The impact of Detective West's strike made him cry out a howl of pain. Jock placed his hand on his throbbing cheek and ran it over his sandpaper skin.

'I warned you about your manners, hmm? You don't get anywhere, hmm, in life without them. Kids these days. I don't know what your parents taught you, hmm, but it's not correct. You wouldn't survive one minute at school in my day, hmm?' Corporal punishment, laddy. They should bring it back. It would make a man out of you, hmm? Now, you mentioned the laptop, hmm?'

191

'Yes. It had the codes to the bank on it,' whimpered Jock.

'Really, hmm? How did you know that?'

'That guy, Wilkinson, tipped us off.'

'And when did that happen, hmm?'

'I don't fuckin' know. Ask Sneaky,' said Jock in irritation.

Detective West struck Jock as quick as a lightning bolt across the other cheek, making Jock's whole face resemble a tomato. Jock's upper torso jerked to the side as he let out another shriek. Detective West watched Jock's upper torso jerk to the side and cower into a fetal position in anticipation of being hit again. It was enough. Detective West had no further questions for Jock but plenty for Sneaky. The noise from Detective West shuffling his chair backwards from the table made Jock flinch.

'And what did you do with this laptop?

'Sold it…sold it….,' cried Jock

Detective West sucked his bottom lip in disappointment. The laptop was a key piece of evidence that had been sold on and lost in the cosmos. There was little chance of finding it and even if the police did, the information on the hard drive would be lost forever.

'I have no further questions for you, hmm?'

Detective West left the shaken Jock behind him and

left the room, walked down the hallway towards interview room one where Sneaky was being held. A constable, who had been standing guard, looked pleased to see him.

'Hello, Sarge. You have to be careful with this one. He's highly volatile and is easily set off. It's taken a few hours for him to calm down after I started to interview him. I didn't get that far to be honest,' said the constable who had been guarding the door.

'Hmm. I see. Thanks, hmm. I can handle the likes of this whippersnapper, hmm.'

As Detective West entered the room, he noticed Sneaky was sitting bolt upright in his seat and looked ahead of him as if he was in a trance. His face didn't look as sore as Jock's but Detective West could clearly see marks from where the duct tape had been. Sneaky remained still. Detective West sat at the table opposite him.

'I'm Detective West and I need your cooperation hmm?'

'Good for you and fuck you,' stated Sneaky.

Detective West could not believe his ears. It was another toe rag. He wondered if there was a factory that produced them and turned them out into the neighbourhood. As much as Detective West wanted to slap Sneaky as he had done with Jock, he took the advice of the constable and chose to ignore it.

'I have been told that you might, hmm, have had something to do with the Copeland robbery, hmm. Is this true, hmm?'

Sneaky shrugged his shoulders.

'If you cooperate, I'll personally make sure that you receive a lighter sentence.'

Sneaky thought about the deal and considered it a way of keeping his reputation somewhat intact if a little damaged. Detective West predicted, through all his years of police experience, that Sneaky would shift the blame onto Jock.

'Yeah. So what if I did speak to Chris?' asked Sneaky.

'What did you talk about, hmm?'

'He came to me about breaking into that geezer's place. Wanted me to kill 'im. Told me about some laptop that had some bank shit on it,' exclaimed Sneaky.

'Forgive me for jumping to conclusions, hmm, but you don't look like a hitman, hmm. Did you agree to do the job?'

'Nah way! I didn't say shit to the tosser. We just decided to break in and steal things and that's it.'

'But that wasn't it, was it hmm? You left Mr Copeland with horrific injuries, hmm, and inflicted a beating on Mr Wilkinson, hmm.'

'They got in the fuckin' way,' said Sneaky without

194

any remorse.

'You went there to kill them both, hmm, didn't you, hmm?

'No. I said, we just wanted them out of the fuckin' way,' said Sneaky, getting more irritated with Detective West's questions.

Detective West sighed and started to control his anger at Sneaky's poor choice of words through taking deep breaths.

'So, hmm, you are saying, hmm, that Chris, hmm, wanted to hire you, hmm, as an assassin, hmm, with the intention of killing Dexter Copeland, hmm?'

'Yes.'

'But you said no, sorry, hmm, correction, you didn't answer him, hmm?'

'Yes.'

'So why did you stab Dexter Copeland and not Chris Wilkinson hmm? It seems to me that you went there, hmm, with malice aforethought, hmm?'

'What the fuck does that mean?' asked Sneaky.

'Please, hmm, do not swear. I told your friend the same thing, hmm. Manners don't cost anything, hmm. Manners. For your information, I am saying that you, hmm, went there with the intention to murder.'

'Nah man! It weren't murder. As I say, we just didn't

want them in the fuckin' way. My stabs were nuffink man. It was Jock that did it all anyway. He hit that Chris bloke,' pleaded Sneaky.

Detective West breathed heavily and gulped several times in quick succession. He couldn't get past his bad choice of words, which offended and irritated him.

'Hmm. How did you break into the house, hmm?'

'The back door was open.'

'Hmm. And you stole the laptop, hmm?'

'YES! For the fuckin' millionth time, YES!' shouted Sneaky.

Detective West raised his hand and slapped Sneaky across the face with an excessive force that almost knocked his interviewee off his stool. Sneaky recovered fast from the strike, raised himself and threw a right hook back in the detective's direction. Detective West ducked as Sneaky's fist flew past his left ear and failed to make contact. The constable and another officer entered the room, rushed forwards and wrestled Sneaky to the ground, restraining his arms and legs.

'You fuckin' pig. You fuckin' bastard mother fucking cunts,' spat Sneaky.

Detective West coughed, retracted his pencil and looked at his fellow colleagues who were struggling to keep Sneaky under control. Detective West watched Sneaky wriggle like a fish on the floor while continuing to use vulgar language.

'Could you make sure, hmm, that he is confined to a secure cell, hmm? We don't want the likes of him, hmm, to incite the other vagabonds here, hmm?'

The constable nodded and Detective West left the room pleased with the new information. He knew he was getting closer.

CHAPTER 16

Jules stroked the back of Dexter's hand with soft tender strokes. It had been a week since she had heard her husband's deep voice throughout their home. The children asked when their dad would be coming home. Jules always replied with 'soon'. She had found it harder to keep a sense of normality in the Copeland house after the attack.

Blip!

The machine's rhythm had not changed. Jules hated its sound; a sound that represented Dexter's struggle to cling to life. He had not moved. He had not made a sound. He had not woken. The movement of his lungs breathing in and out was the only sign that he was alive. Jules looked at Dexter's blemish free face as he lay asleep. His facial injuries had healed and Dexter looked like Dexter again. She ran her fingers down his cheek several times, starting at his eyes that she wished would open and look at her.

Blip!

She wished and prayed that he would wake up so

that they could live happily together again. Jules started to cry, drew her hand away from Dexter's face and thought about the future. She didn't want to envisage every day with a hospital visit but it started to feel as if it was becoming a part of her life. She cursed at those responsible for the attack. They had flipped her family upside down and she hated them for it.

Blip! Blip! Blip!

Out of the corner of her eye, Jules thought she saw a small movement of a finger moving. Was it her imagination playing tricks on her? She looked at the machine that had started to play a different rhythm. The green wavy lines had started to rise, and Dexter's heart rate started to increase. Jules looked at Dexter's still face that showed no signs of movement at all. The doctors had warned her that Dexter's heart rate would fluctuate at times and that it meant nothing but it didn't stop her from her hopes being raised, every time it happened.

Blip! Blip! Blip!

It wasn't her imagination. Dexter's hand started to move, looking as if he was trying to grip something that wasn't there. Jules jumped up from her stool, leant over towards Dexter's face and stared at his eyelids. Dexter looked as if he was having a nightmare. His eyes tightened together and then relaxed again.

'Yuuulsh! Yulsh!'

Dexter opened his eyes like a newborn baby. Jules

looked down at her husband and couldn't believe it. Her husband had awoken from the brutal attack, a feat that the doctors had claimed wouldn't happen. Dexter had defied them against all the odds.

'Dexter? Dexter? Dexter? Can you hear me? My God! I knew you wouldn't leave us, Dexy! I just knew it!'

Jules held Dexter's hand and rubbed the back of it with her thumb as if she was polishing a precious ornament. She looked at the machine, back at Dexter and then at the button to call for medical staff. She didn't know what to do. Her impulses told her to call her parents to tell them the good news first, then Dexter's relatives and then friends and everybody else she could. She imagined the happy look on her sons' faces when she told them the good news that daddy would be coming home again.

'Yulsh! Yulsh!'

Dexter moved his head from side to side.

'Dexter? It's me. Jules. Dexter?'

Dexter turned his head towards Jules and blinked his eyelids as if the batteries that controlled them were failing. The tears from Jules's eyes dropped onto Dexter's bed linen, creating a damp patch. Jules leant forwards and kissed Dexter again, and a nurse entered the room in a hurry, checked the machine and then Dexter. Jules stepped to the side but remained at his bedside.

201

'Is he ok? Will he be ok? Is there anything I can do to help? Is he ok?'

'He seems fine but I'll call for a doctor.'

Jules returned to her seat, as soon as the nurse had left the room, and remained fixated on her husband until the doctor arrived.

*****

'I just can't believe it, Kate. I don't know what to do. I mean, I…'

Jules paused, wiped the tears away from her eyes and listened to Kate's surprised but happy responses. Jules smashed her fork through the crust of the apple pie she had bought from the hospital's restaurant.

'He can't say much at the moment. Just my name. The doctors say to be cautious but at least he knows who I am. I'm just beside myself, Kate. I can't tell you how happy I am right now. We'll do lunch or take a coffee soon. Yep. OK. Bye!'

After Jules had finished her apple pie, she stacked the tray on the cart full of leftover meals and made her way back to Dexter's room again. As she entered the room, Dexter rolled his head to the side and looked at his wife.

'Yulesh?'

'Yes. Dexter. It's your wife.'

Dexter blinked for a second and tried to focus. Jules kissed his forehead and noticed his facial muscles trying to bend his mouth into a smile. The smile was taken away by pain when Dexter started to wriggle and writhe in his hospital bed.

'Aaarggh! Pain. Pain. Aaaargh!'

Jules moved away in sheer shock at the sight of her husband in pain and panicked. She pressed the on-call nurse button by the side of the bed and could only watch her husband shriek. The same nurse, who had attended him earlier, appeared and rushed to Dexter.

'What's wrong? Please nurse, do something for him, please,' screamed Jules.

The nurse checked the machine, Dexter's medication and looked at Dexter whose scream could be heard echoing through the shiny ultra white corridors.

'Please, Mrs Copeland, follow me,' said the nurse and led Jules outside the room and shut the door, 'I want to reassure you that your husband is not in danger. He can still feel the pain from the attack, which is a good thing in some respects. If it appears to be getting too much for him, I will call the doctor who will make a decision on sedation to make him comfortable.'

Jules looked down at the floor and started to cry. The nurse's reassurance made little impact against the sombre setting of the hospital. Jules felt that Dexter's cries of pain were indicating that he would relapse and fall back into a coma again and, possibly, die. The machine, the tubes sticking out of his arms and the mere mention of making him 'comfortable' didn't paint the picture of somebody who was 'doing well'.

'Why don't you come back tomorrow? Try and get some sleep. He'll be well looked after, Mrs Copeland. He'll be fine.'

*****

Jules returned to Dexter's bedside after a night of interrupted sleep. Her husband's screams had resonated in her mind. Despite this, her mood had been lifted by the time she reached the hospital. Dexter had not had any more painful fits of pain and doctors expected a full recovery although the road ahead would be bumpy. Dexter had suffered such a hard blow to the head that the injury had caused brain damage, which, in turn, had caused some memory loss. It would take months, a year, maybe even several years for him to return to normal.

'Wow! I haven't szeen you in agezz, Yulesh.'

'Dexter. I was here yesterday.'

Dexter screwed up his eyes as if he had sucked a lemon and looked away from Jules. She had been there every day since the attack but Dexter couldn't remember it. The extent of Dexter's memory loss didn't even allow him to remember if Jules had left his hospital room to go to the toilet and return. It had upset Jules to the point where she, at times, had to leave the hospital, collect herself and return again.

'Kate will visit you today she said.'

'Kate? God! I haa-vent szeen her for like…. Who iz she?'

'Chris's wife. You remember Chris?'

'Chriz? Yez. Chriz! He got mawwied? Wow! He hazent told me anyfing.. And Liza?'

'Lisa? I haven't heard anything about someone called Lisa. Anyway, I don't want you to think about Chris. Your so-called friend has not been in to see you once. Just concentrate on getting better.'

Dexter screwed up his face again, turned his head and looked away from Jules.

'What happened, Julez?'

The innocence of the question moved Jules to tears. She had told him about the attack the day before and the day before that. Dexter couldn't remember it. It was a test of Jules's patience as she told him again, for the tenth time, about the attack that was the reason for him lying in the hospital bed.

'Two robbers broke into our home while you and

Chris were there, attacked and beat you and stole some items. Don't you remember anything?'

The irritated tone to Jules's question ended her account of the attack. Dexter looked at Jules and remained quiet. He couldn't remember the attack no matter how hard he looked to be thinking about it. After the brief silence had ended, Dexter reached out and held Jules's hand.

'Julez? I think we zhould get mawwied. We're a team, eh?'

Jules breathed out a heavy sigh, dropped Dexter's hand and showed him the huge gleaming rock that tried to sparkle under the fluorescent hospital lights.

'Youz alweady mawwied? What? I alwaiz thought we..'

'We are married Dexter. I married you, Dexter. We have two children for god's sake!'

'We did? I don't wemember. When?'

Jules stood up from her chair and started to cry. She had told him the same information over and over again and none of it had stuck. Jules couldn't understand how he could remember Chris's ex-girlfriend Lisa but couldn't remember their own marriage and, even worse, their own children. Jules fetched a tissue from her jacket pocket, dried her eyes and blew her nose. Jules breathed another heavy sigh, turned around and looked at Dexter.

206

'Wow! I haven't szeen you in agezz, Julez.'

Jules shook her head in despair. She couldn't face going through the same conversation, the same pain, the same anguish as she had continued to do for four straight days. With the room's door open, Jules stepped out into the corridor and walked away without saying goodbye to her confused husband. Dexter turned his head and looked up at the ceiling. He didn't know what he had said wrong.

CHAPTER 17

Chris had not gone straight home after the television network's party. He had not gone straight home to the awaiting Kate and observed the scornful grimace on her face. He had not gone straight home to be with his disappointed son, Chuck. Instead, he had drunk himself into a stupor, helped into a hotel room booked by the television network by fellow partygoers and passed out until the early hours of the morning. As Chris awoke, he became disorientated by the unfamiliar lamp hanging from the ceiling. When his vision started to become clearer, he remembered what had happened the night before. He had been offered a job. A television presenting job for Sunny Days. It wasn't his own chat show that he had been hoping for but he thought it would do in the meantime.

Chris put on his glasses and looked at the clock. The time read twelve past nine. He was late but he didn't care. Chris was supposed to be at Eastern View headquarters for a meeting with Mr Lawson but he could wait. Chris had made an important decision about his future and it didn't include Eastern View.

Today was the day he had decided to quit his job of twenty years and say all the things he daren't have said whilst still being employed by them.

The journey to Chris's hometown would take an hour by train. It was the journey he was supposed to have made after the party had finished but time had run away from him. He had made a promise that he would 'be back in time for the midnight news' but he had had the best reason for not keeping it. Chris looked at his mobile, called Kate and swallowed.

'It's Chris. I'm sorry Kate. Really sorry but I have a good reason.'

'Uh huh.'

'I've been offered a job as a presenter for Sunny Days, you know, it's one of those house hunting programmes.'

'I know what it is.'

'Oh, yes, well, I'll be presenting that show. It's fantastic. Better wages but, of course, it will mean a lot of travel. It's fantastic, Kate. Things are looking up and going my way for a change.'

'Are they?'

Chris sensed irritation in Kate's short sharp answers but continued to talk.

'Yes. Just think - today - Sunny Days, tomorrow - News At Ten, the day after that - Wilkinson - my own chat show. It's the future, Kate.'

'It's your future. Not mine.'

'Come on, Kate.'

'Don't you dare! Don't you dare! You promised you would be home for the midnight news. You promised that you would spend today with Chuck. And where are you now? Probably passed on somebody's floor, half smashed. You have no bloody sense of morality, Chris. I don't care about some stupid house hunting program or how much money you'll be paid. You'll piss the majority of it up a wall. What about us? A family again. You sober. Us happy. Pfff! I…'

'No, Kate. You've got it wrong,' said Chris, interrupting Kate's ranting, 'I couldn't make it home yesterday. There was a problem with the trains and, besides, the HTN's boss talked to me about the job for hours, Kate, hours. I couldn't get away, honest, I couldn't. It was important.'

Chris listened to Kate sobbing on the other end of the line. He wondered if he had twisted the events of the previous night enough to convince her that he had no other choice.

'I even booked a hotel room. I didn't wake up on somebody's floor and I only drank one beer. ONE BEER.'

'One beer, Chris? You expect me to believe that? You promised you wouldn't drink at all. I knew this would happen. I bloody knew it. You're a fucking use-less husband. Everything is just me, me, me all the bloody time. I bet you don't have any idea that Dexter is awake and talking now either. You know why? Be-cause you haven't friggin' well visited him since the attack or asked how he's doing. You don't care about us. You don't care about him. You're just so fucking selfish.'

Chris gulped with concern. Dexter was awake and talking. Chris panicked and it felt as if his insides had started to rot away. If Dexter was awake and talking, Chris wondered what he was saying. Had he told the police his recollection of the night of the attack? Had he told them about Chris's lack of help and how he had behaved that night? Chris's fingers trembled and started to sweat around his mobile as he fell silent.

'There's nothing left for me to say, Chris. Chris? Chris?'

'D..D..Dexter is awake? How? I mean, how is he?.. I meant…'

'Like, all of a sudden, you pretend to care.'

Chris listened to the crackles and pops of his mo-bile's dead air. Kate had hung up on him. Most of her conversation had entered Chris's right ear, bypassed his brain and exited through his left ear but for one snippet of information. Dexter was awake and talking. Chris lowered his mobile down to the bed, raised his shaky hand to his sweaty forehead and started to think of the worst-case scenario. The police would put two and two together, if Dexter described the night of the attack in detail, and make Chris a suspect. Chris ran his hand through his untidy hair, raised himself out of bed and rushed to put on the clothes he had worn yesterday. The plan to quit his job had changed. Now he had to travel back to his hometown as quick as possible to visit Dexter and make sure he wouldn't talk.

*****

The train journey to Easthampton seemed to take an eternity. Chris's restless leg hopped up and down and irritated passengers watched him, puffing out sighs of disapproval. Chris entertained the notion of finishing Dexter off before he had the chance to say anything to the police. He had imagined holding a pillow over Dexter's face, suffocating him into a state of eternal peace but he knew the actual physical act of murder was beyond him. The thoughts continued to spin around in Chris's head as the train pulled up at the station. Chris left the train with gusto, bumping into people waiting on the platform, as he hurried his way towards the hospital, which was nearby.

After a ten-minute dash that left Chris breathless and feeling light headed, he reached the hospital and entered the building through the slow revolving door.

'How can I help you?' asked the receptionist.

'C…Cope..land,' gasped Chris.

'Copeland? Let's see.'

The receptionist tapped the keys on her keyboard and checked the hospital database. Chris leaned on the counter with his arms and tried, in vain, to look at the information on the screen. Chris's heavy panting attracted the attention of the receptionist who looked over at him.

'Have you run here?'

'Yes. Where can I find him?'

The receptionist, taken aback by Chris's sense of urgency, turned her attention back to the screen again.

'He's in the neurology ward. Go down this hallway to your right. Take a left at the cross section and straight ahead.'

'Thanks.'

Chris hurried down the corridors and followed the signs to the neurology ward. He walked past the ward's unmanned reception and started to peer into the rooms as he passed by. Chris looked into a room, and caught sight of Dexter sleeping. Chris opened the door and walked in. The injuries that Chris had seen Sneaky and Jock inflict could not be seen. He looked like the same Dexter he had known before the attack. Chris looked at the pipes sticking out of Dexter's arms and at the electrocardiogram that beeped to the beat of his heart. Chris gulped, approached Dexter's bedside and grabbed one of the tubes in his hand. Chris's heart filled in a beat in between the blips of Dexter's machine as the sweat started to drip off his forehead. With one quick hard determined tug of the tube, Chris believed it would be all over for Dexter. Chris looked behind him at the door to make sure nobody was watching. Dexter opened his eyes and looked up at him.

'Chriz?'

Chris dropped the tube in shock and jumped a couple of steps backwards. Chris put his hand to his heart and looked at Dexter.

'Jesus Christ! You scared the shit out of me. Christ!'

'Chriz? Wow! I haven't szeen you in agezz!'

Chris gulped, swallowed his saliva and tried to act innocent.

'I, erm, yes, well, sorry about that, I have been busy. Lot of work, you know, just had no time to come in and visit, sorry, I would have come in sooner but.. You know how it is!'

'I don't understzand. In sooner? I haven't szeen you in like, erm, yeerz. How'z youz and Liza?'

'Lisa? What are you talking about?'

'Liza. You know, you're girwlfwend.'

'Lisa? Oh! Erm, we split up ages ago. Are you ok?'

215

'You did? I can't wemember.'

Chris could see the strained tension in Dexter's face as he tried to remember the break-up. After a short moment of silence, Chris changed the subject.

'So, how have you been? I mean, since the attack. I'm still suffering from it and have nightmares about it. I have trouble sleeping. What do you remember?'

Dexter's eyebrows stayed glued in position as he tried hard to think of a response.

'Wemember? What attack? I don't understand, Chriz. Do you know what happened to Julez? I haven't szeen her for agezz.'

'You haven't seen Jules for ages? She hasn't been in to see you?'

'Yeah. I thought we'd get mawwied but…'

Dexter started to cough.

Chris stepped outside, fetched a cup of water from the coffee machine and entered Dexter's room again. He lifted the cup to Dexter's lips and he took a sip, which soothed the cough into submission. Dexter placed the cup by his bedside and looked at Chris.

'Chriz? Wow! I haven't szeen you in agezz!'

Chris smiled. Dexter had no recollection of the attack that had hospitalised him or Chris's odd behaviour on the night it happened. Chris breathed a sigh of relief.

*****

"A new twist in the case of the ANA bank robbers happened in court this morning when the perpetrators issued a counterclaim against the police for actual bodily harm. The robbers claim that the police injured them when they removed the duct tape they had used as disguises from their faces. Judge Pinehurst who resided over the case described the robbers as 'a menace to society' and dismissed their claims against the police. The robbers, Paul Andrews and James McCracken, were both sentenced to twenty years each. Martin Lawson, Eastern View."

Chris had entered Eastern View headquarters three hours after he was supposed to meet with Mr Lawson. The mention of Paul Andrews and James McCracken caught Chris's attention as he walked into the department. Martin was sitting in Chris's spot, editing the report. A photograph of Sneaky and Jock's poor disguises flashed up on the screen as Martin continued to edit. Chris laughed out loud at the stupidity of the men he had entrusted with the mission of killing Dexter. The laugh made Martin turn around and look at Chris like a rabbit caught in car headlights.

'Oh. Chris. Hello.'

'What is this, Martin? Are you the big reporter now?'

217

'This? No. This is just a practice report. My grandad says that if it is good enough, I will be a reporter.'

Chris looked at the skinny weakling who had his boney finger on the mouse and knew that he didn't have 'it'. Chris looked at the clump of yellow and red acne on Martin's chin and knew he didn't have "it". The sooner he was told, the better it would be for him. Chris knew, as it was his last day at Eastern View, that he would be the one to break the news to him.

'Look, I don't know what you expect mate. You're just a piffling work experience schoolboy with about as much charisma as a potato. Even if you bulked up, lost those zits, actually washed your hair and spoke with a voice that had fully broken, you still wouldn't be able to do my job like you are pretending to do now. Have you been watching me when I have been reporting? The microphone is my paintbrush. The story is my backdrop. The cameramen are my assistants. Pure artwork, mate. Look. Just go back to school, study something you're really good at and forget about TV. It's not for you. It really isn't.'

As the last words left Chris's lips, Martin's bottom lip complied with gravity and fell towards the floor in shock at what Chris had just said. Every word that entered his ears, seemed to cut and slice into Martin's self-esteem, shaking his confidence to the core. Chris hoped that his insulting description of the spotty weakling was an apt one. Martin turned his head away from Chris and looked at the floor. Other members of staff, who had heard Chris's character annihilation of Martin, shook their heads in disbelief. Chris shrugged his shoulders nonchalantly at them.

'What? What are you looking at? At least I have the guts to tell him the truth. It's what you all think too for sure.'

'CHRIS? GET IN HERE NOW!' shouted the red-faced Mr Lawson from his office door.

It wasn't often that Mr Lawson raised his voice and it made most of the stunned silent staff of Eastern View drop everything they were working on and look in his direction. Chris looked at the raging Mr Lawson's and remained quiet as he walked towards him. A large part of him felt a certain sense of liberation from the job that he had grown bored of but at the same time, he also felt excited by the attention. It wasn't a case of dead man walking through; it was a case of a man reborn. Chris had pictured his glorious resignation on the train, during every day and in his dreams. It was time to light the flaming torch and throw it onto the bridge. Once Chris had stepped past Mr Lawson and into his office, the door slammed behind him, marking the start of whispered conversations between Eastern View employees.

'How DARE you speak to Martin like that? How DARE you. Who do you think you are?' snapped Mr Lawson.

'I'm Chris Wilkinson and he shouldn't be such a

lightweight,' answered Chris.

'I'm sorry. I beg your pardon. What did you just say?' asked Mr Lawson, shocked by Chris's attitude.

'He shouldn't be a lightweight, deaf man. There's not a TV station in the country that would employ Martin looking the way he does, sounding the way he does and being the way he is. It's only because he's your grandson that he's stayed on longer than he should have.'

Chris had got twenty years of built up repression off his chest. All the useless news stories, all the time spent compiling the reports and all the years of going unrecognised were now being addressed. Mr Lawson rubbed the bridge between his eyes and tapped his fingers on his desk.

'Chris. In all my years, I have never heard such ill-mannered insults drop off a tongue of an employee that I actually used to respect. If this is the way you truly feel then I feel sorry for you. Martin looked up to you but after this? I can only assume that his estimation of you will be like mine right now - down in the gutter.'

Chris remained standing in front of Mr Lawson who grimaced. A wry smile started to form on Chris's face. It felt as if it was the first time he had enjoyed himself for years.

'I don't care. The truth is the truth. It's best that he knows now rather than be ridiculed and find out later that his grandad pulled strings for him. What sort of career would you be setting up for him by doing that anyway? It's all false.'

'Don't you dare accuse me of nepotism. Don't you dare accuse me of nepotism. Martin will make an excellent reporter and him being my grandson had nothing - NOTHING - to do with it. He'll make a better reporter than you, I can tell you that.'

The wry smile faded from Chris's face and turned into a frown. It was one of the worst insults anyone had hurled at Chris and it hurt. It was a low blow. Chris couldn't imagine Martin chasing criminals down the street, doing charity bungee jumps or riding in helicopters. Martin didn't have "it".

'Well. What else can I say than fuck it! I don't need to be told by some has been who I am, what I can do or can't do or where I'm going. As from today, I am no longer an employee of Eastern View because I quit. You heard me - I QUIT!' shouted Chris.

The speech had gone almost the way he had imagined it. Chris turned his back on Mr Lawson, put his hand on the door handle and waited for a moment. He waited for the pleas of "I forgive you. Don't leave. You are the best. We won't survive without you".

'Fine with me. Saves me from firing you. I'm calling security to escort you out of the building,' said Mr Lawson without any hesitation.

Chris shrugged his shoulders, pulled down on the

door handle and stepped out into the department. Two security guards approached Chris, stood either side of him and ushered him through the department. Chris smiled and looked up at the employees he would leave behind, some of whom he had worked with for years. Chris winked at Geoff the cameraman as he walked out of the mute, quiet department and out of the doors. He would never have to face any of them, including Martin, again.

*****

Chris rattled the wrong key around in the front door's lock after coming home late. He had walked out of Eastern View and straight into The Belvedere where he had remained for hours until closing time. Chris stumbled over the doorstep and into the Wilkinson home after finding the right key. Chris walked into the living room, threw his glasses down on the table, collapsed onto the sofa and passed out.

*****

A text message beeped Chris awake in the early hours of the morning. He put on his glasses and read the text message about check in times and departures from the airline that would fly the Sunny Days crew to

Spain. Chris wiped his bloodshot eyes with his thumbs and knew that he would have to pack and get ready for the trip.

'Kate? KATE?'

Silence greeted him again. Chris raised himself from the sofa and looked up the stairs for a sign of movement. Nothing.

'Chuck?'

Nothing. Kate and Chuck were not there. Chris scratched his head in bewilderment and started to call Kate on his mobile whilst walking up the stairs to fetch a travel case. An answer-phone. Chris hung up without leaving a message and started to throw clothes into his open, empty travel case. Chris was going to travel to Spain regardless of the state his family was in. It signalled a new beginning and nothing would stand in the way of it, not even Kate and Chuck. Chris assumed they would come around to his way of thinking, and agree that it was all for the good of the Wilkinson family unit for him to become a successful TV personality after all his years spent at Eastern View.

Chris shut the travel case and twiddled the four numbered dials on the padlock around. He checked his watch. Time was running away fast. Although Chris still smelt of alcohol and cigarettes, he dodged a shower and opted to leave for the airport. As Chris stepped outside, a car pulled up by the curb.

'Mr Wilkinson, hmm, I need to have a word with

you, hmm.'

Chris shut the boot and looked startled as Detective West approached him.

'Going somewhere, hmm?'

'Spain.'

'Oh really? Hmm. I see. Escaping, hmm?' asked Detective West.

'Escaping?'

Chris could feel his heart rate increase when Detective West moved closer towards him.

'Are you ok, hmm? You seem a bit rough around the edges, hmm.'

'Yeah, yeah. I'm ok. Yes. I'm ok. Never better in fact.'

Chris spat into his hands and slicked back his hair. He looked at Detective West and waited for him to speak.

'Well. As you probably already know, hmm, we arrested and convicted the two bank robbers who tried to pull the ANA bank robbery, hmm. They've both mentioned you, hmm, as being involved. Have you any idea why they would do that, hmm?'

Chris rubbed his hand over his face and looked at the ground. He hadn't thought of Sneaky and Jock grassing on him. A couple of excuses filtered through

Chris's brain before he looked up at Detective West, and selected one that would be the most plausible.

'Well, I guess they would mention me,' quipped Chris.

Detective West was taken by surprise.

'Oh? And why would that be, hmm?'

'Paul is probably still pissed off about that camera raid story I ran on him. You know, I made him look stupid, you know. It's just revenge. I don't know what reason James would have other than he is his friend and will just agree with whatever he says. I'm not surprised.'

Detective West squinted at Chris. Chris dived his hand into his jacket pocket, pulled out a packet of cigarettes and lit one. Although Chris was holding his ground, he couldn't control how nervous he felt. Detective West shuffled his feet and stepped away from the cloud of smoke that had started to irritate him.

'Hmm. They also mention a laptop that they say had codes to all the security doors in the bank on it, hmm. I have spoken to Mrs Copeland, hmm, and she claims that there was not any sensitive information on the computer, hmm. She claims that if that file existed, hmm, someone must have put it on the machine, hmm, as she certainly did not,' said Detective West watching Chris smoke his cigarette with shaky fingers.

'I don't know anything about her laptop other than

the fact that she had one.'

Detective West raised his hand to his chin and held it. Chris took another drag on his cigarette.

'Hmm. I see. Hmm. Well, hmm, have you remembered anything, hmm, else from the night, hmm, of the attack, hmm? You forgot about the, hmm, memory card, hmm, after all, hmm?'

'No. I have told you everything that I can remember about that night. You have the two criminals that did it. Isn't that enough?'

Chris took one last drag of his cigarette, threw the butt to the ground and stamped it out.

'If there is nothing else, I have a plane to catch.'

'Hmm. No. There isn't anything else, hmm, at least, hmm, for now.'

Detective West turned, scratched his head hard, coughed and walked away towards his car.

'Oh, hmm, there is something else, hmm. I will be giving your friend, Dexter, a visit today, hmm. I hear he is awake and improving, hmm. You must be pleased and joyous, hmm?'

'Sure. Say hello for me.'

Chris reversed out of the driveway and drove past Detective West, who stared at him through the windshield. Chris felt rattled by the Detective's insistent line of questioning but he had disavowed any knowledge of the file on the laptop and knew that Sneaky and Jock's criminal reputations discredited them as witnesses. Chris could relax safe in the knowledge that Dexter couldn't remember who he was, let alone the night of the attack. Chris pressed his foot down on the accelerator, breathed out a relieved sigh and drove down the motorway towards the airport.

CHAPTER 18

Detective West knew exactly where to find Dexter's room. He had been there a number of times before and the walk through the white, polished hallways had become easy. He approached the door to the room, peered through the window and saw Jules weeping by her husband's bedside. Dexter Copeland was asleep. Detective West pushed the door open and entered, attracting Jules's attention.

'Mrs Copeland? I'm sorry to disturb you, hmm.'

'It's ok, Detective, it's ok. Come in.'

'Whatever is the matter, hmm?'

'It's nothing, really, it's…'

Jules lowered her head and started to cry.

'The doctors have said that Dexter will never recover. That he has permanent brain damage. That he will always be like this. I can't..I can't let myself believe that.'

Detective West bit his lip.

'Oh. Hmm. You have my condolences Mrs Cope-land, hmm.'

Detective West's hopes of any improvement in Dexter's condition had been dealt a blow along with his hope of Dexter remembering vital information of the attack. Putting his disappointment to one side, Detective West put his arm around Jules's shoulders and comforted her.

'The doctors are wrong. Dexter is a fighter. He wouldn't just check out on me like this. He simply wouldn't. The doctors are wrong.'

The noise from Jules's cries woke Dexter up. He tilted his head to one side and looked at his wife and the unknown figure beside her.

'Julez?'

'Dexter. I'm sorry, we didn't mean to wake you.'

'Who iz thiz?'

'My name is Detective West, hmm, I'm investigating the attack that has left you incapacitated, hmm.' Detective West turned to Jules. 'Can I ask him some questions?'

'You can but I don't think he will be able to answer them.'

'I'd like to ask you a few questions, hmm,' said Detective West, looking at Dexter.

'Hmm?' asked Dexter.

'Hmm. Yes. Do you feel you could answer them? Hmm?'

Detective West looked at Dexter's confused expression and, despite the news of Dexter's permanent brain damage, had no intention of backing away from his course of enquiry.

'I'll get straight to the point, Mr Copeland. Do you remember anything about your attack, hmm? What was Chris doing?'

'Chriz? Wow! I haven't szeen him in agezz!' commented Dexter, ignoring Detective West's questions.

'He says this all the time, Detective. He just can't remember anything,' said Jules.

'Hmm. Can you please try and remember Mr Copeland, hmm? Can you remember anything about the attack at all?'

'Attack? I don't know know anyzthing about an attack. Who is this man, Julez?'

'Mr Copeland! Please. Hmm. Could you just try, hmm, and think about it. What happened that night? Did Chris help you? Hmm?' snapped Detective West, irritated by Dexter's lack of answers.

'I don't think this is going anywhere, Detective, and I would like you to leave please. You are distressing my husband and he's been through enough already,' said Jules.

'I'm sorry, Mrs Copeland, hmm, I didn't mean to, hmm, upset you or Mr Copeland, hmm.'

'Chriz? Wow! I haven't szeen him in agezz! Or Kate.'

Jules jolted her head towards Dexter as if she had been brought back to life by defibrillators.

'What did you just say?'

Dexter frowned and looked at Jules. She had not understood what he had just said.

'Chriz. I haven't seen him for ages or his wife, Kate.'

Jules started to cry and hugged Dexter tight, which took him by surprise.

'You've never said that before, Dexter. You've never mentioned Kate before. I knew you hadn't left me. I knew it. The doctors don't know what they are talking about.'

Detective West smiled. The evidence he needed was all locked up in Dexter's head like a nut and the small sign of improvement he had witnessed, made him feel confident that he would crack it open. Jules loosened her hug on her husband and reached into her pocket for her mobile to inform everybody of the good news.

'Is it ok to continue, hmm?'

'I don't know, Detective. I'm too.. .. gone.. to even make a decision. What is all this about anyway? Haven't you arrested those responsible and haven't they been sent down?' asked Jules.

'Yes. We they have, hmm, but we need more information, especially from Dexter, hmm, more information on Chris Wilkins.., hmm!'

Detective West cut off his conversation after he realised that he had let sensitive information about the attack slip out of his mouth. He couldn't take it back. Jules blinked and shook her head upon hearing that Chris, her husband's best friend, might have been involved in the attack.

'Are you saying that Chris was involved in the attack? Is that what you just said?'

'No, hmm, not at all, hmm, I, hmm. No.'

'Chris? Really? I would find that hard to believe. What makes you think that?' asked Jules, puzzled by Detective West's slip.

A carrot had been dangled in front of Jules and she looked at Detective West with an expectation that she would get an answer to her question.

'I can't, hmm, tell you any details, hmm, of the case, hmm, but if your husband, hmm, remembers any small detail, ANY small detail, hmm, can you call me immediately, hmm?'

'Yes, but,….'

'Well, hmm, I must be going, hmm. It was nice talking to you Mr Copeland, hmm.'

Detective West backed away towards the door.

'Who iz thiz?' asked Dexter.

'Oh, hmm, there is one more thing, Mrs Copeland, hmm. Are you sure you didn't give your laptop password out to anybody except Dexter, hmm?'

'Yes. I am quite sure about that. Detective West? Is Chris is involved?' asked Jules again.

'I wish you both a good day, hmm.'

Detective West opened the door and left Dexter's room.

CHAPTER 19

Jules had thought about Detective West's comment about Chris. She had thought about all the variables over and over again until it sounded like a broken record. Jules asked herself if Chris could have really done it and why. She couldn't figure out a motive in her mind but the circumstantial evidence was there. Jules spotted Kate enter the bistro. She looked windswept and jagged around the edges. Jules was taken aback by her unkempt appearance and could tell that there was something wrong.

'Hi. Sorry I'm late,' said Kate. 'The traffic was awful.'

Jules noticed black bags under Kate's eyes that were devoid of any make-up. She had combed her hair back and tied it in a ponytail. Multiple creases crisscrossed Kate's blouse and it looked as if she had worn it for days. Jules hugged Kate and sat back down at the table again.

'Have you been here long?' asked Kate.

'No. Not really. Five minutes, perhaps.'

There was a brief silence as they looked at each other across the table. They had not seen each other for some time although Kate had visited Dexter a number of times.

'So, how are things with you and Chris?' asked Jules.

Kate lowered her head, picked up the menu and tried to hide her face from Jules. She started to cry, and the menu shook in her hands followed by uncontrollable sobs. Kate folded the menu, placed it on the table and reached into her pocket for a tissue.

'Things could be worse, I guess, but we have split up again. I don't know what has got into him. He can't control his drinking and had started to come home late again, or not at all. I've had enough. He doesn't care. He doesn't care at all.'

Jules stroked Kate's arm up and down. She didn't like seeing her friend in pain but knew she was better off without Chris, especially if he was responsible for the attack on her husband. She had never liked Chris right from day one but he was Dexter's long time friend. She had made allowances and had tolerated him as best she could.

'Where are you staying?'

'With my parents until we find somewhere. Chuck is in a right state. He's playing up at school and the teachers say he is disruptive. It's all I need, Jules. It's all I need,' spluttered Kate.

A waitress approached the table and asked for their orders, interrupting the women's conversation.

'How's Dexter?' asked Kate

'He's doing so well, Kate. The doctors said that he wouldn't improve and that he would stay the way he is but he's proved them wrong. He remembered you. He mentioned you by name and said who you were. I'm so happy.. and proud in a way. He's a fighter. I knew he had it in him,' said Jules and smiled.

'That's great news Jules. I'm pleased for you and Dexter,' said Kate.

Jules took a sip of wine and started to think about Detective West's investigation and about the conversation they had had at the hospital. She started to wonder if Kate knew anything about the evening of the attack or if Chris had been acting strange that night. She had to find out if he was responsible for causing the immense pain in the Copeland family. She had to know.

'It's all thanks to Detective West that Dexter remembered,' said Jules.

'Detective West? How's that?'

'He came to visit Dexter while I was there. Started questioning him about the night of the attack and about Chris and that's when he mentioned you.'

'Oh. Really? Well, it's a result if anything.'

237

The waitress returned to their table with the steaming hot plates of pasta that filled the air with the smell of basil and Parmesan. Jules pierced her fork into a twist of fusilli and lifted it to her mouth. Jules looked at Kate who picked at her pasta with her fork as if she was a child who didn't want to eat their greens. Tears started to fall from Kate's eyes as she continued to play with her food.

'I'm not really that hungry,' cried Kate and dropped her fork onto the rim of the bowl.

'God, Kate! You really are in a bad way.'

'I'm sorry, Jules. I just haven't been myself since me and Chris split. The last conversation we had wasn't a good one. He's got some new presenting job that he took without talking to me first. Days in the Sun, I think it is called, no, Sunny Days. Sunny Days. Now he's off, travelling the globe, looking at houses and spending more time away. Honestly, Jules. It's as if we don't exist.'

'Sunny Days?' asked Jules.

'It's a property house hunting show.'

'I see,' said Jules.

Jules rested back in her seat and started to connect the dots. Chris had been in the headlines ever since the attack as the hero that tried save his friend. It was starting to make sense. If it hadn't been for the attack, Chris would still be an unknown local TV news reporter. Jules coughed and couldn't conceal the disgust she felt. All the information she had gained from Detective West and, now Kate, all seemed to point at Chris's guilt.

'Has Detective West spoken to you at all recently?' asked Jules, continuing to stab at her pasta.

'Erm, no, not for a while. Does he want to speak to me?'

'Well, he didn't say as much but I got the impression that he is still investigating.'

'Investigating? What, you mean, the attack? I thought they had sent the two responsible down for it.'

'They have but Detective West is thorough, you know,' said Jules, looking at Kate.

Jules leant forward, ate another mouthful of pasta and washed it down with a small swig of wine.

'He'll probably speak to you soon. You know, ask you questions about where you were on the night of the attack or what Chris was doing, how he was acting, you know.'

'I've already told him where I was on the night of the attack. I was visiting my parents with Chuck. I didn't even know Chris had planned to go and see Dexter. The way Chris was acting? What's all this about, Jules?' asked Kate.

Jules had not been subtle and Kate had started to frown at her from across the table.

'Well, Detective West said he was investigating Chris's involvement in the attack.'

Kate's mouth dropped open in shock, followed by a small shake of her head.

'Wha.. What? What did you say?' asked Kate, still in shock.

'He's investigating Chris's involvement in my husband's attempted murder and as far as I am concerned, I think he is right to do so,' said Jules.

'WHAT? You've got to be kidding. Chris maybe many things but he's not a murderer. NO WAY!' shouted Kate.

The well dressed restaurant guests on the table behind stopped eating and turned around to look at the commotion.

'Chris wouldn't attack anyone. He wouldn't attack Dexter. No. No. No. Detective West has got it wrong. YOU'VE got it wrong.'

'No, Kate, listen to me. The evidence points to him. It all points to him,' pleaded Jules.

'HOW exactly? Tell me, HOW?'

The manager of the bistro approached the table, wary of stepping too close to Kate who looked as if she was going to throw the wine glass at Jules.

'Is there a problem here?' asked the manager.

'No,' replied Kate, 'I was just leaving.'

Kate drank the remaining wine and threw the glass onto the table, smashing it into jagged shards and fragments. Jules jumped in fright, looked at the manager and shrugged her shoulders. Kate grabbed her coat and walked towards the entrance with fast heavy footsteps.

'I will clear this up,' said the manager, pointing to the broken wine glass, 'Do you want me to call the police?'

'No. No, thanks. That won't be necessary. I'd like the bill though. I'm sorry about this,' replied Jules embarrassed.

The manager gave a wry smile and called for the waitress to bring the bill. The other bistro guests turned back to their respective tables and continued eating their lunches. Jules paid the bill and left the bistro through the back door to the car park.

CHAPTER 20

"Now this property comes in at under your budget. In fact, substantially under your budget at £595,000."

The stunned house hunters turned and looked at each other in shock. Chris had revealed that their dream house was cheaper than they had expected. The filming of Sunny Days had been much harder than Chris had imagined and the last show in the series was testing his patience. The tight hectic schedule of showing one couple a day around three properties, combined with the hot temperature, had taken its toll on Chris from day one. The punters had been testing his patience. He had heard the phrases "this is chocolate boxy" and "this ticks all the boxes" all too often, making him resent the whole experience.

'I liked the house but the stairs were a bit too up and down,' commented the house-hunting husband.

'Well, that's what stairs do. You either walk up them or you walk down them. What did you expect?' snapped Chris.

'CUT! CUT! Chris? A word?' shouted the producer

from behind the camera.

Chris looked at the film crew and walked towards the producer, leaving the offended customers rooted to the path to their dream house.

'What was that about, Chris? I've told you before to hold your tongue. Staple it to your bottom lip if you have to. You don't insult the guests on the show,' said the producer.

'Well, they shouldn't say such ridiculous things. The stairs are a bit too up and down. I mean, come on.'

'Ridiculous to you but not to the show. You are here to present the show. Full stop. We chose you over other perfectly able presenters who would have given their right arm for this job. Go and fuckin' present and shut the fuck up.'

Chris looked at the angry producer who spat demands at him. Over the producer's shoulder, Chris noticed Rod Parkton in the distance who was leaning up against a wall and watching the proceedings. Chris acknowledged him with a nod of the head but didn't get a response back. Chris gulped. He didn't know whether it was odd for the chief executive of the network to be in Spain with the crew or not. Chris thought that he was maybe on holiday and had passed by to say hello. Maybe he had passed by to check up on his new presenter and to pass judgment. Maybe he had seen Chris insult the house hunters and that he would be fired as soon as the filming had finished. Chris glanced at the producer, turned away and walked towards the house hunters who looked upset.

'I'm sorry. I'm sorry. It must be the sun or something. I didn't mean to snap at you. Shall we continue?'

The house hunters looked at each other bemused whilst the producer whipped the crew back into filming again.

'So, what do you think then? Ha! Ha! This could be your own palace in your dream location, AND, it's UNDER budget! Ha! Ha!'

Rod Parkton stood up straight and walked over to the producer.

'So, every day, you said in your email, every day is like this.'

'I wasn't fuckin' lying. You saw what just happened,' said the producer, 'he can't control his fuckin' mouth. Ends up insulting the guests, insulting us, insulting everything. I don't know where you found him from but I'd like you to put him back there.'

'Hmmm. I see. Well, maybe he's not right for this show' commened Rod.

'Too fuckin' right,' snapped the producer.

'But maybe, he's right for something else.'

'A fuckin' cleaning job, I hope.'

'Don't be like that.'

245

'How else do you want me to be? He's offensive, Rod. Offensive to everybody. There's not one person amongst the crew that likes him. I honestly can't work with him. And he drinks too much. The guy has problems and, despite this, he thinks he is better than everybody else. Even you, perhaps.'

Rod laughed and placed his hand on the producer's shoulder.

'Ha! Ha! Well, so what if he does. It just says to me he would be perfect for Bon Voyeur.'

'Really?'

'Of course. The controversial character. We need someone to antagonise the others on that show. The ratings have been dropping off recently. We need to get them back.'

'And you think Chris is your solution?' asked the producer, aghast at the suggestion.

'Don't you?'

The producer shrugged his shoulders and turned his attention to finishing the episode.

'AND… CUT! That's it everyone.'

'Chris? Can I have a word?' shouted Rod.

Chris walked away from the house hunters without saying a word to them. The crew talked amongst themselves and drank bottles of water from a crate.

246

'Hello, Rod. I didn't expect to see you here. How long had you been standing there?' asked Chris.

'Long enough.'

'Oh. Well. I apologised to them. I didn't mean to bark at them like that. It's just the heat and the crazy schedule. It's taken it out of me,' stuttered Chris.

Rod laughed and put his arm around Chris's shoulders. Chris gave a wry smile and felt confused.

'Don't apologise, Chris, don't apologise. The people we get on these shows are all plebs but do you know what the most important thing is, Chris?'

Chris shook his head.

'We're not plebs, or more to the point, you're not. Listen, I was thinking that Sunny Days is a bit beneath you actually. I was thinking that you might need a challenge.'

Chris remained quiet and wondered where Rod was going. Maybe Rod was about to offer him his own chat show? Chris started to imagine his future where everybody would know his name. All the big celebrities would want to be on his show Wilkinson, a show where they could talk about anything they wanted to talk about. An informal chat show where guests would be respected.

'I was thinking. How about Bon Voyeur?'

'Bon Voyeur?'

'Yes. We are in dire need of someone like you. I actually liked the way you treated those plebs up there on the steps. If you can do that and be like that twenty-four seven, you could see your name in the tabloids, in the broadsheets, everywhere. What d'ya say?'

'Well, I, don't know really. Up there, on the steps, was just a one off really.'

'So modest, Chris, so modest. You don't have to lie to me, Chris. I bet you've always felt as if you've been held back. Always misunderstood. Am I right?' asked Rod.

Chris nodded his head and felt drawn to Rod. He had hit the nail on the head. The world owed him something after years of being an unknown TV presenter. He looked at Rod and remained silent. Bon Voyeur was not the News At Ten. It was far from the fantasy of the Wilkinson chat show. Rod looked back at Chris with raised eyebrows and a look in his eye that was hard to say no to.

'It's a step up from this, Chris. If you want the fame and the glory, you can have it but under one condition.' Rod lowered his eyebrows, dropped his smile and spoke in a serious tone. 'You let that personality of yours off the hook. Let it create havoc. Controversy. Let the world know that you are in it.'

Chris nodded and thought about Bon Voyeur, a show he had not even watched but knew all about. The newspapers could not go one day without an article published about one of the guest's outrageous behaviour. The net was rampant with stories of guests who had been voted off the show. They had all become celebrities almost overnight. Book deals. Documentaries. Interviews. Guest appearances. All Chris had to do was to be himself and that wasn't hard to do. Chris looked at Rod and smiled.

'It sounds great, Rod.'

'Ha! Ha! You'll be the star of the show for sure.'

Chris and Rod walked away from the film crew and towards a taxi that waited for them. Chris started to think about the stories in the newspapers that brandished his name in bold print. He started to think about the opportunities Bon Voyeur would open up to him. He started to think about his successful future. He didn't think about Kate and Chuck. Not even once.

*****

Chris would appear on Bon Voyeur as soon as he landed back in the UK. The airport was busy and packed full of tourists with sunburn who had crammed themselves into the same tourist shop as Chris and Rod. After they had waited ten minutes in a queue, they left the shop and sat down in the waiting area. Rod unfolded the tabloid he had bought and extended his legs, resting them on the table in front of him. A woman with two energetic children shook her head in disgust at Rod's audacity for using the table as his footrest. Chris looked at the front page, which carried the headline 'A Right Royal Shock!' and a photo of a Prince in a compromising position.

'You see, here, right here, this is what it's about.'

Rod showed Chris the middle pages. Chris looked at the screen grabs from Bon Voyeur that showed two of the show's guests naked and having sex. Chris read the words 'EXCLUSIVE' and 'SHOCKING' across the top of the pages followed by the first names of each guest.

'You see, even in Spain they are famous. Even in Spain.'

'Yeah, I guess. But they probably don't sell this newspaper anywhere else other than this airport,' quipped Chris.

Rod scrunched the newspaper down on his lap, an angry grimace took over his smile.

'That's not the point. We are in Spain and so is this story. Can't you imagine how many people had read this or just looked at the pictures? Can you? It's a big fucking show!' shouted Rod.

The woman sitting opposite rounded up her children, tutted in Rod's direction and moved to another section of the waiting room, far away from Rod's foul language. Chris noticed Rod's irritation towards him and turned away. Rod straightened out the newspaper and turned to the centre pages again.

'Just remember. You can have it all. You can have it all.'

The words repeated themselves in Chris's head on the flight home. He could have it all. He could have it all. By the time they had landed and had passed through the gates into the main section of the airport, Chris had convinced himself that he could have it all and that nothing would get in his way. That was until a photograph of Dexter on the front of a film magazine caught his attention. Chris's walk ground to a standstill as Rod strode ahead of him, unaware that Chris had stopped by the newsagent's stand. The article focused on Dexter's attack, how it was a miracle that he had survived and how he was improving day by day despite the doctor's initial bleak outlook. The film manuscript that he was working on would be completed and shot.

'What the hell are you reading?' said Rod who had turned around and approached Chris.

'Erm, oh, erm, nothing, really. Nothing.'

'Why waste your time on nothing? We have things to do, Chris.'

Chris skim read the rest of the article and placed the magazine back in the rack. The doctors now expected Dexter to make a full recovery and regain 75% of his memory. Chris gave out a nervous cough. There was a 25% chance that Dexter wouldn't remember anything about the attack and Chris started to feel uneasy about those odds.

'Come on! I've got a taxi waiting. Come on!'

The news shot shivers and goose pimples down Chris's spine. His stomach had started to feel as nervous as it had on the night of the attack. Rod's constant conversation sounded like a foreign language, rebounding off his ears, failing to find a way into his distracted mind.

'Are you listening to me, Chris? CHRIS? HELLO?' barked Rod with irritation.

'Oh, erm, sorry, I was *cough* miles away there.'

'Shit. You'd better not be like this on the show otherwise..'

'No. No. It's ok. I'm ok,' stuttered Chris.

'You'd better be.'

Chris and Rod left the airport and got into the taxi bound for the set of Bon Voyeur.

*****

The Bon Voyeur house had been built in the middle of a disused industrial estate, a perfect spot that members of the public wouldn't recognise. A large security team guarded the house day and night, to stop any contestants from escaping over the barbwire fences and out-side crowd of film extras wanting to get in. The pro-duction crew had received the news that Chris would be arriving and had rolled out a red carpet in front of the door to the Bon Voyeur house. The crowd, stand-ing either side of the carpet, would welcome him with an abundance of fake energy. Loud cheers. Deafening whistles. Sparkling fireworks. It was the treatment a member of the royal family would receive on a visit. Rod and Chris's taxi had pulled up alongside a stretch limo that would take Chris to the house.

'Now, remember what I said. You are there to cause trouble. You are the troublemaker. I want you to spread rumours and create arguments between the contestants,' urged Rod.

'Ok. I guess I can do this if it will, as you said, open doors for me.'

'It'll open doors. It will open doors. No guessing, Chris. As I said, just let that personality of yours off the hook. You can even hurl a few insults out as all swearwords are automatically detected and bleeped. Controversy, Chris. That's all I want.'

Chris breathed out a nervous sigh and fidgeted in his seat.

'Look, you'll have a kind of script to follow. It'll be fed to you when the cameras are focused on another participant in the house. You don't have to worry. As I said, all you have to be is yourself!'

Chris opened the taxi door, walked across the road and into the stretch limo that drove him to the entrance of the Bon Voyeur house. The fake crowd that had been waiting for hours began to scream when the limo drove slower than a snail's pace to the edge of the red carpet. Chris stepped out of the limo and onto the red carpet as fireworks exploded to mark his arrival.

"And here we introduce, Chris Wilkinson, a forty-three year old TV presenter from Easthampton. Some of his interests include; drinking, women and topical events," announced a voice over a tannoy.

The crowds cheered as Chris smiled and waved whilst walking up the red carpet to the door. The door opened and Chris stepped inside to the sound effect of a loud thud behind him.

Once inside, Chris continued to walk towards the kitchen were all the contestants were sitting, enjoying drinks. One of the contestants, Denise, a woman of Jamaican descent, stood up and extended her hand for a handshake.

'Hello. I'm Denise.'

Chris looked at her and shook her hand.

'I'm Chris.'

Some of the other contestants followed Denise's example and introduced themselves whilst others remained seated and nodded.

'What brings you to this happy home?' asked Marilyn, a post transgender patient.

Chris looked at Marilyn and was shocked at the overwhelming amount of make-up on her face.

'Erm. The challenge, I guess,' said Chris.

'Ha! Ha! Challenge? What challenge would that be then, baby?'

Chris felt uncomfortable being called 'baby' by Marilyn and winced at her. Her question went unanswered. Chris nodded at the other contestants and looked out of the kitchen window at a climbing frame in the garden.

'What's that for?'

'The climbing frame?' said Roger, the oldest contestant of Bon Voyeur, 'that's for our physical challenges and general well-being.'

'Are you sure you are up to that?' asked Chris.

Roger's mouth dropped open as he reeled from hearing the insult roll off Chris's sharp tongue.

'I'll have you know that I am as fit as a fiddle. I might be old but I'm not decrepit,' quipped Roger.

Chris smiled and looked at the kitchen. It was a bog standard kitchen made up of cheap plywood cupboards and hard plastic work surfaces. No expense had been spared on the house's decor and it made Chris wonder if his bedroom would be the same.

'As a new tenant in this house, there are a few rules that you should be aware of,' said Brenda, an over-weight woman in her mid-forties, 'anyone new to the house must do the washing up and the hoovering for the first three days from their arrival. We don't tolerate mess in this house. We also require new guests to tell all the other guests about themselves. It helps to break the ice. So .. Go ahead, Chris, tell us who you are.'

'I know who he is,' piped up Mark, a stocky guy featuring tattoos, 'he's the guy that filmed that attack. That film director guy. What's his name? Copeland. That's it. Copeland. How's your mate doing?'

Chris fell silent. It seemed he could not escape the mention of Dexter Copeland, note even in the Bon Voyeur house. He had not expected to be asked any questions about Dexter let alone answer them.

'He's doing ok.'

'Oh yeah! I thought I recognised you. You're that guy!' said Marilyn fluttering her mascara thick eyelashes at Chris.

'Uh hmm! I'm Chris Wilkinson. I am married to Kate and have a son called Chuck. I have worked as a local television news reporter for many years and have presented Sunny Days.'

Chris stopped talking and waited for a reaction. After a brief moment of silence, Denise stood up and spoke.

'Can't you tell us more about the attack? How you filmed it and lived to tell the tale?'

Chris could only think about the image of Dexter lying in his hospital bed telling Detective West everything. The housemates of the Bon Voyeur house had already started to get under his skin and their line of questioning showed little sign of easing.

'Well, you know, it was rough. It's hard to talk about actually. I'd rather not go into it. The people responsible are in jail and that's all that matters really,' said Chris hoping to deflect Denise's questions.

'Well, I think you were brave, what you did, secretly filming the attackers in an effort to get them caught,' said Denise.

Chris raised an instant smile. Denise had called him brave and the other housemates seemed to sympathise. Chris leant back on the kitchen surface's countertop and started to suck up the adoration.

'Well, you know, when faced with a situation like that, you just do what you have to do, you know. I felt it was the best thing to do under the circumstances. I knew I couldn't stop the attackers but I knew I could help get them arrested. I didn't think too long about making that decision either. I knew what I was doing and the risks but did it anyway.'

Every moment was being caught on camera and he knew that even more people would now view the infamous footage of the attack. Soon Chris would be known right across the country and not just in his hometown of Easthampton.

'And you said that your friend is doing ok? Dexter?' asked Denise.

Chris gave a nervous cough and looked down at the floor, avoiding eye contact.

'Er. Ok. Tell us about your family then,' said Denise.

Chris took a deep breath and exhaled. He wasn't in the mood to talk about a happy family when there wasn't one to speak of. Chris took off his glasses, gave them a quick polish with his shirt and put them back on again. Denise stared at Chris in anticipation of an answer, which heightened his irritation. He hadn't had a drink for twenty-four hours or smoked a cigarette for at least the same amount of time. Chris breathed out a deep breath and couldn't contain himself any longer.

'What? Do I really have to answer these questions? F**k's sake. Ok. Look. Me and my wife are separated, ok? My son lives with her and, to be honest, I'm glad of that.'

Denise's head jolted backwards as if she had been sprayed with water.

'It's my wife's fault anyway,' snapped Chris.

Denise looked at Chris with an unhappy smirk. 'What's her fault?'

'Chuck. I told her to have an abortion but she refused. What a bitch!'

The contestants looked at each other and started to whisper. Chris had started to follow Rod's instructions and had let his personality off the hook in the biggest way.

'Who are we dealing with here?' whispered Mark.

'What? Come on, like you're all shocked. It's the 21st century people,' stated Chris.

'What we are shocked at is your frank point of view, Mr Wilkinson,' said Brenda.

'Really. Well, I guess this is who I am, isn't it? It was you who wanted to 'break the ice' wasn't it? Well, consider it broken. Now, where's my bedroom? I have to settle in.'

Brenda shook her head at Chris as he walked out of the kitchen to find his bedroom. It had been an introduction to beat all introductions. Chris Wilkinson had arrived.

CHAPTER 21

CREEPY CHRIS BLASTS WIFE!

WILKO'S WIFE'S RAGE!

CHRIS'S SHOCKING REVELATIONS!

WHO IS CHRIS WILKINSON?

Kate read the headlines and watched the news. It had been a shock that her estranged husband was taking part in a reality show that she didn't ordinarily watch. It was even more of a shock to read his comments about herself and Chuck. The insults jabbed her with hurt and made her cry.

'Mrs Wilkinson! Mrs Wilkinson! Have you got anything to say about your husband's comments? A reaction?' yelled a reporter through the double-glazing.

'Go away! Just FUCK OFF!' shouted Kate and rushed to the window and drew the curtains, 'you're all BASTARDS!'

A pack of reporters had found Kate's new address

and had started to camp outside, ready to pounce with lights and cameras as soon as she opened her front door. Chuck had left for school before the convoy had formed but it wouldn't be long until he returned home. Kate threw the newspaper that carried the repulsive headlines to the ground and cried. She tried to ignore the reporter that banged on her window, each knock sounding louder than the last. Kate rushed upstairs to her bedroom, tiptoed to the window and peered out through the net curtains. It was worse than she could have imagined. Television network vans, multiple cameras and crowds of people had gathered outside her house to catch a glimpse of the angry wife, who would provide them with a hot exclusive story. Kate retreated into her bedroom and sat on the edge of her bed.

Kate opened her bedside cabinet drawer and retrieved Detective West's card. Although Detective West had stated that he wanted her to call him in connection with Dexter's attack, Kate was desperate.

'Detective West.'

'H..Hello detective. This.. is..Kate. K.K..Kate Wilkinson. I need help. Please. I n..need help.'

'Calm down, hmm, calm down. How can I help, hmm?'

'I'm scared. There's a l..l.lot of p..p..people outside my house. Rep..porters. They're all shouting. Screaming. Banging on my w..w..indows. Help me, please, help me. I need the police,' stuttered Kate through her tears.

'I see, hmm. Listen to me, Mrs Wilkinson. Stay where you are. Don't move, hmm. Draw the blinds or curtains. Lock all the doors. We'll be there as soon as we can, hmm.'

'T..thank you, thank you.'

Kate placed her mobile on her bed and started to cry again. She had locked all the doors and drawn all the curtains but nothing could block out the noise of the people outside.

'KATE! KATE WILKINSON! COME ON! TALK TO US!'

Kate raised her hands to her ears to block the noise from outside and looked at the baby picture of Chuck that she had hung on the wall. A flicker of blue reflected off the glass of Chuck's picture and off of the walls. Kate peeked out of her bedroom window and noticed that the police had arrived. They had started to usher people away from her house and urged them to leave the street. Detective West stepped out of an unmarked police car and walked towards the path to Kate's house where he found a keen reporter kneeling down by the letterbox.

'Haven't you got anything better to do with your time, hmm? Leave!' barked Detective West.

'Why should I?' asked the reporter.

Detective West produced his identity from his jacket pocket and flapped it open.

'Here's why, hmm. You can either leave or I can have you arrested for harassment. I'm giving you a choice because I am feeling kind today, hmm.'

The reporter stood up, looked sheepish at Detective West and left Kate's front garden through the gate. Detective West knocked on the front door and waited until Kate opened it enough for her eye to show through the thin gap.

'Hello Mrs Wilkinson. It's Detective West.'

'Thank God!'

Kate opened the door and showed Detective West into the front room where a number of cardboard boxes were stacked three high. Detective West looked around the room that was devoid of any decoration and furniture.

'I'm sorry. I've just moved in. I'll fetch you a chair,' said Kate.

'That won't be necessary, hmm.'

'Do you want a cup of tea or coffee?'

'Hmm. A cup of tea, thanks.'

Kate walked into the kitchen, pressed the switch down on the kettle and delved into a box of teabags. Detective West followed her and noticed how much her hands shook as she dropped the tea bag into his cup.

'Are you ok, Mrs Wilkinson?' asked Detective West.

'Yes. I think so. I… er.. Now that you are here..Will they leave me alone now?' asked Kate.

'For now, hmm, but you need to find somewhere else to stay.'

'Like where?'

'If you have parents you can stay with until this blows over, hmm, then I would suggest that you do that.'

'I've only just moved out of their house….'

Kate started to cry and looked at Detective West.

'I think you should sit down, hmm.'

'Yes, I.. er.. guess..this is all Chris's fault. All his fault. I don't know how he could say such hurtful things about me and Chuck.'

'Oh, hmm. You mean this reality television show business. I can't say as I really understand why anyone would want, hmm, to watch a group of people in a house for twenty-four hours, hmm. What has the world come to when that can be called entertainment, hmm? Depraved gutter television, hmm,' commented Detective West.

Kate dried her tears, stood up and finished off making the tea.

'I didn't even know Chris was going to be on the show. We haven't spoken for weeks, maybe over a month now. I can't remember anymore.'

Detective West stared at Kate as she concentrated on pouring the boiling water into the cup, trying her best to control her shaky hand.

'Mr Wilkinson. Yes. Hmm. I wanted to talk to you about him actually.'

'I heard that you are investigating him for the attack on Dexter. Is this really true?'

'Oh, hmm, yes. Well. It's more, hmm, eliminating him from our enquiries, hmm.'

Kate fell silent.

'Can you remember if he was acting strange, hmm, on the night of the attack?'

'Do you really think he would do something like that? I mean, attack Dexter?'

'Mrs Wilkinson. Please calm down, hmm. We have to investigate the claims made by Paul Andrews and James McCracken that your husband was involved in the attack, hmm. We just want to eliminate him from our enquiries. How did you know we were investigating your husband?'

Detective West sipped his tea.

'Jules, Mrs Copeland, told me.'

'Oh, hmm. Yes, well, as I said, hmm, it's something we have to investigate. Now, hmm, can you remember anything about the night of the attack?'

'I've told you everything I know. Please, this is difficult right now.'

Detective West paused, took a sip of tea and continued.

'I'm sorry, Mrs Wilkinson, but I have to ask again, hmm.'

'I took Chuck to my parents house where we stayed until I heard about the attack. Then I went straight to the hospital. That's it. That's everything. Is that all?'

Detective West raised his hand to his chin and rubbed it.

'No, hmm, that's not all. Can you remember anything before you left the house?'

'NO. For the last time, NO! Chris was not acting oddly. He was not acting out of character. He was just being Chris as far as I can remember,' snapped Kate.

Kate sat back down on the chair and rested her head in her hands.

'I thought you were here to help me, not interrogate me.'

'I'm sorry, Mrs Wilkinson, hmm.'

A patch of uncomfortable silence passed between them until Kate spoke. Detective West drank his tea down to the bottom of the cup.

'So what happens now? Will the media continue to

267

hassle me or us, I should say?'

'It seems, as long as Mr Wilkinson has his spotlight, hmm, the media will have an interest in you.'

'This is all his fault. That arsehole of a husband's fault.'

Detective West's face shrivelled upon hearing Kate's bad language.

'Sorry, but I really can't bear to think about him right now.'

Detective West shrugged off Kate's bad language after her apology and started to listen.

'I don't know what has got into him recently. He's like a different person. He doesn't care about us. He only cares about himself and how successful he is. He's only visited Dexter once, I think.'

'Really, hmm. Please continue.'

'After the attack on Dexter, he tried to change. He said he had given up drinking and things were good between us but now, after this,.. I….,'

Detective West put his arm around her shoulders and consoled her as she started to cry again.

'Do you truly believe that my husband was involved in Dexter's attack, I mean, truly believe?'

Detective West took his arm away from Kate's shoulders, placed his cup on the kitchen countertop, turned and walked towards the front door.

'Thanks for the tea, hmm.'

'You didn't answer my question.'

Detective West turned back, looked at Kate and sighed.

'Speaking as a detective, anything is possible, Mrs Wilkinson. Anything.'

*****

A pack of reporters waited outside the Copeland residence after Chris had called Dexter a 'nigger' on Bon Voyeur. Jules had closed the driveway's gates to keep the media at bay. She had been following Bon Voyeur since its inception and was shocked to see Chris on the show. She had been appalled by his behaviour and even more appalled by his wicked comments against Kate. When the word 'nigger' left Chris's lips, Jules had switched her television off and sat in silence, trying to comprehend what she had heard. Jules wondered if Chris had ever been Dexter's best friend if he could just dismiss him in an instant. Jules agreed with Detective West and knew Chris was guilty.

Jules walked into the kitchen, where the two Copeland boys were playing on the floor, picked up a plate from the draining board and thumped it down

269

on the countertop in anger. The noise made the boys stop playing and look up at their mother who continued by banging a mug down on the countertop. A glint of sunlight rebounded off a kitchen knife on the draining board, which caught Jules's attention. It was within easy reach of the kids and Jules knew that she had left it there after preparing her dinner last night. She picked up the blade, looked at it and paused. The Copeland boys watched in silence as she slipped the knife into its plastic sheath and placed it into a kitchen drawer that she locked.

Jules picked up her mobile and thought about calling Kate. They had parted on bad terms when they had met for lunch but that was before Chris's rants on Bon Voyeur. Chris had wronged both of them on so many levels that it could only serve to unite them.

'Hello, Kate. It's Jules.'

'Oh.. and?' remarked Kate.

'I just wanted to say sorry for, you know, before.'

'Oh. Ok.'

'I wanted to see if you were ok after everything that has happened on Bon Voyeur. I can't believe it.'

'Thanks. I'm ok. The police are here, controlling the crowds outside.'

'Crowds?' asked Jules.

'Yes. After Chris said what he said, my house has

270

been under siege, Jules. I feel like I am living under house arrest.'

'Oh God! Not you as well.'

'What do you mean?'

'The media had collected outside my house too, wanting to catch a photo of me or something I say.'

'I don't understand. Why are they there?'

'Your husband is why. He called us the 'n' word, Kate. The 'n' word.'

'Oh Christ, no. I had no idea about that. That bastard.'

It was the first time Jules had heard Kate call Chris a bastard. It filled Jules with the notion that Kate had had the good sense to reconsider her opinion of her estranged husband and admit that he was guilty of Dexter's attack.

'So now do you believe me?' asked Jules.

'Believe you? What are you talking about?'

'That Chris is guilty. I mean, look at the way he is acting. It's awful, Kate. It makes me wonder if he was ever Dexter's friend based on what he has said about him. He wouldn't be on Bon Voyeur if he hadn't filmed the attack and got the attention from it.'

'No. No. You have called the wrong person if you think I share the same opinion, Jules. You're wrong. I still can't see Chris having anything to do with Dexter's attack. Detective West was here and said they were just trying to rule him out, not arrest him.'

'Rule him out, Kate. Rule him out. It means he is a suspect. Listen to me, Kate.'

'I've had enough for one day. I'm done with listening, Jules. I don't feel well.'

'How do you think I feel? My husband is still laying in a hospital....'

Click!

Silence.

Kate had hung up. Considering all of Chris's insults and bad behaviour, Jules didn't understand why Kate would still defend him. Jules looked at her sons who had started to play with toy cars on the floor again. She would soon have to get them ready to visit their father in hospital whose condition improved day by day.

CHAPTER 22

Bon Voyeur's ratings had shot through the roof after the introduction of Chris to the show but had also created controversy. Politicians wanted the show to be cancelled; the broadsheets and television standards agency had called the show 'the epitome of societal depravity' and opinion polls suggested that the general public also had had enough of Chris the creep. Even Rod had started to become one of the haters. He hadn't expected Chris to be as outrageous as he had been. If Chris continued to be in the show, Rod faced a consequence of Bon Voyeur being cancelled permanently and he wasn't about to let that happen.

'That nigger stole my ideas. That's why he is so fucking well known. It's all my work. If it hadn't been for us being at university together..' said Chris.

'You have a nerve using that word,' said Denise, 'Where do you get off?'

'What's the matter? Getting upset over one sodding word? Get a fucking grip.'

The other contestants remained silent and felt uncomfortable. Chris had caused shockwaves since he had entered the house and outside it. Denise got up off the sofa, shook her head in disgust at Chris and stomped off down the hallway to her room, muttering uncomplimentary words.

'That's it. Run away. You baby!' shouted Chris.

Marilyn tutted.

'And what's your problem, faggot?'

'Is there a time when you actually think before you say something? Do you have the capacity to be nice to your fellow man? Do you? .. And for your information, I'm not a faggot,' argued Marilyn.

'Woah! Listen to the tranny's complex lingo… 'Do you have the capacity…,"

'Would you just shut up?' snapped Marilyn frowning at Chris.

'Why don't you, faggot? People like you should all be lined up against a wall and shot.'

The small camera mounted in the ceiling, turned and focused on Marilyn. She got up, snatched her cup of hot tea up off the table and threw it at Chris's head. Chris raised his arms in time to block a majority of the beverage from hitting his face but felt the heat burn his arms. Drips of tea ran down Chris's glasses as he lowered his arms down to his lap and rubbed his hands on his jeans.

'Ow! FUCKING BITCH!' shouted Chris.

The producer raised his hand to his neck and made a slicing motion.

'Ok. Ok. Cut! CUT! We have to stop it here. Roll adverts. We have to stop it, everyone. We've been told to stop filming. What's the plan, Rod?' asked the producer.

'Ok. There's only one thing to do, we'll bring the vote forward and Chris is out. He has to go and preferably before lunchtime. We are cutting his mic. I don't want this to get any uglier,' said Rod.

'Gotcha!' said the producer who spoke into his headset, 'Can we get Marilyn and Denise back in here?'

Chris was busy wiping himself down with a towel as Marilyn and Denise returned to the living room. His t-shirt had been painted sepia and his arms stung red by the cup of hot tea.

'Here's the new plan, straight from management. We are to go directly to the vote and, Chris, you are the one who had to leave us. Everybody got that?' stated the producer.

'Hey! But, hold on a minute. I'm doing what you told me to do. Why am I being voted off? Do you have any idea who I am? I am Chris Wilkinson.'

The member of the crew ignored Chris's pleas and checked with the control room that everything was in place.

275

'Ok. Everybody. In.. 3…2…1… Go!'

The loud voice of the voyeur started to boom through the Tannoy system installed in the house.

"Contestants. You have executed all of your chores to an adequate standard apart from a select few who know who they are. You now have a decision to make. Who should be the next person to leave Bon Voyeur? Make your decision and state your reason why in the confessions booth."

'What the hell? Hey! HEY! This isn't fair. This show is a scam. A front! A fake! A phony. It's all scripted people. All scripted….' shouted Chris.

Chris's lips moved but nobody, apart from the people in the room, heard his comments that blasted the show. One contestant after another entered the confessions booth and had one name on their minds.

'Chris.'

'Chris.'

'Chris.'

'Marilyn because she, he or it is a fake - just like this fuckin' show..' said Chris.

"Thank you for your votes. We have a result," said the voice of the voyeur, "Chris Wilkinson, you must leave the house. Thank you for your participation."

'Hey! Wait a minute! I don't fuckin' believe this… Rod Parkton is a liar everybody. A liar. Do not trust him…I'm Chris Wilkinson. Chris Wilkinson! You can't get rid of me!' pleaded Chris at the top of his voice.

The Bon Voyeur guards moved in to collect Chris whose shouts could not be heard on the air.

'Are the crowds in place?' asked Rod.

'Roger that,' said the producer.

'Get rid of him,' snarled Rod through gritted teeth.

The guards held Chris firmly by the arms to the cheers of the other contestants. They were glad to see the back of Chris the creep who had insulted each and every one of them. The guards led Chris down a hallway towards the front door of the Bon Voyeur house, a walk that had been christened the 'walk of shame'. The front door opened to camera flash after camera flash that blinded Chris through his tea stained glasses. The same crowds that had welcomed him with cheers on day one, now booed, hissed and chanted 'moron', 'bastard' and 'arsehole'. Chris looked from side to side at the angry mobs and protested his innocence but nobody could hear him over the deafening noise. A car waited for Chris at the end of the path to take him to wherever he desired as a final gesture of goodwill on the show's behalf. The noise from the crowd was shut out as Chris got in the car and shut the door behind him.

'Where to?' asked the driver.

'I want to speak to Rod,' stated Chris.

'I can't make that happen, mate. I'm just here to drive.'

'Fuck's sake. You must be able to contact him. You're part of the show.'

'I'm only a part of my taxi business, mate. I drive people from A to B and, sometimes, B to C and that's it, mate. Now, where do you want to go?' asked the driver.

Chris breathed a sigh of despondency and put on his seatbelt.

'Take me to The Belverdere, Easthampton. Just… take me there. Whatever.'

'Right you are, mate.'

*****

Chris stepped out of the taxi and looked at The Belverdere's front. The familiarity of the pub reassured Chris that he had made the right choice of destination after being evicted from Bon Voyeur. Chris opened the heavy door and walked towards his usual bar stool with the intentions of drowning his sorrows with alcohol. Time had passed since Chris had drunk his last pint but today was the day when he would be reunited with a beer.

'The usual,' said Chris to the barman.

'I'm surprised to see you in here, Chris,' commented the barman.

'Why's that?'

'After what you said and did on Bon Voyeur. I'm almost reluctant to serve you if I'm being totally honest.'

'Oh that? Did you really believe that? It's all put on. All scripted. They told me to say and do those things. Honest.'

'Really? I thought it was all live. It looked real to me.'

'Can I have my usual?' asked Chris.

'Yeah, ..well,… ok.'

The TV, mounted above the bar, showed Eastern View's report about Chris's involvement on Bon Voyeur. Chris listened close to the voice of the reporter. He swore he recognised it. He continued to listen until the penny dropped. It was Martin Lawson. Chris shook his head and looked down at a crumpled, stained bar mat. He couldn't believe that Martin had been promoted at Eastern View and taken his job. Chris sipped his beer and tried to comprehend what had happened to him. He had followed Rod's instructions of creating controversy and trouble to the letter and couldn't understand why he had been evicted from the Bon Voyeur house. He was Chris Wilkinson.

279

A natural talent in front of the camera and presenter extraordinaire or so he thought.

'Chris? Chris Wilkinson?' asked a voice by the side of Chris.

'Yeah, that's me..' replied Chris.

'This is for Denise…'

Before Chris had had a chance to look up from the bar mat, a fist flew through the air on a collision course with Chris's jaw. A man, who had clocked Chris on his way into The Belverdere, looked as if he wanted ed Chris's head on a stick. Chris dodged the right hook and fell off his barstool and onto the floor. The barman looked across at security who were quick to pull the livid man away from Chris and show him the door to the street. Chris picked himself up, dusted himself down and sat back on his stool.

'Are you ok?' asked the barman.

'Yeah. I think so.'

'If I were you, I'd lay low. You've riled up a lot of people, you know.'

'I told you. It's all made up. All made up. All of it. As soon as I talk to the press, everyone will stop watching that show. I'll expose it for what it is,' snarled Chris.

'Well, I dunno, mate. I guess you know better than I do.'

Chris sipped his beer and glanced at the television that was still showing Eastern View. A photograph of Dexter appeared on the screen with a caption of 're-covery' written underneath it.

'Hey! Could you turn it up?' asked Chris.

The barman obliged.

"Dexter Copeland, the victim of a brutal assault and the county's film hero, is to make a full recovery according to the doctors who had originally given him a slim chance of survival. Sources close to the movie scriptwriter say that his memory is improving all the time and although he may never be the same again, Dexter Copeland has made a miraculous recovery and is expected to return home within the next couple of weeks. Martin Lawson, Eastern View."

Chris's fingers started to go cold and stiffen as if rigor mortis had set in.

'Is….is it ok, if I..I, erm, go out into the..the..the courtyard?' stuttered Chris.

'Yeah.. Sure. Are you ok?'

'Yeah, yeah, erm, yeah. I'm just a bit sh.. shaken after that..that guy attacked m..m..me.'

Chris walked out into the courtyard, lit up his ciga-rette and took quick drags as if the world was going to end. Chris couldn't fathom how his life had gone from fantastic to being flushed down the gutter as fast as it had and now there was a chance he would serve a jail sentence, thanks to Dexter.

I can't go to jail. I won't go to jail, thought Chris, lighting another cigarette. I have to do something but what can I do? You have to finish Dexter off. He's onto you, don't you understand? But I'm no murderer. Yes you are. You were halfway to doing it before. Just a tug of the pipes and he would have been done. Why didn't you do it? I'm no murderer.. Or am I? Do it now.

Chris finished off his second cigarette, stamped it out and lit a third. He walked out of The Belvedere's courtyard gates and in the direction of the hospital where he believed he would visit Dexter for the last time.

CHAPTER 23

Mr Tyler sipped on an ice-cold lemonade and watched the local news. It had been something he had done for as long as he could remember ever since moving to the estate with Mrs Tyler thirty years ago. They had seen a lot of things come and go. A majority of the families around them that had moved into the area with them, had moved out when the council gave people the option to buy the houses. Although not prejudice against any particular group of people, Mr Tyler had noticed a larger number of poorer families moving in, giving rise to graffiti, vandalism and theft. It wasn't the neighbourhood that they had signed up for but they didn't want to move, especially after they had taken great care in cultivating their prize-winning garden. They had worked hard with the difficult soil and steep incline, creating a garden from seeds to flourishing plants. They had nurtured their plants from day one, using organic fertilisers, home made weed killers and even talked to them with love. The garden rewarded them with vivid colours, magnificent scents and maintainable vegetables that they ate with their dinners.

They weren't going to leave it, regardless of how the housing estate seemed to be deteriorating.

Mr Tyler looked out of the back door and into the garden. He knew he had to go out into the heat of an unusually warm spring day and finish tending the garden. Mr Tyler finished his lemonade, put on his sun hat and walked out into the garden again. He was a tall, thin man who had kept himself in shape but not by choice. It didn't seem to matter what he ate or how much he ate, he never put on any weight. Mrs Tyler, who sat on a deckchair on the patio, was reading a book and sipping the same lemonade that she had made. It was the latest murder mystery written by a prolific crime writer that she couldn't get enough of. She had read the other twenty-two books in the series and had just reached a juicy part of the latest novel. It could wait.

'Dear? Can you make sure the runner beans are ok in this heat? They can wither up so quickly. Pick them off if they are on the turn and we can eat them tonight,' said Mrs Tyler, waving her pointed hand towards the bottom of the garden.

The heat was starting to become unbearable and Mrs Tyler was worried about the affect it would have on her plants and vegetables. The sweat had started to soak into Mr Tyler's sun hat as he wiped away the excess sweat from his forehead with his hand. If he was suffering, the plants must have been suffering twice as much. Mr Tyler walked down the steps towards the runner beans, checking each row of plants as he went. He pressed down the soil with his fingers and realised it was hard and dry. The whole garden was gasping for moisture. The good condition of the runner beans surprised Mr Tyler but other plants in the garden were starting to look thirsty. The strawberries needed a refreshing spray of water thought Mr Tyler as he picked a strawberry from the stem and tasted it.

'I think I'll go and fetch the hosepipe, dear. The plants are looking a bit dry.'

'We can't use a hosepipe because of the ban, dear. It said something on the news about it.'

The hosepipe ban had been enforced last week but had been lifted. Mr Tyler's ardent observation of the news had kept his finger on the community's pulse. When the clock struck the hour, Mr Tyler always rushed indoors to catch the news headlines, regardless if anything had changed or happened. He watched every news story even though he had probably seen each one before several times. He had signed a deal with a cable network that supplied him with a 24-hour news channel but he drew the line at watching the news at night. Mrs Tyler complained about his insistent watching of the local news but it didn't make any difference to Mr Tyler. He continued to watch regardless.

'The hosepipe ban has been lifted, dear. That was only last week.'

'Was it? Oh, ok then.'

Mr Tyler held down his sun hat and prevented it from blowing off his head in a freak breeze. He opened the garden gate and trundled towards their garage. The yellow metal garage door had been damaged by dents made by the youths of the estate that kicked a football against it. It annoyed Mr Tyler every time he heard a loud bang accompanied by the shouts of those responsible for the noise. He had complained to the police but they did nothing, informing him that he would have to put up with it for now. It was the Tyler's garage and they had paid their mortgage every month to be the owners of it. Mr Tyler did not want dents in his garage door or any future dents.

Mr Tyler inserted the key into the garage door lock and twisted it open. A stale smell of old grass and compost filtered out as Mr Tyler stepped into the Aladdin's cave of gardening equipment. Two lawn-mowers, one new and one old, sat at the back that had chunks of old grass stuck to the blades. A bottle of fox scent had sprung a leak, which had filled the garage with a pungent earthy smell. Mr Tyler had regretted the day he took the advice of a neighbour who had recommended it as a cat deterrent. Mr Tyler had planted sticks in the garden, lined with the repellent, with the expectation of seeing cat's tails point to the sky, disappearing into the horizon. It hadn't worked. He remembered a cat that had strolled up to one of the sticks and licked it, treating it as if it was a stick of candyfloss made for cats. Now Mr Tyler was left with a bottle of repulsive brown liquid that repelled more humans than it did felines.

Mr Tyler picked up the old hosepipe up off the floor and hooped it onto his arm. He knew that he would have to invest in a new one, as it tended not only to spray the garden, it also sprayed the neighbour's gardens too through all the holes and leaks. Mr Tyler plugged the hosepipe into a tap located in the garage, unravelled it and noticed a piece of paper flutter to the ground. Mr Tyler picked up the piece of paper and examined it. It was a photograph of a man that had been bleached by the sun. He flipped the picture over and discovered some text written on the other side. Although the rain had made the ink run, Mr Tyler could still read a time, date and address. He looked at the photo again with a concentrated stare that made his brow wrinkle and eyes turn into slits. The face of the man started to resonate with Mr Tyler and, after thinking hard, he knew who it was. It was Dexter Copeland, the screenplay writer who had been attacked and almost killed by robbers. Mr Tyler gasped at his discovery and dropped the hosepipe on the ground in shock. He couldn't fathom how the photograph had ended up in his garage but assumed the wind had blown it under the door. Mr Tyler locked the garage door and rushed back into his garden as fast as his old thin legs could carry him.

Mrs Tyler jumped out of her chair as she watched her husband run up the steps, through the gate and towards her. It was unusual athletic behaviour for her husband who rarely moved fast. Mr Tyler came to a stand still on the patio, clutching the photograph in the one hand and caught his breath.

'What ever is the matter dear?'

'I… *gasp*.. found…'

'Calm down dear. Take a seat. Here,' said Mrs Tyler, pointing to the other deckchair.

Mr Tyler gave the photo to his wife, who looked at it and shook her head.

'Who is this? I don't understand, dear.'

'It's Dexter Copeland. The poor man who was attacked.'

Mrs Tyler looked at the photograph again, shook her head and was still none the wiser.

'The scriptwriter. The film director man. On the news.'

Mr Tyler had a good memory and if he said that the photograph was of Dexter Copeland, Mrs Tyler had to believe him.

'I have to call the police. It could be important. Any little detail.'

'Yes, dear. It's like this book I am reading now. The attention to detail is just…'

Mrs Tyler could not tell her husband about the book she was reading in detail. He had ducked inside

their house and called the police before she had had
the chance.

CHAPTER 24

CHRIS THE CREEP VOTED OUT!

MAKING BON VOYEUR BON!

SHOW BROUGHT TO A STAND STILL!

ONE STEP TOO FAR FOR REALITY SHOW!

Detective West tutted at the headlines that graced the pages of the newspapers. He had not watched any of the Bon Voyeur show but was well aware that Chris had rubbed a large percent of the British population up the wrong way.

'I really don't understand why people watch this, hmm,' said Detective West shaking his head.

'My wife and daughter are addicted to that show and talk about it all the time,' replied the constable.

'Well, I guess I will remain bemused by my puzzlement, hmm. Tell me. Do you happen to know what Chris is talking about, hmm, when he described Mr Copeland as 'stealing his ideas?''

'I'm really not sure, gov. They went to university together so they probably worked together on projects. Maybe one of those projects is similar to the screenplay Mr Copeland is, or was, writing. In all likelihood, there's probably no truth in it.'

'Probably, hmm? That's what I like to hear, hmm, - certainty!'

The constable smiled and returned to typing information into a computer. Detective West glanced at another newspaper that showed photographs of Chris leaving the Bon Voyeur house. He had bought a copy of every national newspaper including the tabloids that he usually avoided. He trusted the broadsheets and preferred his news to be from a sound source, impartial and newsworthy. Detective West had also seen recent episodes of Sunny Days featuring Chris as the presenter.

'Hello. I have something to report,' said Mr Tyler with the faded photograph in his hand, 'it concerns the attack on that poor Dexter fellow.'

Mr Tyler was standing by the front desk. Detective West's ears pricked up like a startled horse and stood up to greet Mr Tyler.

'Yes. Hmm. How can I help? I am Detective West.'

'Mr Tyler. I found this in my garage. I think it could be important.'

Mr Tyler handed over the damaged photograph to Detective West who examined it. Although the photo was the worse for wear, Detective West could see the photograph was of Dexter Copeland and the text on the back corresponded with the day and time of the attack.

'You found this, hmm, in your garage, you say? Where do you live, Mr Tyler?'

'Stonebrook Road on the eastern estate.'

'Stonebrook Road, hmm? I see. That's interesting, hmm.'

Detective West paused and smiled. Sneaky and Jock had been telling the truth after all. Sneaky had mentioned Stonebrook Road as the spot he had met Chris to talk about the deal. Detective West now had some evidence in his hand to arrest Chris but knew the photograph would not be enough on its own.

'Hmm. Interesting. It appears this photograph is only one half of the whole picture, hmm. We need to find the other half, hmm, or the actual photograph and run a hand style comparison check, hmm, on the other side,' said Detective West to the constable who took the photograph away to process.

'I hope that helps,' said Mr Tyler.

'Yes, hmm, it helps immensely. Thank you very

much, Mr Tyler.'

Detective West shook Mr Tyler's hand and watched him leave the station.

'Could I have your attention, hmm? We have just received some new evidence in the Copeland attack case and we need to act as fast and efficiently as we can, hmm. While Constable Jones processes the photograph, hmm, I want, you and you,' said Detective West pointing to several colleagues, 'to join me in searching the Wilkinson home, hmm.'

Detective West fetched his coat and left the police station with a small team who would make light work of searching the Wilkinson home.

*****

'There's nobody home, guv,' said the constable, turning away from the Wilkinson's front door.

Detective West looked up at the second floor windows that all appeared to be shut tight. The constable looked through the letterbox and saw a pile of unopened and untouched mail that sat on the hallway's carpet. It appeared as if the house had not been lived in for some time. Detective West had a hunch that the original of the damaged photograph lay within and was a key piece of evidence that would seal the arrest of Chris Wilkinson. He ran his hand through his white ruffled hair and knew there was only one solution: to ring Kate.

'Mrs Wilkinson? This is Detective West, hmm.'

'Hello.'

Detective West paused and collected his thoughts. There wasn't an easy way of tackling the subject of her husband's guilt but he knew she would have to be told.

'I don't know how to say this, Mrs Wilkinson, hmm, but some new evidence has come to light that implicates your husband in the, hmm, attempted murder of Mr Copeland.'

Silence. Dead air. The slight noise of fuzzy static hid Kate's breath from the ear of the detective. Kate gave a dry cough and swallowed before responding.

'And.. How do you know that? I mean, what evidence do you have that would possibly implicate him? I'm sorry.. I'm finding this hard to take…'

Detective West could not fathom whether Kate was still on Chris's side or not. If she was still on her husband's side, Detective West couldn't understand it. The alcohol problem. The neglect. The appalling behaviour on Bon Voyeur. Now, the attempted murder of Dexter Copeland could be added to the list.

'I'm not at liberty to tell you what the evidence is, Mrs Wilkinson. I can only reiterate that your husband was involved in Mr Copeland's attempted murder, hmm. As part of our continuing enquiry, hmm, we now need to perform a search of the family home, hmm.'

Kate fell silent again.

'We need to gain access to your house, Mrs Wilkinson, hmm. Do you have a key?'

'Erm, .. I see, well, I do, but…'

'Good, hmm. Can you let us in?'

'I'm at work but, I, erm..' stuttered Kate.

'Tell them, hmm, you are officially helping the police with their enquiries, which, hmm, is precisely what you are doing.'

Detective West and his team of investigators waited ten patient minutes until Kate arrived. She parked her car off-road. Detective West raised his hand to his chin and made a mental note about her fatigued appearance.

'Thank you for coming, Mrs Wilkinson, hmm. I hope that you are feeling much better after our last meeting,' commented Detective West.

'That's ok. I'm doing fine thanks. We have been staying with my parents, Chuck and I, until everything blows over,' said Kate.

Kate paused and looked at the detective with a wry smile on her face.

'Do you really think he is involved in Dexter's attack? I mean, they are, or were, best friends. As much as I hate him right now, I just don't think he would do this.'

'I'm sorry to say that we believe it to be so, hmm. If you could open the door, Mrs Wilkinson, we'll be as quick and discrete as we possibly can, hmm.'

Kate shook her head, breathed out a dejected sigh, fished the front door key out of her jacket pocket and opened the door. Detective West had started to feel some sympathy towards Kate and it wasn't the first time he had informed someone that his or her other half was a suspected murderer.

The investigators encountered a dry patch of old vomit on the living room's floor, a remnant of when Chris was last in the house. Empty beer cans lined the floor and lay strewn about on the dining room table. Detective West could smell the stale odour of cigarettes as he stepped into the kitchen. The sink had been used as a jumbo sized ashtray with cigarette butts doubling up as an unintentional plug. A loaf of bread that had been left out had turned green and become a home to fruit flies that filled the air with jerky flying. Kate held her arm up against her nose, looked around at what was once her family home and started to cry.

'Maybe you should wait outside, Mrs Wilkinson, hmm?'

Kate nodded her head and walked with at a fast pace through the living room and out of the front door.

'We found it, guv,' yelled the constable from upstairs.

Detective West turned his attention away from the filthy kitchen and rushed upstairs. The constable had found the folder of photographs on the Wilkinsons' computer desktop and had found the same image that Mr Tyler had found in his garage. The arm that Detective West had spotted on the edge of the damaged photo belonged to Chris Wilkinson. Detective West smiled and knew that he now had the evidence to arrest him.

'Good work, Constable, hmm. Impound that computer. We've got him!'

Detective West walked down the stairs and out of the front door. Kate was sitting on the curb with her head in her hands, crying.

'Mrs Wilkinson? I'm sorry but I, hmm, need to know where Chris is,' stated Detective West.

'How would I know?' replied Kate.

'Mrs Wilkinson. I'm sorry about what your husband has done to you, hmm, but I need your help.'

Kate kept her head bowed while she tried to compose herself.

'I want you to call him, hmm.'

Kate lifted her head up and looked surprised by the

detective's request. She rubbed her eyes and stood up from the curb.

'We haven't spoken for weeks and I'm not about to start now. That man has caused me nothing but problems. I don't know what I'm doing or where I am half the time. You're the police. You call him. Don't shift your detective work on me,' argued Kate.

'Mrs Wilkinson. Please calm down, hmm. I want you to call him because he's more likely to answer the phone, hmm, if it is you. He's avoided answering all of my recent phone calls, hmm. I need to know where he is, right now, hmm.'

'No. I don't want to do it,' said Kate and stomped towards her car.

'MRS WILKINSON! I do have to remind you that if you don't help, hmm, you will be charged with perverting the course of justice, hmm. You could be tried,' shouted Detective West.

Kate's key ring dangled from her car door as she slammed it shut. Detective West's direct threat had stopped her in her tracks and had made her reconsider driving away. Kate muttered a swearword under her breath and retrieved her mobile from her jacket.

'What do you want me to do?'

'I just want you to find out where he is, hmm. I don't want you to argue with him. Just try and have a normal, civil conversation with him, hmm. Say that you are not angry and that you want to meet him, hmm. Say you want to work things out with him, hmm. Put it loud speaker, hmm.'

Kate called Chris and shrugged her shoulders at the detective.

'Chris? It's Kate. How are you?' stuttered Kate, 'I've seen the newspaper reports about you.'

'Kate? I can explain everything...'

Kate looked at Detective West who nodded his approval and waved his hands to signal that she should continue.

'Listen...where are you? Have you got time to meet? Chuck says he misses you.'

'I'm on my way to the hosp... to do a job. After I'm done there maybe we can meet. I don't know if I have the time....'

'Right. Really? And that's all you have to say is it? You haven't changed a bit. What the hell were you doing on that show and how could you say that about us?'

'Listen Kate, I can explain...'

'How could you say that about Dexter? You really are a bastard, Chris, YOU HEAR ME? A BASTARD!'

Kate threw her mobile to the ground, which caused the thin plastic casing to eject away from the electronics.

'The hosp?' Detective West felt the blood drain from his head to his feet, which left him cold, 'Chris Wilkinson is heading for the hospital, hmm. We need to get there as fast as we can. Let's get a move on!' shouted Detective West at his colleagues.

The piercing noise of the klaxons howled and echoed across the neighbourhood, which caused neighbours to stare out of their windows. Detective West reversed out of the Wilkinson driveway, span the steering wheel and sped down the street with his team following behind. Detective West caught an image of Kate in his wing mirror as he approached the end of the road. She was sitting on the edge of the curb with her head in her hands. Detective West turned his attention back to the road and threw his unmarked car around the corner.

CHAPTER 25

Chris had stopped off at a newsagent on his way to the hospital and bought a bunch of wrinkled grapes, a packet of cigarettes and a six pack of beer. Newspapers and magazines lined the front of the shop's counter where a man started to add up Chris's bill. Chris took of his glasses and gave them a quick rub on his t-shirt and read some of the headlines.

BON VOYEUR CANCELLED!

PROTESTS RAGE OVER TV SHOW.

PUBLIC OPINION DIVIDED OVER REALITY SHOW.

BON VOYAGE to BON VOYEUR!

CHRIS THE CREEP HAS DESTROYED RE-
ALITY TV!

Chris couldn't believe the headlines. He was glad
that the show had been cancelled but he would be buried alongside all the other previously voted off contestants.

'That'll be £17.54 please,' said the shop owner, disturbing Chris from reading the headlines.

Chris handed the shop owner a twenty-pound note
and examined the change that returned.

'It is all there, sir, I assure you.'

Chris raised a smile, ripped a plastic bag from a roll
and placed his shopping in it.

After Chris had walked away from the shop, he
found a bus shelter where he stopped and lit a cigarette.

Fuckin' Rod Parkton. I did and said what he told
me to do. It was all in my brief. Now I'm being treated like scum thanks to that fuckin' show. Just a short
while ago, people were treating me like a hero, like a
God and now... I was on my way to Wilkinson, my
own chat show and now... Dexter still gets more positive press than I get. Bloody typical. Hmm... Dexter.
Yeah, well, he'll get what's coming to him. Or at least I
think he will. God! I don't know. I don't know if I have
the nerve to go through with it. Maybe I should just

head back home and drink these beers…. But if I do that, Dexter will talk. He will tell. Put me in jail. Then my career will truly be over. Shit! Dexter needs to go. I have to stop him from talking. I can recover from the bad press and bounce back. I'm Chris Wilkinson after all…. I'm no murderer though. I can't go through with it. Best to turn back now…. No! No! I have to go to the hospital. I've bought grapes, the perfect camouflage. Nobody would expect a murderer to carry a bunch of grapes, would they? You have to do it. Do it. Do it. Do it.

Chris walked away from the squashed cigarette butt and rushed towards the hospital. Goosebumps raced up his spine and down his arms, making every hair spring up and stand to attention. His heart beat faster. Droplets of sweat fell to the ground from his forehead. He was going to do the unthinkable.

Chris stopped to catch his breath by a pay and display machine in the packed hospital car park. An ambulance had parked outside the entrance where medical staff were carrying in a patient wearing an oxygen mask on a stretcher. Chris grabbed the grapes and the six-pack of beer and headed towards the hospital. Once Chris had passed through the revolving doors, he noticed hospital staff dashing through the corridors and past the reception desk. A large number of stretchers with injured people lying on them littered the reception's waiting area. Chris could see the bloody bandages of those who had been attended to and the injuries of those who had not. A serious accident had happened and Chris was shocked at the sight of so many injured people.

What has happened? So many people. So much blood. Blood. Turn back now. You can't go through with it. Look at the mess in front of you. Do you really want to do this to someone? thought Chris. I have to do it. I won't leave any mess. It will be painless. There will be no blood. Dexter has to go. I have to do it and this is the perfect time while all the staff's attention is somewhere else. Do it.

Chris walked past the reception, clutching the grapes with his left hand and six-pack of beer in his right. He knew where to go. Chris reached Dexter's room without a hitch. The TV in the corner of the room was showing a game of snooker in progress while Dexter lay asleep in his bed. Chris felt his nerves start to shake his body as if he was about to perform a play to thousands of people for the first time. He felt a coldness sweep over his sweaty hands. Chris looked to the right and then to the left, making sure that nobody in the department or other patients were watching him. The coast was clear.

The noise from Dexter's snores drowned out the blip from the heart rate monitor. Chris crept into the room, placed the grapes and beer down on his bedside cabinet and wiped his forehead clear of sweat. An array of get-well cards stood on the bedside cabinet where Chris had placed the grapes. A card from Kate caught Chris's attention and had been scribed with: "We will be praying and hoping for your speedy recovery. We send you our love and best wishes, Kate & Chuck." Chris picked up the card, ripped it into shreds and threw the pieces on the floor. Chris turned away from the cards and looked at Dexter. There didn't seem to be anything wrong with him. He looked the same as he usually did. Not a hair seemed to be out of place, his designer stubble had been trimmed to perfection and all of his bruising had vanished. His old friend had recovered despite the odds and looked as if he could wake up and strike up a normal conversation as if nothing had happened.

Chris blew out a huge breath through pursed lips and tried to steady his shaky nerves. It was now or never. Chris plucked a grape off the stem and gripped it between his shaky cold fingers. With his other hand, Chris tried to prize open Dexter's mouth with the intention of popping the grape down the back of his throat. Chris fumbled open Dexter's bottom lip but let the grape slip out of his cold boney fingers.

'Fuck.'

Chris picked up the wrinkled grape from the duvet and, once again, tried to force open Dexter's mouth with his other hand. Once he had opened up enough of a gap, Chris leant forward with the murder weapon, a grape, clenched between two fingers. As Chris brought the grape closer and closer to Dexter's mouth, the noise from his snores changed from uniformed exhales of breath to snorting. Dexter moved his head to the side making Chris retract his arm and abort his mission.

'Who's that? Oh. Chris? Wow. I haven't seen you in ages!' said Dexter.

Chris pulled his hand away with fright, his body froze. Dexter had caught him red-handed. He moved his hand down below the level of Dexter's sight and relinquished his pincer grip, sending the grape towards the sterile hospital floor.

'How's Kate?'

'Oh. Erm. Kate's ok, mate. She's ok,' spluttered Chris.

Dexter smiled at Chris and looked at his bedside cabinet adorned with get-well cards and Chris's wrinkled grapes and six-pack of beer.

'Are you ok, mate? Is something wrong?' asked Dexter.

'Yeah, yeah. Erm. I just need the toilet. I'll be back in a minute.'

Chris turned away, left the room and entered the toilet. Chris exhaled a deep breath and walked up to the washbasin. The nervous jitters had spread to his legs, making them feel heavy and cumbersome. He could feel his heart beat twice as fast and there was an uneasy feeling in his stomach. Chris took off his glasses and threw them down by the side of the basin and ran the hot tap. Chris cupped his hands and warmed them with hot water and splashed his face. After Chris had scraped his face dry with a rough paper towel, he put on his glasses and looked in the mirror at his reflection. A would be assassin stared back. Chris breathed out and looked himself in the eye.

'You can do this. Dexter knows. He knows. You'll find yourself in jail once he speaks to the police. You have to do it. And he stole your idea. He stole your idea. You have to do it. Just take a deep breath and do it. DO IT!'

Chris continued to stare at his reflection. The murder was not as easy as he had imagined and had been made worse by Dexter awaking. Chris gulped, breathed out and left the toilet to rejoin Dexter. Chris reentered Dexter's room and walked towards his hospital bed, casting a shadow over him. Dexter turned his head towards Chris and noticed that his friend's face was soaked with water.

'Are you ok, mate?'

'Yes. Yes. I'm good. I'm good.'

The sight of Dexter and Chris started to think about the memories of being at university together. Chris shook his head and deleted them like a file on a computer. His hands had started to feel like blocks of ice again. The colour in his face had drained away to a pale complexion. Chris squinted at Dexter and summoned up the courage that would allow him to strike.

It was now or never.

'You don't look so comfortable, Dexter.'

Chris grabbed the corner of Dexter's pillow and pulled it out from under his head.

'What are you doing?'

'I'm going to make you..' Chris paused, '.. comfortable.'

Chris fluffed up the pillow in the air and scrunched the ends into the middle as if playing an accordion. When Chris stopped, Dexter leant forward in anticipation of receiving a soft place to rest his head. Instead, Chris placed the plump pillow firmly over his friend's face and pressed down hard. Dexter's muffled screams for help emanated from under the pillow, his arms and legs flailed around in attempts to beat off Chris. Chris applied more pressure to the pillow and started to drain the life from his former best friend. Chris gritted his teeth and allowed the anger and rage that had built up inside him out. He could see Dexter's limbs start to lose their buoyancy as each attempt to hit him failed.

CHAPTER 26

Detective West kept his hands loose on the steering wheel as he cut his way through the traffic that moved out his path. When he reached the hospital, a large number of ambulances were blocking the hospital's entrance.

'Ditch the cars as close as you can to the entrance. Ditch the cars as close as you can to the entrance,' spoke Detective West into his radio mic.

'Roger.'

Detective West pulled into the hospital car park and made an emergency stop, coming to a standstill next to an ambulance. The medics, who were lifting an injured person on a stretcher, stopped and looked at the police run into the hospital.

'Follow me,' yelled Detective West running towards the neurology department.

Detective West looked through the window of Dexter's room and stopped for a split second before he realised that Chris was standing hunched over Dexter's bed. Detective West burst through the door with a force that almost wrenched it away from its hinges. Two constables followed behind.

'CHRIS! STOP!' shouted Detective West.

Chris did not turn around. Detective West looked at the twitching movements under the bedsheets.

'I told you to STOP,' shouted Detective West, and removed his taser from his belt.

Detective West lunged forwards and stabbed the taser into Chris's side. Chris grimaced in pain and fell to the floor, crippled by the shock.

'ARRGH! It's his fault. He made me do it. He made me do it' whimpered Chris.

Detective West tasered Chris for a second time making Chris writhe around the hospital floor. The two constables attached handcuffs to Chris's hands and picked him up off the floor. Upon hearing the commotion, a doctor and two nurses entered the room and looked at the unusual sight of the police in the room.

'What on Earth has happened?' asked the doctor.

'Please, hmm, attend to this gentlemen here,' said Detective West, pointing at Dexter.

The doctor and nurse rushed to Dexter's bedside and began checking his vital signs.

'Chris Wilkinson, you are hereby arrested, hmm,

for the attempted murder of Dexter Copeland. You do not have to say anything, hmm, but it may harm your defence if you do not mention when questioned, hmm, something which you later rely on in court. Anything you do say, hmm, many be given as evidence. Take him away.'

The two constables dragged Chris towards the door.

'AAARGH! He made me do it.. It's all his fault..'

Chris's screams echoed down the hallway and could be heard by everyone. Detective West ran his fingers through his sweaty hair, turned and looked at the doctor and nurse who were attending to Dexter. The force from the nurse's CPR made Dexter's head bounce off his pillow. His lifeless limbs flopped around the mattress like spaghetti. The doctor examined Dexter's heart rate monitor.

'How is he?' asked Detective West.

'We're doing what we can.'

Detective West raised his hand to his forehead and wondered if he had been too late. If he had arrived ten minutes earlier, the situation would have been very different. The nurse continued to press and pump Dexter's chest hard. Detective West looked down at the floor, turned away and walked out of the room.

'You ok, guv?' asked a constable.

'Yes. Hmm. Yes. I guess I am.'

Detective West walked down the hallway towards the hospital entrance. He knew Dexter Copeland was no stranger to staring death in the face but wondered if his luck had run out.

CHAPTER 27

Detective West's day had started with a smile that wrinkled his cheeks. He had arrested Chris Wilkinson thanks to Mr Tyler's vigilance. Barbara Perkins, an acclaimed psychologist, had joined him to witness Chris's interviews. They had known each other for some time and Barbara was the only psychologist Detective West trusted. Dressed in a smart jacket and skirt, Barbara could have been mistaken for a lawyer.

'Thanks for being here, hmm, Barbara. I appreciate it,' said Detective West.

'You're welcome,' said Barbara, looking into the interview room at Chris, 'how has he been?'

'Subdued today but has been, hmm, irrational.'

'Irrational in what way?'

'He keeps repeating the same line, hmm, 'he stole my ideas'. If I didn't know better, hmm, I would say he's insane.'

'Well, it seems I can go home if you've already analysed him.'

Detective West looked at Barbara and took her comment as a joke.

'Hmm. Well. See what you make of him, hmm. I don't want this one getting away.'

Detective West jiggled the keys in the door of the interview room and walked in. Chris looked up, lifted his hands from the table, leant back in his chair and stared at Barbara who stared back at him and smiled. Chris raised a smile back, making Barbara scribble down her first notes of the interview on a pad in front of her.

'Now, hmm, let's start from the beginning. Can you explain to us, hmm, the story behind the photograph of Dexter Copeland, hmm, with a time, date and address written on the back, hmm?'

Detective West slid the zip-bagged evidence towards Chris who remained motionless. Chris kept his focus on Barbara and ignored the items that incriminated him. Detective West tapped his fingers in the table, looked at Barbara and then back at Chris again.

'Maybe, hmm, I should introduce Barbara Perkins.'

'Barbara,' said Chris, 'that was my grandmother's name. She looked a lot like you.'

'That's nice, Chris,' replied Barbara.

Detective West tapped his fingers on the table again. His previous question had not been answered and his patience was starting to run out.

'Chris! Chris! Could you, hmm, answer my question please? Can you explain these items here?'

Chris broke from his hypnotic trance and looked down at the table. The polythene bags reflected the fluorescent light, highlighting the ripples and creases. Chris moved his face closer, spat at the photo of Dexter and withdrew his head.

'Bastard! He made me do it. He stole my ideas. MY ideas. Everything. He deserved it. He wanted me to do it. Bastard!'

Barbara scribbled down notes, observing every reaction.

'That didn't answer my question, Chris. I'm going to put something to you now, hmm, and you can react to it any way you want, hmm, but the fact will remain that you are still guilty, hmm, of two attempted murders of Dexter Copeland, hmm. I put it to you that you gave these items, hmm, to Paul Andrews asking him to murder Dexter, hmm. It's exactly the way he said it happened, hmm. What is your response to that, Chris, hmm?'

Chris looked at Detective West and, without warning, slammed his fist down hard on the table. Chris stood up, picked up his chair and threw it at the window, which bounced back and broke when it hit the floor. Before Chris could pick up the table Barbara and Detective West were using, two constables walked into the room and pinned Chris to the wall. Barbara

317

and Detective West raised themselves to their feet and walked out of the room.

'Hmm. This is what we have had to deal with, hmm,' said Detective West.

'I think I should talk with him alone,' suggested Barbara.

'I don't think that is a wise idea, hmm.'

'He said I remind him of his grandmother. I think he will feel comfortable talking to me.'

'I'm not sure, hmm.'

'Please. Just let me interview him.'

Detective West nodded his head, allowing Barbara to walk back into the room. Barbara picked up Detective West's chair and replaced Chris's broken one. Barbara looked up and smiled at Chris who was still being held by the constables. Chris relaxed the muscles in his body and allowed the constables to release him. Barbara nodded her head to the constables and they left the room.

'You and me now. You and me. It should always be like that, Barbara.'

'Yes, Chris. It's just us now. You can tell me anything you want to tell me. I'm here for you.'

Chris nodded his head.

'Maybe you can get me some cigarettes. Maybe a

beer? I'm desperate for either.'

'Unfortunately, I can't help you with that. But what I did want to ask you about something and it's up to you if you answer this question. You mentioned that he stole your ideas. Somebody stole your ideas. What did they steal?'

'He stole my ideas. All of them.'

'Yes. Who stole your ideas?'

'Dexter Copeland stole all my ideas. The bastard! I am Chris Wilkinson. Eastern View. I tell the truth.'

Barbara placed her pen on her pad and leant towards Chris.

'What ideas were they? I believe that you are telling the truth. You can trust me.'

'Manuscripts. He stole them and made them his. The bastard!'

'Ok and how did that make you feel when you found out?'

'Bastard. He didn't have to do that to me. He didn't. I couldn't trust him afterwards. No. He wasn't as good a friend as I thought. He deserved it.'

Chris spat at the table again and slammed his head into the edge, leaving a straight line that marked his forehead. The constables that had subdued him earlier, looked through the room's window and were about to enter when Barbara raised her hand to stop them.

'Chris. I want you to calm down, ok. Calm down. I understand what you are saying.'

'Yes. You understand. You've always understood me, right from when I was little.'

'Exactly, Chris. I just have to leave the room for a short while but I'll be back. Is that ok?'

Chris nodded his head and watched Barbara leave the room, closing the door behind her. Barbara approached Detective West who was standing next to the coffee machine, sipping from a flimsy plastic cup.

'Well? He's insane isn't he, hmm?'

'Well, I'm not so sure. He seems to have some conviction in what he is saying.'

'And, hmm, what is he saying, pray tell?'

'He claims Dexter stole his manuscripts and ideas. We need to check if that is true.'

'Are you quite serious, hmm? Do you actually believe him? The man is insane. You can't trust a word he says, hmm.'

Barbara remained quiet but raised her eyebrows.

'Alright! What do you need, hmm?' asked Detective West.

'Copies of Dexter's work and Chris's work if you can find them. If the two don't match in any shape or form, I might be able to get a good sense of Chris's character from his writings.'

'Fine. Fine. Hmm. We'll go over to the Wilkinson and Copeland houses again, hmm, and you'll hopefully have everything by this afternoon, hmm.'

*****

Barbara had spent an evening and an early morning reading through all of the information retrieved by Detective West and his team. She had come to the conclusion that although one of Dexter's manuscripts had not been copied direct from Chris's manuscript, the general storyline was almost identical. She had not expected to find such a similarity but there was no denying that it existed. Dexter had stolen Chris's ideas and by doing so, given Chris the motive to murder him. Barbara chewed on the end of her pencil. The case had started to intrigue her. The inquisitive streak within her started to analyse the night of the attack and she wondered how Chris could have even contemplated such an elaborate murder.

'Have you got something for me, hmm?' said Detective West, walking into Barbara's quiet office.

Barbara stopped chewing her pencil.

'Yes. I have actually. Chris is right to say that Dexter stole his ideas.'

'What? Are you sure? Hmm.'

'I've read through everything you found and it's true. Chris wrote this manuscript in 1994 whilst Dexter wrote his manuscript in 2008 at the very earliest. Dexter hasn't copied it word for word but the story is exactly the same. Change the character names. Bend the plot slightly. It's essentially the same but much better written.'

'Oh. Hmm. That really does flummox me.'

Detective West couldn't accept that Chris had been revealed as the intelligent and creative one behind Dexter's manuscripts.

'So, hmm, in your expert opinion, is Chris sane?' asked Detective West.

'Saner than you and me.'

'I simply can't believe it, Barbara, hmm. You mean to tell me that Chris arranged the night of the attack, hmm, roped in Paul and James to do it, hmm, and tried to murder Dexter not once but twice? And he is sane?'

'For the last time, Derek, yes!' snapped Barbara.

The sharpness of Barbara's voice and being called by his first name caused Detective West to sit down at Barbara's desk and refrain from asking any more questions relating to Chris's sanity. He frowned, took off his glasses and rubbed the bridge of his nose in an attempt to relieve his lack of understanding.

'Look on the bright side, you have a motive and he's not insane which means you can try him like any other criminal. I would, however, like to make a suggestion.'

'Which is?'

'That I go and talk to him again. I can make him drop this charade of playacting insanity. It's not the first time I have seen it.'

'No, hmm, I guess it can't be. Ok. You do what you have to do, hmm.'

Detective West stood up and walked out of the office, leaving Barbara to finish her psychoanalytical report.

*****

'Hello, Chris. How are you today?'

Chris was lying on his bed when Barbara had walked into his cell. The guards had reported that he had spent most of the night balanced on the end of the mattress, bouncing his leg up and down. Chris raised himself up and looked at Barbara.

'I've been waiting for you to come back,' said Chris.

'Oh really? And why is that?' replied Barbara.

'Did you bring my cigarettes? My beer?'

'No. Sorry. I have told you that I can't do that.'

'Oh. I'm still glad you are here because you listen. Not like that West guy.'

A constable watched through the window of the door.

'Bodyguard?' said Chris, nodding his head towards the door.

'I wanted to talk to you today about what you said to me in our last conversation.'

Barbara interrupted Chris's attempt at a joke and cut to the chase.

'You were right. Dexter did steal your ideas. So now I can understand why you were so angry about that.'

'See. You listen. You've always listened to me. I told you, didn't I? What a bastard!'

'I also want to ask you to do one thing for me. Can you speak slower? Just try to calm yourself down. It'll help you relax.'

Chris nodded and started to speak slower.

'As you said, he stole my ideas. He was my friend and how can friends do that?'

Barbara smiled and knew she had had a minor breakthrough. Chris had begun to talk to her like a normal human being again, as if she had flicked a switch.

'We went to university together and used to write many of our stories there. We would always bounce them off each other. It was hard for me to take when Dexter got his first screenplay made as a short film. That was my idea. My story. Do you want to know what I did when I found out?'

'Go on.'

'Nothing. I just overlooked it and carried on as if nothing had happened. I felt our friendship was worth more, which it clearly wasn't.'

'You must have felt some anger towards him. Bitterness? Resented him?'

'Yes. You know, I did. I just suppressed it.'

Barbara could not smile at Chris any longer. It had all been said. All the evidence pointed to Chris and now, he had admitted to having a motive for murder.

'What will happen to Dexter once he recovers? I mean…the truth is out now. He should be punished for what he did to me. Everything he has is down to me. Me!'

'Yes. Well, it's certainly a case for the courts to decide.'

The empty promise of court action against Dexter had canned Chris's anger from reaching boiling point and flowing over. Dexter would get what was coming to him or so he thought.

325

'Well, if there isn't anything else that you want to talk about, I must be on my way, Chris.'

'On your way? But you just got here. I thought you were here to help me?' asked Chris, with panic in his voice.

'Yes. I am here to help you, Chris, but I have to go.'

'But when will you be back?' asked Chris.

'Soon.'

Barbara gathered her belongings and headed to the door. As the door shut behind her, Barbara looked through the peephole to Chris's cell. Chris had stood up from his bed and was pacing. Barbara flicked the peephole cover back and walked down the corridor towards Detective West's office.

'Ah! Hmm. Barbara. Well, did he confess?'

'In a roundabout way, yes.'

'Good. Good. I guess that we're all done here then, hmm?'

Detective West and Barbara exchanged a hand-shake.

'The force won't be the same without you on it, Derek,' said Barbara, looking into Detective West's eyes.

A tear ran down Detective West's face when he realised that the Dexter Copeland case was to be his last before retiring. Barbara gave Detective West an extended hug and left his office stating that she would keep in touch. He wiped away the tear, sat down at his desk and sipped a cup of tea.

CHAPTER 28

The reporters that had annoyed Kate were back in larger numbers outside her house. She had read the headlines and news reports about Chris's attempted murder and it made her feel sick to her stomach. She had tried to shield Chuck from hearing about his father through the media but had failed.

Kate nudged the net curtain to the side and looked out of the window. A barrage of media vans and reporters holding microphones were waiting for her to leave the house. Chris was due to appear in court in the afternoon and his journey from the police station to court was something she didn't want to miss. She had planned to use the occasion to vent her anger.

Kate walked into the kitchen and flicked the switch on the kettle. She looked at her mobile phone on the counter top and wondered if she should call Detective West again for help but decided against it. As Kate poured boiling water onto a tea bag, she looked out at the garden. There were two gates at either side of the house with the back gate leading to concealed off-road parking. Kate picked up an old jacket and a baseball cap from a box that she hadn't sorted through after moving and put them on. She didn't know if she would come face to face with anybody outside her back gate but she had to leave the house. Kate opened the back door. Noise from the activity on the street echoed off the alleyway between her house and the neighbour's house. Kate poked her head out of the door and looked around. She listened for the sound of anybody lurking in her garden, anybody who had scaled her fence and was lying in wait to ambush her with multiple snapshots.

It was quiet.

Kate lingered on the doorstep and looked one last time at the kitchen. She had forgotten her mobile. Kate stepped inside, grabbed her mobile and stuffed it inside one of her jacket's inside pockets. She took a pair of sunglasses that were by the side of her phone and put them on before stepping into the garden.

The garden's lawn had been neglected and had overgrown to such an extent that weeds looked like plants Kate wanted to keep. Kate looked from side to side to make sure nobody was tracking her movements. She put her ear close to the gap in the gate and the fence and listened. There didn't seem to be anybody standing on the other side of the back gate. A large tree, that had dropped a multitude of pinecones, overhung the fence, which made the gate difficult to open. Kate tugged at the gate's handle and forced a gap large enough for her to pass through. Once out into the parking area, Kate looked around and scanned the houses opposite. There didn't seem to be anybody watching her. She walked fast towards a small path that crossed an allotment. Once Kate had passed through the allotment and was on a main street, she headed in the direction of the police station, keeping her head bowed towards the pavement, trying her best not to be spotted. She could feel her heart pound more and more, every step she took. When the police station was in sight, she heard the sound of car horns beeping and people shouting at each other. The media had secured the pavement outside, waiting for Chris to be led out. A reporter looked in Kate's direction, which made her jolt to a stop. The reporter looked away and carried on with her preparations, unaware that it was Kate. A sigh of relief left Kate's mouth as she found a wall to stand behind. She looked at her watch. It was coming up to midday and there was no indication when Chris would leave. Kate breathed heavy breaths and decided to sit by the base of the wall to collect her thoughts. She looked at her watch again. When would Chris arrive? Kate started to worry about her presence outside the police station. She didn't know if her disguise was good enough to avoid the media's scrutiny even though it seemed as if she had fooled one reporter. She didn't want to be stopped. She couldn't afford to be surrounded and hounded by reporters. She had had enough. She would have to be bold, fend them off and beat them away if need be.

331

Kate looked at her watch again.

She hoped Chris would be led out soon.

CHAPTER 29

'Where's Barbara? She said she would be here to help me.'

The constable guarding the door to Chris's cell had been given strict instructions not to answer any of his questions. Chris missed his heart to heart sessions with Barbara and without them he felt at a loss of what to do in his small cell. She had made him relax and had lifted the burden of years of jealousy and hatred towards Dexter off his shoulders.

'Where's Barbara?'

The constable stood motionless by the door and failed to acknowledge that Chris was speaking to him. He didn't answer. Chris stepped back from the door, sat on his bed and looked up at the frosted window, complete with a heavy-duty lock on its handle. Chris took off his glasses, breathed on them, rubbed them with the bed sheet, put the back on and looked around the cell. He looked at the ceiling and, in particular, the corners of the room, expecting to see a small camera filming him. He had been locked up for over a week and the same irrational thoughts spun around and around in his mind, day after day. His rise to stardom through Bon Voyeur had made him wonder if his time in jail was being filmed for entertainment. The public had started to tune in to watch Chris the creep in action. Who was to say that his time in the small cell was his own show where people could watch him 24/7? Chris squinted his eyes and focused hard on a black stain in the corner of the room. It could have been a camera.

'Where the hell is Barbara?' shouted Chris, thumping his fist on the blue metal door. He looked through the small window.

The constable stood as still as a pillar. In the distance, Detective West was walking down the corridor towards his cell.

'Finally! Hey! Detective! Detective! Where's Barbara? She said she would be here.'

Detective West jangled the key to Chris's cell and pushed it into the door's lock.

'Please, hmm, step away from the door.'

Chris stepped away from the door and looked at Detective West as he entered his cell, locking the door behind him.

'Where's Barbara? She said she would visit and talk to me again,' asked Chris again.

'Did she, hmm? Well, Barbara has been very busy

recently, hmm, and hasn't had the time.'

'I really need to talk to her. Really have to. It's urgent,' said Chris flapping his arms around.

'Urgent, hmm? What do you need to talk to her about?'

'About today and my counterclaim.'

'Counterclaim?'

'Yes. About Dexter stealing my work. Something has to be said about that. It has to.'

'I see, hmm, well, I guess that will all be made clear when are in court.'

'Good. Good.'

Chris strode towards his cell door and pulled down on the handle to get out. Detective West looked on in astonishment as Chris pulled down hard on the handle several times.

'What are we waiting for? I want to speak to her. Why did you lock the door?'

'Chris, hmm, I want you to calm down and listen to me, hmm,' said Detective West, raising his right palm to form a stop signal, 'there is an abundance of media outside this police station, hmm, and I want you to do what I tell you do, hmm, OK?'

'Really? An abundance? Well, I should have expected that because I am Chris Wilkinson.'

'Chris! Listen to me! Hmm!' said Detective West, picking a blanket up off of Chris's bed, 'I want you to put this blanket over your head, take my arm and I'll lead you to the van, hmm, that will drive you to court. Do not say anything. Just let me guide you and avoid the media, hmm.'

Chris walked over to the sink, wet his hand under the tap and ran his fingers through his hair. He ignored Detective West's instructions and had started to imagine the articles the media would write about him.

UNJUSTIFIED TREATMENT OF TV STAR, CHRIS WILKINSON.

CHRIS WILKINSON, THE BRAINS BEHIND DEXTER COPELAND'S BLOCKBUSTER.

TV STAR CHRIS: CLEARED OF ALL CHARGES.

'Chris? Did you hear what I said? Hmm?'

Chris was busy prepping himself for the media frenzy that he thought would jump at the chance to speak to him. It had been some time since Bon Voyeur and Chris was sure that journalists would have been curious about him. He was ready to yell at the top

336

of his voice that Bon Voyeur was scripted and fake, Dexter Copeland was a fraud and the two murder attempts had been justifiable under the circumstances. Chris looked in the mirror above the sink and adjusted his glasses. He was almost ready.

'Chris? Please. Hmm. Put the blanket over your head, hmm, and we can make our way to the court.'

Detective West outstretched his arm to give the blanket to Chris. Chris turned around and paused while a blank expression formed on his face.

'What do you want me to do with that?'

'My word, hmm. Have you listened to anything I have said? Wear this on your head.'

'Why would I want to do that?' laughed Chris. 'Nobody will know it is me. Chris Wilkinson, star of Bon Voyeur.'

'Chris. This is not another TV opportunity, hmm. Have you any remorse at all? You almost killed a man, twice, hmm.'

Detective West lowered his hand and shook his head.

'Just as a matter of interest, hmm, did you sleep well last night?' asked Detective West.

'Yes. Why?' replied Chris.

The question seemed to confuse Chris.

'Hmm. No remorse at all.'

Chris shrugged his shoulders and returned to the mirror to make some final touches to his appearance before facing the media. Detective West placed the blanket back on the bed, frustrated by the man who had taken up most of his time both at work and at home. Detective West lunged forward and grabbed Chris by the arm.

'Hey! Get off me!' yelled Chris, trying to break free, 'I'm not ready.'

'Chris! It's time to go.'

Chris stopped struggling against the detective and relaxed. Detective West unlocked Chris's cell and led him down a long hallway, towards the reception and the entrance. Chris could see the van that would take him to court, parked in the car park with the back door open. The sound of a large crowd of people could be heard even before Detective West opened the entrance doors to the station. The sound was louder than Chris had anticipated. Detective West opened the entrance doors to a hail of jeers and boos from the crowds. Chris panned the crowd from left to right, smiled and started to wave, soaking up the attention he was receiving.

'Hello everybody! Bon Voyeur is fake! Dexter stole my ideas!' shouted Chris at the top of his voice.

The crowd booed louder and started to hurl cutting insults at Chris. The angry reaction rocked Chris. It shattered his bravado and reversed his smile. Nobody seemed to believe a word he had shouted. Nobody seemed to be listening to him. Nobody. Nobody was interested anymore. Chris Wilkinson was a nobody.

'Chris! Hey! Chris!' said a voice to Chris's left.

Chris stopped walking towards the van and listened to a familiar voice that called his name. He knew the voice but couldn't place it.

'Keep moving!' shouted Detective West, nudging Chris in the back.

Chris took a small step forward, stopped again and looked in the direction of the voice. It was Martin Lawson. Chris's eyes bulged open at the sight of the intern. He couldn't believe the person who he had described as 'having as much charisma as a potato' was standing in front of him, doing his job for Eastern View.

'Hey, Chris! This will make a great story! Thanks!' said Martin with a smug smile on his face.

Chris grimaced and pointed at Martin the stick insect.

'Fuck you!' shouted Chris, taking strides towards Martin, 'fuck you!'

'Chris! Get in the van!' shouted Detective West who yanked Chris by the arm.

The crowd booed even louder and had started to

throw projectiles at Chris with one clocking him on the head. Chris yelped in pain and raised his hand to his forehead as Detective West kept pulling his arm. Martin continued to film with a smirk on his face. Chris was too busy shouting obscenities at Martin to notice a woman who had broke through the police defence and was running straight at him. Detective West, distracted by Chris's rage towards Martin, had also failed to spot her.

'You've ruined everything!' shouted the woman.

The woman screamed at Chris and thumped her fist into his chest as hard as she could. Chris doubled over and fell to the ground as if she had winded him. Two police constables rushed in and intervened, pulling the woman away from Chris who lay on the ground, moaning. The woman dropped a small bloody kitchen knife that bounced on the tarmac, coming to a standstill near Detective West's feet. Chris's blood started to seep into his shirt, spreading like an inkblot on blotting paper. Gasps could be heard from the awestruck crowd including Martin, who lowered his camera out of shock. Other reporters continued to film.

'Get an ambulance!' shouted Detective West.

The detective kneeled over Chris's body that had crumpled up into a fetal position.

By the time the ambulance had arrived, it was too late.

Chris Wilkinson was dead.

340

CHAPTER 30

Three years had passed since Chris Wilkinson's death and Martin Lawson felt that the real story was long overdue to be told. It was his story to tell. He had given up his job at Eastern View to tell it. He had fallen out with Eastern View executives who kept showing Martin's footage of Chris's murder at every opportunity they got. Martin couldn't stop them from using it and to address the balance, Martin had decided to make a documentary based on what really happened and why. He didn't owe Chris Wilkinson anything apart from his influence on choosing his profession. That was all. There was a story to be told about all the other people who had been affected by him and what he left behind. The lies. The deceit. The heartbreak.

Martin glanced down at the clipboard of questions he would ask Chris's assassin. The prison board had made an allowance for the film crew to set up cameras and lights in the prison hall, which was a rare occurrence. The bold headlines and footage surrounding the murder of Chris Wilkinson had sparked debates between politicians who had agreed, after lengthy discussions, to curb the media's presence at high profile court cases.

The first interview was with the most obvious person. Chris's killer. The prison had been her home for the past three years and one of those years had been consumed by court appearances and appeals. None of the appeals had been successful and she had been sentenced to twenty years. Martin sat across from the woman who had killed his former idol and looked at her. He noticed how calm she was, as if she had removed all trace of the incident. The shock of discovering her identity was still difficult for Martin to process. She had acted out of character and nobody, including her own family, believed that she could have been capable of such a crime.

'Are you ready?' asked Geoff.

'Yes. I think so,' replied Martin and turned to the killer, 'Are you ready?'

Martin watched the murderer nod her head towards him as if she was saving all of her breath for the actual interview. She had been led into the prison hall without any hitches and was now waiting for the interview to commence. Her face was devoid of make-up. Her hair was imperfect. The professional portrait shots, taken in happier times, did not match the woman in front of Martin. They didn't match Jules Copeland.

'Action!' shouted Geoff.

'I know the next question is an obvious one but I

342

have to ask it. Why did you do it?'

'Why does anybody do anything? I can't explain exactly why I did it. I just did,' stated Jules.

'But you must have said to yourself that "this is wrong".'

'Of course. I knew it. I guess it was anger.'

'Anger?'

'Yes. Dexter was recovering until,' Jules paused, 'that man put us back to square one. Something took over and I couldn't control my inner rage.'

Jules shifted on her seat and looked down at the floor for a moment. The mere mention or thought of Chris Wilkinson irritated her.

'You must have some regrets,' said Martin.

'Yes. Not being able to be with my family.'

'How are they?'

'They're as good as they can be, thanks.'

Tears started to trickle from Jules's eyes.

'Are you ok? Do you want to continue?'

Jules nodded and soaked up the sadness from her eyes with a tissue Martin gave her. Martin felt sympathy for Jules who had been just one of the many who had been affected by Chris Wilkinson. Martin thought back to his time spent with his mentor where fond memories were few and far between. It had not been easy for Martin to report on the story, especially when he knew some of the people involved. When Jules had settled down, the interview continued.

'If you could say whatever you liked to all those people who have called you a cold blooded murderer, what would it be?' asked Martin.

Jules flopped her arm holding the tissue by her side and glared at Martin with contempt.

'I would say it was unfair given the facts,' snapped Jules.

'And what are the facts, in your opinion?'

'Chris tried to murder my husband, not once but twice and left him with brain damage. He was supposed to be his best friend, for God's sake. What person would come up with a scheme to murder their best friend just so they could film it and create a news story? I will admit what I did was wrong. Very wrong but I'm not a cold-blooded murderer. I'm not.'

Martin handed Jules another tissue.

'So, if you started all over and had to do things again, would you do things differently?'

Jules rested her head on her hands and seemed to give her reply some considerable thought.

'Yes. I would. It was a moment of madness and I regret it deeply because I can't be with my family.'

Jules dropped the soggy tissue to the floor and

cried into her hands. Martin gave a signal to Geoff to stop filming. It had been enough. He didn't need to ask any further questions to make her feel worse than she already did. She had murdered Chris Wilkinson and now she was paying for it.

'Thanks, Mrs Copeland. I really hope things get better for you in the future,' said Martin.

'Thank you.'

Martin watched two wardens approached Jules and ushered her back in the direction of her cell. He felt an overwhelming sense of empathy towards Jules Copeland and questioned whether he would have done the same thing under the circumstances.

*****

Martin's documentary suffered a setback when he received an email from Kate stating that she did not want to take part. She had moved abroad with Chuck, had remarried and was happy. Martin shrugged his shoulders and respected her wishes of wanting to remain estranged from everything related to her first husband. It was a blow but at least he was having more luck with the rest of the Copeland family. They had not objected to being part of the documentary and Dexter was more than able to cope with a few questions.

The Copeland house looked the same as it did on

the night of the attack. Miles was looking out of the living room window as Martin and Geoff pulled into the driveway. Excited to see the guests arrive, Miles shouted a patch of steamy breath onto the window, ran to the front door and opened it.

'Hello. You must be Miles. Is your dad home?' asked Martin.

'Yes.'

Dexter walked through from the kitchen and greeted Martin at the doorstep.

'Hello, Martin. Nice to see you. Do come in.'

Martin nodded to Geoff to fetch the camera and lighting equipment. Martin followed Dexter into the living room where the carpet was hidden by paperwork and toys. An array of coffee and teacups lined the living room table that looked as if they had been there for some time.

'Well, this is my home. Would you like a tea or coffee or something?' asked Dexter.

'Oh. Erm, no, thanks Mr Copeland,' replied Martin.

'Please, call me Dexter.'

'Ok.'

'I think I will have one if you don't mind.'

'No. No. Go right ahead.'

Geoff walked into the living room and placed a lamp down on the floor next to the living room table. Miles and Marcus were mesmerised by all of the equipment laid out in front of them. Marcus walked up to the camera and started to look at the screen on the back.

'Hey Marcus! Don't touch anything! Expensive equipment, ok?' said Dexter, walking into the living room with a cup of tea, 'Now then, where do you want me or us?'

'Your sofa will be ok, Dexter. We're all ready when you are.'

Dexter sat down on the sofa with one son either side of him. Sausage, the dachshund, plodded into the living room, jumped up on the sofa and laid down. Geoff gave a signal and started filming.

'Dexter Copeland, how nice it is to see you alive and well after all of the traumatic experiences you have been through. The first question is, really, how are you?'

'I'm much better now thanks. It's been a long recovery process but I feel better every day that passes.'

Dexter gave Sausage a pat on the head.

'In all honesty, you shouldn't be here at all, should you? Do you remember anything about either attack?'

Dexter stopped giving half his attention to Sausage and thought about the answer to Martin's question.

347

His eyes looked up to the ceiling, trying to summon a divine intervention that would bring his memory back.

'Well, I remember the attack in the hospital. I remember Chris coming in to see me. He'd brought some grapes. He then pretended to puff up my pillow and then it went dark as he held it over my face.'

'That must have been scary,' commented Martin.

'Yes. It's unimaginable. Not being able to breath or have the strength to fend off your attacker. I was at the mercy of somebody else to come and rescue me.'

'And they did. Detective West,' said Martin.

'Yes. Thank God! I owe my life to that man.'

The two children remained quiet as Dexter answered Martin's questions.

'Do you remember anything about the first attack that took place here in this very house? And have you seen the footage?'

Dexter paused again and rolled his eyes up to the ceiling again for some answers. His smile faded and his face started to wrinkle when he remembered the violence. His eyes squeezed into crosses. Dexter shook his head and opened his eyes again.

'No. Sorry. I don't remember anything. Not seen the footage and don't want to. Next question. Next question,' said Dexter.

Martin was disappointed that Dexter did not want

to talk about the first attack but understood why. Martin decided that he didn't want to put Dexter through it again, especially with his children sitting next to him.

'If I mentioned Chris Wilkinson, what would that mean to you?'

'Uh hmm. Well, I just feel numb. Numb. To think that he used to be my best friend. I still have trouble coming to terms with what he did.'

'Is there any part of you that has moved on from this traumatic experience?'

'I think it's hard to move on but we are doing our best. We are selling this house as it represents too much hurt for us. We visit Jules at every opportunity. So we're doing our best.'

'What are your feelings towards Jules, your wife?'

Dexter paused. 'Love. That's all I can say.'

'But there are some that say that it's wrong to love a murderer.'

'Murderer. That's such a strong word. It is a crime of passion. Passion for us.'

'But surely you must know what Jules did was wrong?'

'Yes, of course, but I understand why she did it.'

Martin leant back in the armchair and absorbed the full force of Dexter's love for his wife despite her label as a murderer. The children remained still, listening to all the questions and answers Dexter gave. Martin wondered if Dexter had told his children that murder was acceptable under certain circumstances. He wondered if Dexter had told them the same thing during prison visits with their mother. He wondered what the children thought.

'If I may, can I ask your children a question?'

'Sure. I guess.'

'What do you want to be when you grow up?' asked Martin, turning to Miles.

'Erm… an arthur!'

Dexter tutted. 'He means an author. He's really into writing!'

'And you?' asked Martin, turning to Marcus.

'Fireman!'

'And what about you Dexter? How is the blockbuster coming along?'

'With help, I finally got that script finished and now it's being filmed. It should be out next year some time.'

'Congratulations. I can say on behalf of all our viewers that we admire your courage and determination. Thank you, Dexter Copeland.'

Martin shook Dexter's hand. The interview had gone well but Martin had wanted and expected more from Dexter.

Martin and Geoff packed up the lights and camera equipment and bid the Copelands goodbye.

*****

The final interview had been booked with Detective West over lunch at his house. The sun was beating down on Martin and Geoff's car and even though they had opened the windows, it still felt like a greenhouse inside. Detective West was in his garden tending to some plants when Martin and Geoff pulled up outside. He looked up and waved at them.

'Come in, hmm, come in. Watch out for the wasps, hmm, we have a nest somewhere.'

Mrs West stepped out of the house with a tray of cold drinks complete with ice cubes and placed them on the garden table under a huge parasol.

'Here, hmm, I thought this would be a good place, hmm. We've prepared some beverages for you.'

'Thanks, Mr West. We'll just set up our equipment and join you shortly.'

After setting up the equipment, Martin sat down in the shade and wiped away the sweat from his forehead with his arm.

'It feels as if the tables have turned, hmm.'

'I don't follow, Mr West.'

'I'm the one being interrogated now, hmm. Ha! Ha!' laughed Detective West.

Martin was taken aback by Detective West's comical demeanor and had imagined him to be the man he had met with a stiff upper lip. Detective West's retirement from the force seemed to have lightened his personality as if it had been weighed down by the criminals of the world. Detective West combed his thin layer of white hair and took off his shades. Mrs West reappeared and placed a tray of freshly baked fruit scones on the table in front of them.

'My wife's infamous fruit scones, hmm. You won't find any better, hmm.'

A wasp hovered in the air before landing on one of the scones. Detective West batted the wasp away, took the scone and bit into it, licking the crumbs away from his lips.

'If we could start, Mr West.'

'Derek, hmm, Derek. Call me Derek,' interrupted Detective West.

'Derek. Ok. Is it ok if we start?' asked Martin.

'What will you be asking me, hmm? I would have thought it was perfectly obvious to the world what happened, hmm?'

'Yes. That's true, Derek, but we are coming in from a human angle. We wanted your personal thoughts on the case. For example, what was your opinion or view of the people involved. We'll be asking those kind of questions.'

Derek bit into the scone again and placed the remnant on the plate.

'Can I have a look at your clipboard, hmm, there's a good fellow.'

Martin handed Derek his clipboard and he started to read.

'What kind of question is this, hmm? If the police had had more resources, hmm, could Chris Wilkinson have been arrested earlier or his death prevented, hmm? Hmm?'

'I'm sorry. It's one of the questions that people or the viewers wanted to ask. It was born out of research that we did before we set up the interview with you. If you feel uncomfortable answering any of those questions, then we can take them out.'

Martin tried to appease Derek West whose jovial mood on his arrival was starting to turn sour. Derek ate the remaining morsel of scone and washed it down with a gulp of fresh squeezed orange juice.

'Hmm. I see. Well. No. I will answer it. Hmm. Just give me time to formulate an adequate response, hmm.'

'Certainly. Whenever you are ready, Derek.'

Martin breathed a sigh of relief and pointed at Geoff to start filming.

'Can you tell me your feelings towards this case. Why did you suspect Chris Wilkinson as being responsible?'

'The case was tricky, hmm. I knew there was an anomaly when processing the initial attack on Mr Copeland, hmm. The back door had been left open. Only a laptop had been taken although the two criminals had raided most of the upstairs level of the house, hmm. It didn't seem to add up.'

'And when did you start to suspect Mr Wilkinson in being involved?'

'I suspected him when he started acting arrogantly towards the police, hmm. He didn't help us, hmm. He didn't seem concerned. He hardly visited Mr Copeland in hospital and he was supposed to be his best friend, hmm. They were not the actions of an innocent man.'

'So you went on gut instinct?'

'Yes. If you want to call it that. Hmm. I call it a detective's intuition, hmm.'

'Now. After Mr Wilkinson had been arrested and he confessed, you must have been pleased?'

'Of course. It's always good to get a dangerous criminal off the streets, hmm.'

'Many people watching have commented on security being lax and unorganised, which, unfortunately, led to Mr Wilkinson's murder. How do you respond to that?'

'It's regrettable that something like that happened under my watch, hmm. But Mr Wilkinson had refused to be led to the van covered, hmm, opting instead to face the crowds of people that had gathered that day, hmm. He stopped walking on several occasions to talk to the press, hmm. It was all like a big media show for him, hmm.'

'If he had followed your advice and worn a cover, would he still be alive today?'

'Certainly. His bad decisions ultimately led to his murder, hmm.'

Detective West slurped his orange juice.

'Do you have any sympathy for Mrs Copeland?' asked Martin.

Detective West stopped drinking and put his glass down with a thud.

'No. I don't.'

The sharp direct answer almost made Martin lose track of where he was in the interview. A recent poll of the community had revealed that many of them felt sympathy towards Jules and would have done the same thing.

'Look, hmm, I've said this before and I'll say it again, hmm, if everybody with a grudge or those who seek vengeance went out tomorrow and did what Mrs Copeland did, hmm, where would we be? Hmm. We would be living in a society with vigilantes out there without any regard for the law, hmm. She committed a murder and punishable under the law, hmm. Can I understand why she did it? Hmm. To a certain degree, hmm, but for someone who is well educated and an upstanding citizen like Mrs Copeland, hmm, I have trouble understanding her actions completely, hmm.'

'Thank you, Derek.'

Martin had found Derek West an easier man to get information from than expected. He had lost some of his rigidity compared to the time when he was a detective but, at the same time, was still a man of principal.

Martin and Geoff finished their orange juices and scones, packed up their equipment and left the Wests to tend to their garden in the soaring summer heat.

*****

Martin and Geoff returned to their studio to edit the material together. Martin had scribbled down 'A Story To Remember' as the title of the documentary on his clipboard whilst waiting for Dexter to answer some of his questions. The title didn't seem to fit. It didn't seem catchy enough to attract people to watch it. Martin raised his head from his clipboard and stretched. He needed to come up with another title. A tabloid newspaper that had been left on the coffee table in front of him featured the headline 'TV-star to divorce'. Martin tutted at the news story but it had given him some inspiration. He grabbed his pen, looked down at the clipboard and wrote 'Making Headlines'. It was perfect and it made Martin smile with delight. It was what the story was all about.

EPILOGUE

Martin Lawson won the "best documentary" award for "Making Headlines" about the Dexter Copeland case. It propelled Martin's career as an investigative journalist into the international spectrum as well as making him one of the best journalists England had ever produced. Ten years later, Martin interviewed the Copelands again for his documentary series "Whatever Happened To…". The series won Martin Lawson several further awards and cemented his place in journalism history.

Dexter recovered to the point where he could use 80% of his memory. It had been a far cry from the man who had almost died and many, including his own wife, could see the changes in him. Dexter's film had not been the runaway success he had hoped for but it opened up the door for him to write more screenplays. After Dexter had recovered, he wrote a book called "Lightning Strikes Twice". It provided a detailed account about his attacks and recovery from his own personal perspective. The book went on to sell by the thousands and was featured on daytime shows as the book to read. Chris Wilkinson's allegations of plagiarism never saw the light of day.

Jules's jail sentence was reduced after good behaviour and she was released after serving fourteen years. She rejoined her family and they continue to live together in a new house in another part of the country. Jules chose not to talk about her past to the press but helped Dexter with his book, filling in some of the details he couldn't remember. To this day, Jules has remained silent about murdering Chris Wilkinson.

Kate Wilkinson still lives abroad and is still happily married. Despite the best efforts of the press to interview her, Kate remains evasive and refuses to talk about the past. Chuck became a property developer and also avoids talking to the press.

Derek West passed away in the one place he enjoyed the most - his garden. He died in his sleep, sitting under the parasol in the garden with the book Cat Amongst The Pigeons on his lap. His death filled the police community with sadness but it was a fitting end for a man who had been responsible for protecting the community for so many years.

Chris Wilkinson was cremated in a ceremony where few people showed. The Wilkinson family had long since departed from England and as a result, no family members were there to witness the occasion. A handful of die-hard fans and a handful of die-hard loathers turned up to the funeral but were ejected by security. Barbara Perkins, who felt it was her duty to represent the police, decided to go to the funeral. She felt only sadness as the curtains were drawn around the coffin, shielding it from view. She felt sad for Chris Wilkinson because he was a man who had it all and could have had it all. He had had a good career, a loving family, good friends he could trust and work colleagues who could have been the same to him. She wondered why he had thrown it all away.